ILLICIT DESIRES COMPLETE SERIES

APRIL CROSS

LACEY CROSS

EMILY'S SECRET DOM

AN MMF ROMANTIC BDSM EROTICA SERIES

CHAPTER
ONE

EMILY

My bedroom is stifling hot. I'm a sweaty mess and daydreaming about the cool mist of our showerhead and wishing I was under it right now. Instead, I'm in reverse cowgirl riding my husband, Nate, and staring at the wall opposite the bed, wondering how much longer he's going to take. I piston my hips faster, hoping to speed this up.

Nate just turned 45 and I swear the older he gets, the slower he comes. Some women might consider this a bonus, but I miss the fast fuck days of our 20s. We'd be watching a movie together, and he'd turn to me, press me into the cushions of the couch, and have his way with me. I'd get a brief fun thrill and we'd finish the movie. Later, he'd lick my pussy and drive me wild until I came. I'm 35 and we've been together for 12 years—married for 10—and he's licked nothing below my breasts in the last 3 years.

I might have forgotten what oral sex feels like, but he can't say the same. He doesn't overtly demand it, but he still gets his Saturday morning blowjobs because the few times I skipped it when I wasn't sick or out of town, he pouted all day. Sometimes it's easier to spend a few minutes on your knees than waste an entire day with a cranky man-child.

Glancing at the clock on the wall, a flash of annoyance ripples through me. Jesus, we've been at this for 20 minutes. Would he just freaking come already? I'm bored with riding him and tired of fake moaning. His cock creates a pleasant friction inside my pussy; adequate to keep me horny and desperate to come, but not enough to get me close to an orgasm. It's just one long edge session and I'm ready to be finished, one way or the other.

Nate stills and grasps my hips to stop me from moving. He sighs. "Emily, I don't think it's happening tonight. I'm just too tired."

Halle-fuckin-lujah! With my back towards him, I don't need to temper my expression and I'm betting I look pretty happy to be done.

I try to soothe him and show him it's not a big deal. "I think it's too hot in our bedroom. That probably didn't help."

He murmurs in agreement as I climb off him and snuggle against him for a moment. Our sweat-sticky bodies make it miserable, so I quickly roll over to my side of the bed to lie on my back and stare at the ceiling. Within a couple of minutes, Nate is snoring softly next to me, and my pussy is an angry buzz of need. Shit, I really needed to come tonight.

Nate travels a ton for work and he just returned yesterday from a two-week trip. His company flies him around to different locations to help set up satellite offices or to troubleshoot when there's a management problem at a site. He's usually only gone one week at a time, but he ran into some complications and had to stay an extra week. I really needed the physical connection of a shared orgasm with him tonight, but our sex life is less than stellar, so deep down I knew I was asking for too much.

I spread my legs and reach down to my slick folds. God, I'm so wet. I slip a finger in and moan softly, but cut off my sigh when Nate shifts in his sleep. I'm not sure I can relax without coming. Gingerly, I crawl out of bed and tiptoe out of the room, using my cell phone's soft flashlight feature to make sure I don't hit anything on my way out. Since Nate hasn't been asleep that long, I know he's in a light phase. But I need to visit the bathroom before I fall asleep anyway, so it isn't uncharacteristic of me to get up after sex, and I could use that excuse if he wakes up.

Escaping to the bathroom, I lean against the counter, spread my legs, and massage my clit with three fingers. My tiny moans echo in the small room, but the walls are thick enough between the bathroom and the master bedroom that I don't care. We also sleep with a white noise machine going, so it would take more than some moaning to bother him.

I focus on my clit for a few minutes, and then press my fingers inside my slick cave, alternating between rubbing and finger fucking myself in a sexual haze. I need something more than I'm getting and my mind drifts to him—the guy I was trying to avoid thinking about tonight while with my husband.

I stop caressing myself and pick up my phone, swiping at the app I use for my friends when I play online games with them. I click on the picture of a sexy grey-haired fox named Aiden and stare at the voice message icon. Knowing I shouldn't do it, I press on the voicemail and let the message play out loud. Aiden's deep voice entrances me as I listen to him.

Emily,

I know you've been thinking about me. I know that my words have been making you restless, making you want to hear more.

You're just discovering that you like being told what to do. That's because you're a natural submissive.

And a sub like you needs someone to guide them, teach them, show them how to obey.

Already you know I have an effect on you. As you listen to this, I know you're squirming, maybe even wanting to touch yourself. You're wondering just what serving me would be like.

So I'm going to make you an offer.

I will give you what you need, even though you don't know what that is yet. I will teach you to serve, teach you to be obedient, teach you to do as your Sir tells you.

And in return, all I ask for is your total surrender to me.

So if you want me to be your Dom, all you have to do is reply.

And say "Yes Sir."

I listen to the message again. The third time through, I realize I've been rubbing my clit the entire time and I'm about to come. I let the audio play one last time while I finger myself, and when he tells me to say, "Yes, Sir," I come so hard my legs turn to Jell-o and I slide to the floor, panting. Aftershocks of pleasure ripple through my body and I stare at myself in the full-length mirror on the wall across from me. I'm wanton, naked, and sprawled with my legs wide open.

I sigh and let the phone slip out of my hand onto the linoleum with a gentle thud. Nate being at home should have solved any temptation from Aiden. Yet, here I am, on my bathroom floor after an intense orgasm from listening to his voice and offer. The same as I've done every day for the past five days since he left the message.

～

NATE

I'm startled out of a light sleep by the bedroom door clicking closed. I wish Emily hadn't been so obvious about wanting sex tonight. We need to chat and not being able to orgasm didn't put me at ease. Something has been going on with her for weeks, and I hoped being gone would give us some time apart to realize how much we mean to each other. But as soon as I got home yesterday, I could tell nothing had changed and things might be worse. Maybe when she gets back to bed, we can really talk.

Realizing I'm thirsty, I get up and head to the kitchen. When I pass by the bathroom, the door is closed and I pause when I hear moaning. *What the fuck.* Is she masturbating in the bathroom? I put my ear against the door, feeling slightly like a peeping Tom, but curious if she really is touching herself.

Through the thin wood, I hear some guy offering to teach her how to obey while she moans. I stand there in shock. When the recording ends and she plays it again, my cock springs to attention. The other guy uses her name at the beginning, so this is a personalized message just for her.

I turn back to the bedroom, close the door behind me, and lie down in bed—forgetting the water. I stroke myself to the image of Emily playing with herself in the bathroom to a random guy offering to dominate her. She never told me she wanted that, and I don't know that I could even do it if she asked. It only takes a minute of rubbing my shaft and squeezing my balls before I come super hard at the thought of her on her knees for another guy.

Jesus. I clean up my mess with some tissues from a box on the nightstand. When Emily comes back into the bedroom, I pretend I'm sleeping until I actually fall asleep.

CHAPTER

TWO

EMILY

My husband makes a good income, so I only have to work part time at a craft store to help feed my crafting addiction and buy supplies with the employee discount. This leaves my days mostly free and boring.

We own a three-story house, and the top floor is a weird mother-in-law apartment with a studio bedroom, a kitchenette, and a bathroom. Nate and I considered renting out the room since none of our family comes to visit, but we don't need the money and we're too lazy to hunt for a renter that might trash our house. Cleaning the house takes a fair bit of effort, but other than that my days are free.

To pass the time, several years ago I started playing an online multi-player fantasy game, and I hate to admit it, but I'm obsessed with it. Nate doesn't know how addicted I am since I play when he's at work. I joined a guild that raided on UK hours, so I'd be raiding during the day, and the game is a second job for me. I am the recruitment officer in my guild and play an elven cleric named Sunshine. I'm continually helping with plans for the guild and acclimating new members to the schedule and requirements.

Two months ago, a necromancer named Dreznar joined the guild.

He was a quiet guy, but not a pushover. He knew his role and played his character well, so he quickly brought attention to himself for his dedicated playing style. I'm a flirt and attracted to quiet and shy guys, so I teased Dreznar a bit. He responded positively, and we forged a budding friendship. I quickly found out he wasn't shy and was only quiet. Once he opened up, he flirted just as much as I did, and our interactions gave me tiny thrills.

The more Dreznar and I talked, the more restless I became. Something about him attracted me like a moth to a flame and I woke up every morning thinking about him. Every night he was my last thought before I fell asleep. We started private messaging each other in an app the guild uses to communicate outside the game. Sometimes we'd just chat on the app all day, without even logging into the game first. We finally got comfortable enough to share our real names. His name was Aiden and from that point on, I mostly thought of him with his real name and not as his character.

Two weeks ago, things changed. Our conversations had taken on a flirtier tone in the week or two leading up to that night. Nate was out playing cards with some friends and I admit I was feeling horny and being more sexual than normal in my messages.

Occasionally Aiden would take the flirting into character roleplay in the game where we would pretend it was just our characters talking and immerse ourselves in the moment. But that night he took it to a whole new level. Before I knew it, we were touring player housing, and Dreznar was bending Sunshine over a table. I was a willing participant and egged him on. I wanted to see how far he would take it. He pushed as far as I would go, which was Sunshine giving him everything she had to offer.

I'm no saint. Twice in my marriage I took flirting too far and ended up sexting another player. But each time it was a one-off type of deal and the other guy always left the game for mental health reasons after I wouldn't continue on with a cyber affair. My guild leader joked I needed to avoid sexting the new guys because I was chasing them off. It was only two men, but in a way it was true, and after that I was careful in my dealings with people until I met Aiden. He changed everything.

Aiden rocked my world. After that first night bent over a table, I really couldn't stop thinking of him all day, every day. His sexting differed from anything I'd ever experienced. He just… took control, and I didn't have to do anything but sit there and touch myself and type occasional sentences about what I was doing or how I felt.

Aiden worked nights, so we had all day together in the game. We grouped, explored, did quests, and found time to sext daily. I was having so many orgasms that I didn't feel the need to have them with my husband. Not that Nate was asking for sex often, but even our weekly weekend sex was rote and more boring than usual. I wanted him to take control and become a wild beast with me, like Aiden was in text, but Nate is all about making love. His softness left me craving Aiden's roughness even more.

During this time, we opened up more about our real lives. It was a scary thrill the day I found out Aiden lived in my state. What are the odds of that? I tried to be cagey about exactly where I lived. I don't need a psychopath showing up on my doorstep threatening to talk to my husband. Aiden was more open than I was, and he told me he lived 30 minutes away from me. The sane part of me knew this kind of temptation living so close is a bad idea, but it's only online, right?

Until I got the voicemail.

CHAPTER

THREE

EMILY

What the fuck am I going to do about Aiden? I'm in the breakfast nook off the kitchen while Nate makes food. Our first attempt at sex after his trip didn't go well, so what does this mean for our marriage? It doesn't help that the orgasm from listening to Aiden's voice message had me seeing stars, highlighting the difference with my husband.

After listening to the voicemail for the first time five days ago, I messaged Aiden and told him I needed a few days to consider the offer. He replied that he'd give me a week and that I can't drag it on forever. I need to decide today so I can give him my answer tomorrow.

Nate brings me scrambled eggs, toast, and a small bowl of strawberries and sits down across from me. He flashes me a smile, and we both dig in wordlessly. Guess he doesn't want to talk about last night, which is fine with me.

"Emily, did you have plans for your day?"

Nate and I usually do our own thing on Saturday mornings after I give him his weekly blowjob, and then watch a movie together in the evening. When Nate got out of bed before I could even attempt the blowjob, it reinforced that something was off with him. He's the type of guy you can't press for answers and have to let come to you when he wants to discuss an issue, so I'll bide my time and wait.

I swallow my bite of egg before responding. "No, not really. Might log in and play my game."

When he doesn't respond, I take a sip of water before continuing. "Do you have plans?"

This is about as scintillating as our Saturday breakfast conversation gets. We eat, see what the other is doing, and then go our separate ways.

Nate scrapes the last of his eggs onto his fork, shoves it into his mouth and talks with his mouth full. "Nope, probably just yard work."

Eww, he knows I hate it when he chews while talking, but he gets up to rinse his plate off in the sink so he misses the dirty look I toss in his direction. Watching him at the counter, I know I've made my decision.

Before Nate leaves the kitchen, he comes over, kisses my forehead, and says he'll see me later. I only wait a few minutes before dumping the rest of my eggs in the trash, laying my plate in the sink, and scurrying to my computer. My hands are shaking as I type my password into the game's log-in screen, eager to find Aiden online. I'm hoping he's in the game because I want to give my answer while my little elf is in front of him. I press enter, and pray.

Sunshine enters the world in her house and breathes a sigh of relief when she sees Dreznar online. She can't tell what part of the world he's exploring, but it doesn't matter. She can say hello from a distance. Sunshine has a funny greeting for Dreznar, and it made him laugh the first time she used it, so she continues to greet him that way.

SUNSHINE

Yo, what's up?

Sunshine waits patiently, wondering how long it will take for him to reply.

He doesn't respond for a solid minute, and I rub my clammy hands on my fleece pajama pants while I wait. Maybe he's away from his computer? Usually he greets me with, 'Good morning, Sunshine,' which I find adorable every time he says it.

Sunshine finally gets a message.

DREZNAR

Hello, Emily. Do you have an answer for me?

I get a zing straight to my pussy when he types my real name and I'm instantly wet. Calling me Emily is hot. I know my answer, but his greeting throws me into a mental tailspin. I try to buy some time to think.

Sunshine rebuts,

Uh, I have one more day.

And receives no reaction.

The longer I stare at the screen waiting, the wetter my pussy gets. Is he doing this on purpose? Does he know how turned on I'm getting when he makes me wait?

After a few minutes, he finally announces to Sunshine.

Okay, Emily. I am logging off. When you have an answer for me, you can find me on the app. I won't talk to you until you do.

Sunshine panics, and quickly messages him before he can leave.

WAIT!

Dreznar doesn't respond to her for a good minute, and Sunshine checks her friends list again to verify he's still in the world. He's there, so why isn't he talking to her?

Yes, Emily? I'm waiting.

Oh, fuck. He was expecting Sunshine to continue.

Um, I have an answer.

The shaking has moved from my hands to my entire body and my clit is throbbing and demands attention. Hoping if I rub myself the shaking will stop, I slip a hand under the waistband of my pajama pants and underneath my panties. I'm so dang wet. My fingers glide easily between my silky folds and I massage gentle circles around my bean while I wait for him to answer.

When he hasn't typed after a couple minutes, I close my eyes and lean back in my office chair, spreading my legs further so I can finger fuck myself easier. Everything Aiden does turns me on, so I don't know why I'm surprised his lack of response is working me up.

I sigh and arch my hips up as I press my fingers downward. My mind clears of worry and thought, and a calm slips over me as I keep my eyes closed and lose myself in the sensation. Aiden and I have shared several selfies, including nudes, so I know what his cock looks like. I imagine my fingers are his thick shaft and that he's in my office fucking me this very moment. The daydream is enough for me to come and my body quivers while I moan loudly and buck against my hand. Waves of ecstasy ripple through me and my pussy clenches as the pleasure peaks.

I'm not sure how long I sat there with my fingers in my snatch before removing them, wiping them on my pants, and opening my eyes. I'm relaxed, content, and ready to face Aiden.

And I am literally facing him.

Dreznar stands in front of Sunshine in her house and at some point he spoke to her.

> Don't make me wait much longer.

Fuckity, fuck, fuck, fuck. How long has he been there?
Sunshine squirms and blurts out,

> Shit, I'm sorry. I'm back.

Dreznar doesn't reply, yet again, and Sunshine realizes he probably won't. Taking a deep breath, she sits down right in front of him and speaks.

> Yes, Sir.

~

NATE

My mind is a whirl of thoughts and emotions after I finish breakfast with Emily and go outside to do yard work. Usually manual labor clears my head, but I keep wondering who the guy in the message was. Where did she meet him? I had a friend in college who was into BDSM and told me stories, so I knew what the guy was offering. But does she?

This is an entirely new side of Emily. She didn't just find this guy yesterday, and based on how loudly she was moaning, she wants to take him up on his offer. I can't wrap my head around what has obviously been going on for a while. A ball of dread lodges in my gut when I realize she could be talking to him right now.

I want to run inside and tell her I love her and to stop talking to the other guy, but I'm reminded of what my father told me after my first girlfriend left me for another kid. He said you can't force someone to stay with you. And while, yes, this is true, shouldn't I fight for Emily? I realize things haven't been good for a long time, but how did I miss something this big?

My thoughts continue in circles as I weed the flowerbeds I'd planted because Emily loves flowers. As I work on clearing the debris around my symbols of love to her, I start violently hacking away at the dirt. I'm tense and my heart is pounding, but not from the physical exertion. The tightness in my chest won't ease and my mind races, searching for answers. I shouldn't be the only one fighting for our marriage. She decided to not talk to me, and has made that choice for god knows how long.

By the time I'm done weeding, I'm more angry than anything else. As I put the yard tools in the shed and clean up, a plan forms. When she's at work tomorrow, I'll snoop on her computer and find out who this guy is. She usually goes in for a couple of hours in the evening on Sundays since the craft store closes early. I won't have to wait long until I can get answers—assuming she hasn't hidden or deleted everything.

CHAPTER

FOUR

EMILY

Almost every Sunday morning, Nate takes his mother to church. Nate and I aren't religious, but his mom doesn't like to drive, and it's their bonding time after his father passed away. It also lets him keep eyes on how she's doing and make sure she's taking care of herself. Unless she's sick she never misses a Sunday, so I usually have the house to myself for a few hours.

Once Nate leaves, I slink into the office to log in and look for Aiden. I giggle at myself for sneaking around since I'm alone. Everything seems more real with Aiden now. After I accepted his offer, he told me training would start today. I don't know what that means, but he had to log off and said he would explain today.

Dreznar is in Sunshine's house when she enters the world and she jumps in fright. He's one of the few people who can enter her house, but she still wasn't expecting to see him there.

SUNSHINE

Yo, what's up?

DREZNAR

Emily, that's not how you will greet me anymore.

Uncertain what he means, Sunshine comments,

Oh?

You chose to call me Sir, so I want you to use it. Some variation of 'good morning, Sir,' is what I expect.

Well, that's hot. I reach down and give my pussy a brief rub through my pajama pants before I continue typing on Sunshine.
Sunshine replies,

Okay.

No. Okay is what you say to your boss when they ask you to serve a customer. When talking to me, you say, 'yes, Sir,' and show me the respect I am due.

Uh... Sunshine is at a loss for words.
I'm not sure how I feel about where this is going, but my traitorous pussy clenches and is wet, which tells me I like it more than I want to admit. It feels wrong to be talking to Aiden this way, but also incredibly right. When I don't immediately echo his words, he types again.

I'm waiting.

Oh, shit! Sunshine answers, "Yes, Sir," but almost fucks up the wording in her haste and has to correct it. She doesn't want to get in trouble for being sloppy.

Good girl.

His use of 'good girl' pings a part of Sunshine's brain briefly, and she wants to shout. See, I did something right!

> Emily, your training starts today.

Oh, now we're getting to the good stuff.
Sunshine responds,

> Yes, Sir.

> I'm going to give you some simple commands and I want you to follow them.

Huh...I'm confused, so I have Sunshine get clarification.

> Wait, Sir. Is this in-game commands, or is this stuff I will do for real?

> I'll give you a combination of both, but eventually more real than game. But for now, I want you to think as if Sunshine is submitting to me and we'll work on training you this way.

Oh. Sunshine knows she's about to get toyed with, but her body tingles and her heart rate speeds up so she knows she wants it. Sunshine is a powerful, good cleric and submitting to this evil necromancer is the perfect kind of naughty for her.

> Emily, kneel for me and open your mouth.

Oh, shit. He's not wasting time. When he continues to use Emily instead of Sunshine, I squirm in my seat. Since this is all virtual, it won't matter if I'm touching myself through this, so score on it being in-game only.

> Oh, and Emily?

Yes, Sir?

While you're doing this, you can't touch yourself in real life unless I give you permission.

Fuck. How did he know what I was thinking? Him telling me I can't touch makes me want it all that much more. I mean, he won't see me, right? I'm tempted to reach down, but stop myself. If I misbehave, it's possible he won't teach me. The need to learn more keeps me from grinding my pussy against my hand.

I'm breathless and my hands shake when I continue in the game.

Yes, Sir.

Sunshine kneels and opens her mouth.

I don't understand why this is so fucking hot since it's not real, but I want to spear my fingers inside my wet hole while he's typing to me.

Today, Emily, I'm only giving you a small taste. Every day you please me, I'll teach you more. I want you to imagine me sliding the tip of my cock into your mouth, and just holding it there so you can lick and suck on the tip. Can you do that for me?

Sunshine's heartbeat thunders in her head.

Yes, Sir.

Good girl. Now, rub your clit for 30 seconds, and 30 seconds only, while thinking about sucking on me. Start now.

Fuck! I frantically shove my hand down my pajama pants, knowing I'm wasting precious seconds. A guy needs to give a woman a little warning. It's not like my privates are jutting out and hitting the desk, ready for action at all times.

As I rub my fingers against my clit, I relax and moan softly. I'm down for this type of training every day. Unfortunately, 30 seconds is nowhere near long enough. Just as I'm getting into it, he tells Sunshine to stop. That felt longer than 30 seconds, so he might have accounted for the time it would take to get my hand down my pants.

> How do you feel, Emily?

Sunshine doesn't know how to respond to him. Turned on? Needy? Wanting him to press his cock further into her mouth to give her more time to touch herself?
   She goes for the simple answer.

> Wet.

> Good girl.

My brain goes a little fuzzy at hearing 'good girl,' again. Jesus, before long I'm going to be a drooling mess whenever he says that to me.

> Now say goodbye to your Sir. I need to log off.

Sunshine bites her lip and rubs her arms, wishing he could stay longer.

> Goodbye, Sir. I'll talk to you later.

> Have a good day, Doll.

Dreznar smiles at Sunshine when he logs off.
My pulse speeds up and I'm breathless when he calls me Doll. I hope he plans to keep calling me that. Aiden didn't say if I could touch myself after he left the game and I don't know what to do. I'm aching and desperate to finger fuck myself while reviewing the chat log, but I hold back. I don't want to get into trouble. With half my training in-game roleplay and the other half in real life, I'm tied up in knots, but I'm loving every minute and don't want to stop.

~

NATE

I try to avoid Emily for most of the afternoon and only briefly kiss her goodbye when she leaves for work. She seems distracted, so she doesn't notice I'm not talking much, which is just as well. After she leaves, I pace and watch the clock. I want to wait at least five minutes to make sure she doesn't come back before I start the hunt for her secrets.

As soon as it's safe, I rush to the computer. My heartbeat is strong and steady and I'm leaning forward, intent on the screen as I scour around on her desktop and in folders. I'm not expecting this to be an easy search, and I slowly shake my head when I find what I'm looking for within a couple of minutes.

Oh, Emily, I expected a challenge. Instead, she has a folder on her desktop labeled "To Keep," and inside are screenshots of her character in the game with some dark elf in a robe. My stomach clenches and nausea hits me as I read the text chats. The two of them are sexting and most of the time she's calling the dark elf by his character name—I can tell because it's also visible in the screenshots—but occasionally she says Aiden.

I close all the open browser windows, turn off her computer and straighten her desk to make it look exactly how it did. Time slows down as I go about the house, not really seeing what I'm doing. It sounds like his real name is Aiden, but having found the information so easily, I'm now at a loss for what to do about it. I'm not ready to confront her, but what I saw leaves no doubt at what she's doing. I don't want to talk to her tonight, so I send her a text message that I have a headache and I'm going to bed early. Popping a sleeping pill the doctor gave me for a bout of insomnia I had last year, I make sure I'm asleep by the time she gets home.

CHAPTER

FIVE

EMILY

I swear I blink and it's already two weeks since I agreed to obey and serve Aiden. Saying yes increased the time I'm spending with him during the daytime, but it's less time in-game and more time over the app. It's been non-stop sexual gratification. Every day he's teaching me a tiny bit more, and it's funny how I had zero clue what I was getting myself into.

He quickly learned that I enjoy being controlled, so he started asking me to do little things, like take photos with my phone of my panty choices in the morning so he can choose which one I wear—or tell me to not wear any and go without for the day.

One training session involved me looking at pictures of different ways to kneel and snapping photos of myself in the positions and emailing them to him so he could evaluate how I was doing. This progressed to him giving me an assignment to kneel for five minutes every morning after Nate leaves for work, and to spend that time thinking about Aiden and how I want to serve him.

Every little thing he does makes me a wet mess. I've been changing my underwear multiple times per day. The days I don't wear any, my inner thighs are damp most of the day, and I just laugh at myself. This craziness has to die down eventually, right?

Nate wasn't feeling good last weekend, so we missed our weekly sex —not that I cared—but now it's Saturday night again and as we're snuggling on the couch watching a show, he moves my hand over his sweatpants so I'll rub his hard cock. Guess it's game on tonight.

I turn my head towards him, smile, and he leans over and kisses me deeply. As our tongues swirl, my stomach flutters and my pussy throbs and tingles. Aiden's sexual teasing and thrilling me has kept me horny and Nate is about to benefit.

We abandon our show, and I grasp his hand and lead him to the bedroom. I've got to strike while the iron is hot. My pussy demands a cock inside of her.

~

NATE

I resolve to not make love with Emily until she and I talk about her online cheating. But two weeks have gone by and I still haven't talked with her since it never seems like the right time. What makes it worse is that she's blossoming before my eyes. She moves with more confidence, smiles easier, and her restless spirit seems soothed. I'm seeing brief hints of an emerging sexual goddess in Emily and knowing that it's another guy bringing this out is killing me.

I waste most of my days trying to not think about Aiden and wonder what's so special about him. My head spins and my mouth goes dry whenever I focus on my failures in our marriage and what possibly led Emily to this point. The fear that I'm not good in bed crossed my mind, and I thought that would make my sex drive disappear, yet I've been masturbating daily thinking about this new Emily. If she wasn't so damn tempting, I could resist her.

That second Saturday my resolve finally breaks. We start our Saturday night movie and she's wearing gray shorts with no socks. Her bare legs and pretty red pedicure distract me as I imagine them wrapped around me with her doing her cute little moans in my ear. My cock twitches and throbs, growing harder the longer we sit close together.

Finally, I can't stand it and I move her hand to my hardness, encouraging her to stroke me. My mind blanks a little and sexual need takes over. When she leads me to the bedroom, a small part of me wonders if I should hold firm to my plan of no sex, but my cock is in control and there's no way he's passing up this chance.

SIX

EMILY

Nate is especially eager tonight, and as soon as we get into the bedroom, we both rapidly strip and fall onto the bed together. I moan as he kisses me and runs his hands along my ribs and cups my breasts. It's hard not to close my eyes and imagine I'm in bed with Aiden, but I promised myself I would keep my two lives separate and give Nate the attention he deserves when I'm with him.

Nate nibbles down my stomach. Time slows down and I go dizzy when he kisses past my belly button. *Is he finally going to go down on me again?* A gush of wetness leaks from my pussy at the thought and I moan and arch my back towards him. *Oh please, god, yes.* I'm craving his tongue on my clit and I want to beg him to lick me, but something holds me back.

He kisses along the line of my bush, but goes no further. I moan in frustration as he moves his mouth up my body. I'm aching and needy for him to fuck me, but every touch is a gentle caress. When he finally brings his hand between my legs and slips his fingers between my silky, wet folds, his softness is too much for me to take. I close my eyes and picture Aiden's hand instead and imagine him rubbing me roughly. I pinch and pull my own nipples while Nate does his sweet and sensual thing, and the added harsh pleasure from manhandling myself propels me towards an orgasm.

Before I come, Nate removes his hand and climbs between my legs. In my head, it's Aiden's cock fitting against my entrance and when he presses into me, I picture Aiden doing it tenderly to drive me wild before he ravishes me. Nate sets a steady, loving pace and I sigh and moan from the joy I'm getting from my vision of Aiden. Maybe I need to think of Aiden all the time. I'm getting double the pleasure from imagining both men.

Nate doesn't talk and I hear Aiden's voice in my head calling me a dirty little slut for thinking of him while having sex with my husband. The delicious naughtiness drives me into a frenzy, and I almost come from the thoughts of Aiden. As I soar closer to my orgasm, a moment of clarity hits me.

It's time to tell Aiden where I live and ask him to fuck me in real life. There's no reason to keep it online-only when he lives close and can give me what I'm craving—what my dear husband cannot with his softness.

Making the spontaneous decision to bang Aiden pushes me over the abyss and my orgasm is stronger than it has been in months. I cry out, and in my head I'm chanting for Aiden to fuck me harder.

As I convulse around Nate's cock, he pauses and stops moving. I buck against him, desperate to get every ounce of enjoyment. Suddenly, he grabs my wrists, pins them to the bed above my head and turns savage. He pounds into me, and my body responds in delight. I was already blissfully spinning from the first orgasm but this sensual raw power removes all thoughts of Aiden as Nate slams against me, sending shocks of pleasure straight to my toes.

My first orgasm had peaked and I was coming down, but as Nate drills repeatedly into my core I crest and come again. I scream out, while the room spins and stars explode behind my eyes from the force of my climax. Wave after wave of ecstasy washes over me. Nate must have come when I did because he goes limp on top of me as my orgasm trails off to just tiny shivers of rapture.

Holy shit. Where did that come from?

~

NATE

Whenever I make love to Emily, I want to worship her body. She's soft in all the desirable places, and I love her tiny moans when I touch her in just the right spot. And tonight, when I push my cock into her, she's more animated and eager for sex than she's been in a while. I bliss out while I leisurely press against her, loving how her warm, tight cave molds against every inch of my cock.

I can tell Emily is getting close to her orgasm, and it pushes me towards mine. I love coming when she does. When Emily comes, the intensity of her quaking and rocking against me shocks me a little but gives me a nice sexual zing. Guess I'm not bad in bed after all. She cries out and moans loudly, ending it with a plea for Aiden to fuck her harder.

I freeze.

My wife just said some other guy's name in bed. My mind goes momentarily blank before a pounding in my ears and a rush of adrenaline spurs me on. I grab her wrists, not caring if I hurt her, and pin them above her head. Determined to make her unable to think of anyone but me, I fuck her more roughly than I ever have before.

I pound my cock into her box, chanting in my head everything I wish I could say to her, as I fuck her with total disregard to her pleasure. "How do you like this, Emily? Is my cock just as good as Aiden's? Can he do this to you?" With each thought, I slam harder into her.

Emily comes again and as her pussy milks my cock, I explode load after load of cum into her quivering core. I collapse on top of her and roll off in disgust. I can't believe what I just did. Peeking over at her, I expect to see her upset, but she's lying on her back, eyes closed, and a dreamy smile on her face. She looks content and more satisfied than I've ever seen her after a round of sex.

Well, fuck. Now what do I do?

The End

MASTERING EMILY

AN MMF ROMANTIC BDSM EROTICA SERIES

CHAPTER
ONE

EMILY

Aiden plunges his thick, meaty cock into my sopping wet hole so forcefully it feels as if he's ripping me in two. The intense pain along with the pleasure has me begging for more. He's tied my legs to the bed, wide open, so I can't do anything but lie there while he fucks me. My hands are free and I can touch him, but when I hit a sensitive spot on his neck, he pins my wrists with his hands. My eyelids flutter as I try to stay focused, and I fight to keep them open so I can watch his expression as he comes inside of me, but it's a losing battle.

Aiden growls. "Emily, look at me."

I force my eyes open wider and Aiden has a feral look as he fucks me hard.

"Can your husband make you feel this way?"

Oh, god. I hate it when he asks me about Nate, but I thrill whenever he makes me compare them. It's immoral and he knows it makes me come harder.

I pant out, "No. No one but you can, Sir."

"That's...right..." Aiden punctuates both words with sharp thrusts into me while I moan louder.

The room spins as I edge closer to my orgasm. I can't hold it back much longer, but Aiden hasn't said I can come yet. He only has several firm rules, and the main one is that good girls don't come without permission. But the pleasure is too intense. I need permission now.

"Oh, my god. I'm going to come! Can I please come, Sir?"

Aiden gives a raw, harsh laugh, taunting me, "No, not yet," and he reaches his hand between us to rub my clit while still slamming into me. Within a few seconds of him caressing my hard bean, I can't stop myself from coming. I scream out, convulsing against his hand and cock, while shocks of delight ripple through my body in waves. I ride the orgasm while Aiden grunts on top of me and comes with a roar, painting my cave walls with ropes of his warm, sticky cum. We're both panting as he relaxes his body into mine. He rolls to my side to snuggle close. I'm barely coherent, and still buzzing from the orgasm.

He whispers in my ear, his breath tickling me. "You know you're going to be punished for that."

A rush of excitement hits me from his words. So far, I've enjoyed the punishments, and that orgasm was worth it. As I relax and drift, I think about how crazy it is that it's only been a month since I told Aiden we should meet in real life. A month of meeting Aiden in secret at his apartment twice a week and having dirty, wild sex behind my husband's back.

∼

NATE

I walk back to my car after watching Emily and Aiden fuck. Today Aiden had the bedroom window open, and I could hear them through the screen. Aiden's bedroom is on the ground floor in a quiet complex of duplexes and his apartment is on the edge of the property. It's isolated and I can creep around the side of his apartment without anyone noticing me. If the blinds aren't closed, a person can see most of the bottom floor. Aiden rarely closes the blinds all the way.

The stain on my crotch is a testament to how amazingly hot it was to peek in and watch Aiden fuck Emily hard. Her cries of ecstasy were more than I could take and I furiously rubbed myself to completion when she came.

I sit in my car for almost 10 minutes. I'm in no shape to drive yet. My cheeks burn and I'm shaking, while self-loathing and disgust wash over me. How did my life get to this point?

When the shaking dies down to a soft tremble, I sigh and start the car. I need to get back to work. Emily thinks I'm working longer hours, when in reality I told my boss I have mental health appointments. He's letting me take longer lunches and working later to make up the time difference. I tell myself 'never again' as I drive off, but I know I'll be back. I say I'm going to stop every time and I never do.

CHAPTER

TWO

EMILY

Last month, when I told Aiden I wanted to meet in real life, I woke up the next morning with butterflies in my stomach. Aiden was usually awake by the time I got up every morning, so that day I rushed to my computer to log into the game. I slumped into my chair with a sigh when I didn't see him. He somehow should have known I was desperate to talk to him that morning and been waiting. I shot a message to him on the app we use for communication outside of the game.

EMILY

Sir, I need to talk with you when you have a moment.

I expected a quick reply, so I busied myself with light housework while I waited. When Aiden hadn't answered two hours later, I was a jumble of nerves and found myself pacing around the house. This was the first time he hadn't gotten back to me within half an hour when he wasn't at work. And maybe he'd spoiled me, but I couldn't help feeling like he wasn't answering on purpose. He said he would train me, so maybe this was to teach me patience.

My mind briefly flashed on the idea that he could be on a lunch date with another girl, and I muttered under my breath about how it would have been nice if he told me he was dating. She's probably younger than me, and prettier. Aiden struck me as the type who might go for a girl in her 20s if she was hot for older men.

My thoughts swirled for a moment about this imaginary girl and how I was going to overthrow the competition. I stopped pacing and chuckled. I needed to calm the fuck down. Who knew if he was on a date? There were easily a hundred things he could do that didn't involve another woman. I had bigger problems to worry about anyway, like what I should do about the online game.

Once Aiden and I reduced our playtime, I stepped down as recruitment officer. The guild leader wasn't happy, but I never felt like logging in anymore. Whenever I was online and talking to Aiden, my head spun and my brain went fuzzy. It's impossible to play a cleric on a raid effectively if you're mentally a pile of mush. The time for a hiatus from the game had come, and I needed to post on the forums about my break, but the guilt of leaving sucked. Well-geared clerics don't grow on trees and my absence would hurt the guild.

I stewed about my goodbye post until my phone app dinged with a message. When I saw Aiden's name, I became lightheaded and breathless.

AIDEN

Busy morning, Doll. What's up?

A delicious thrill ran down my back whenever he called me Doll, but it wasn't a conversation to have when he's busy.

EMILY

Uh, nothing that can't wait, Sir. I'll talk to you later.

I assumed the conversation was over and contemplated my house. What should I do this afternoon? Even my craft projects held no appeal for me anymore. Other than crafts and my online game, what did I do with my free time before Aiden? My phone beeped again with another incoming message.

No, tell your Sir what you wanted to
say. NOW.

Oh, shit. We'd already kicked off this conversation on the wrong foot, so I quickly started typing.

Sir, I have some information I withheld from
you about my location.

His reply didn't take long.

I'm waiting…

Sir, when you told me what city you live in, I
knew it was about a 30-minute drive from
my house.

The app showed me Aiden was typing and it seemed like he'd been typing for a long time, so it surprised me when his message was brief.

Interesting. What are you saying?

I paused and took a deep breath. My hands shook with my next text.

Sir, I want to meet you in person.

*Good girl. When I get home, let's talk about
the details.*

I squealed and wanted to do a happy dance around my living room, but remembered to respond to him first and said I would talk to him later. When he said goodbye to me, I was flushed and turned on. I spun in place with my arms flung out. The room revolved a little, causing me to stumble. I sat down on an ottoman in the living room and put my head between my knees. I took several calming, deep breaths.

Holy fuck, was I really going to do this?

~

NATE

It was only two days ago that Emily said Aiden's name while we made love, but I've become paralyzed with fear that she will leave me. The logical part of my brain asked me if I wanted to be married to someone who cheated online and was doing...whatever they were doing. Could someone call it BDSM if it's just online? How that worked was beyond me, but there was a difference in Emily since meeting Aiden. Also, if she said his name during sex, she had grown attached to him.

I became sick to my stomach most days when I thought about Emily, and I needed to confront her and talk with her. Was it too late for marriage counseling? If we went to therapy, I'd have to admit what I've been doing when she's at work and I was too disgusted with myself to tell anyone.

Every time Emily worked, I snooped on her computer. I found out that she and Aiden used their guild's communication app to talk about non-game stuff. The computer desktop version synced with her phone and all the messages between them showed up when I logged in. Another stupid move on her part was not using a different four-digit PIN to open the program. She used the same one we jointly used for most anything that required a code, despite how security experts said never to do that.

So far, all I'd seen was a bunch of sexting and Aiden commanding her to do random shit. The day I saw him tell her to kneel for him and she posted a picture of her doing it, my head spun and my cock stiffened. I ended up masturbating to the picture of her kneeling. The self-loathing and waves of shame when I came hard didn't deter me from checking the app again.

Most days when I logged into the app, they shared new pictures. Aiden's cock was bigger than mine, but not enough for me to feel inadequate. The petty part of me wished his cock was smaller, but I don't know that it would even matter. She fell for this guy without even touching his cock in real life.

The humiliation on the days I masturbated to the pictures of Aiden's cock was the worst. I've never admitted to anyone, but I had a crush on a guy friend in high school and we shared a weird drunken night together where we sucked each other off. Neither of us spoke about it again and we drifted apart as friends, but occasionally over the years I've thought about him and beat off to the memory of that night. Emily wouldn't care since she's admitted she's on the bisexual spectrum, but I've never had the guts to tell her about my past. The thought of Emily and Aiden together tormented me because it sickened me, and yet it turned me on.

When Emily went to work that night and I opened the app, it wasn't only sexting and pictures. My eyes widened and I had to look away from the screen for a moment when I saw them talking about meeting in person...tomorrow. I had a brief insane thought that maybe I read it wrong, but when I turned back to the monitor, it was there in black and white.

Aiden said he'd leave his door unlocked and gave Emily instructions to come inside when she arrived. He wanted her to take off all her clothes and set them on a side table. Then he told her to go to the living room and stand in a display position, naked, so he could "inspect" her. Inspect her? What in the hell does that even mean? He included a picture from a BDSM website of the position he wanted her to stand in so she could practice.

My cock sprung to life, hard as a rock, when I thought about Aiden fucking Emily in real life. I slid it out of my pants and rubbed it while I kept repeating in my head that I couldn't believe she would cheat on me. The idea had me stroking harder and faster. I had seen enough pictures of Aiden naked to have a good mental image of him plowing into Emily. When I thought about Emily being inspected and then Aiden forcing her on her knees while he shoved his cock down her throat, I moaned and climaxed hard. Four shots of cum hit my shirt before I was done.

I milked the last bit of cum out while I finished reading their messages. They ended with Aiden giving Emily his address and they agreed on a meeting time. My head still spun from the orgasm, and my hands shook when I pulled my phone out to enter the address into my GPS mapping program. I was breathless and my fingers tingled when I realized they were meeting during my lunch break.

Was she really going to do this?

CHAPTER

THREE

EMILY

I was an emotional wreck on that first visit with Aiden. He messaged me the night before and told me to strip naked when I got to his apartment. I didn't knock, but called out when I walked in.

"I'm here, Sir, and doing what you instructed."

I got no response and I didn't expect one. A table next to the door held mail and keys and I was shaking like a leaf as I removed my clothes. The sundress I wore slid off easily, which saved some hassle. My hands trembled badly, and I had problems folding the dress, but eventually got it halfway decent and laid it on the small table. He said his living room was through the entryway to the right, and my bare feet were silent on the carpet.

His apartment wasn't fancy, but the complex he lived in was well-maintained for an older building. The duplex had a second floor, and was an enormous apartment for one guy. Did he have a roommate? I knew so little I know about Aiden, which made what I was doing sound stupid. How could I only know a person for a couple of weeks and yet be this addicted to him and the control he offered? I should have realized that as soon as I found out he lived close, a meeting in person was inevitable.

Aiden wasn't in the living room and I stood in the middle, attempting the pose in the picture he sent me. I stood there with my legs spread and my hands raised, touching the back of my head. He wanted to inspect me, and the pose was for that purpose. The room wasn't cool, but my body continued to tremble and my nipples puckered. With no visible clock, I didn't know how much time passed. It felt like a couple of minutes before he entered the room.

Aiden was more attractive in person than in his pictures. I would estimate he was in his early 50s, with short silver hair and a clean-shaven jaw. His chin had a tiny dimple in it that I wanted to kiss. He was about six feet tall, and only wore black basketball shorts. He had a tiny bit of a belly, but otherwise was in good shape for a guy his age. I wouldn't toss him out of bed for eating cookies, that's for sure.

"Hello, Emily."

A tingle ran down my spine when he said my name, and I shook harder. He circled me slowly and visually inspected every inch of my body while I yearned for his approval. Never one to work out much, I was soft but still on the slender side of average, with generously sized breasts that age hadn't taken a toll on yet. I joked with Nate that he had a few more years to enjoy them being perky, but he swore he would love them well into old age, no matter what. According to him, there were no bad boobies.

The longer Aiden didn't speak, the more nervous I became. I attempted to hold back my trembling, and my teeth almost chattered. No one had ever examined me so thoroughly. I flushed and was desperate to squirm or hide under a blanket. Aiden said the purpose of the inspection was to inspect what was his, what he owned. He needed to make sure I took care of myself and it reminded me I gave myself to him completely.

This was worse than baring my soul during our online chats, especially because I tried not to fidget. He didn't specifically say I'd get punished if I moved, but he wanted me in this pose, so changing positions without permission seemed unwise. When the room spun, I gasped and inhaled sharply, not realizing I'd been holding my breath.

Aiden cried out when I wobbled. "Oh, shit. Emily!"

He scooped me up, carried me over to the couch, sitting down with me cuddled in his lap.

"Oh, you poor thing. You're shivering."

He pulled me into him and I laid my head on his shoulder with a sigh. When he kissed my forehead as if I was a child and rubbed my arm soothingly, I tucked my head down and smiled. This wasn't how I envisioned being in his arms for the first time, but seeing this side of Aiden was reassuring. Online he was always so forceful with me. I thought I wanted that, but meeting someone for the first time while also being naked was a bit much.

After a few minutes, the shaking stopped. I relaxed and noticed more things about Aiden. A faint whiff of leather surrounded him as if he recently wore a leather jacket, and it was pleasant. Bringing my hand up to touch the dimple in his chin, I could tell he shaved recently. My pussy pulsed with the thought that he might have shaved just for me.

He smiled down at me and pretended to bite my finger. I giggled and moved my hand to his neck, lightly stroking it. His skin was soft, like he just got out of the shower and dried off, though there was no moisture on his skin.

Seeing that I felt better, Aiden spoke.

"Emily, I'm really sorry. I didn't realize you were so nervous. You only seemed excited."

I murmured, "I'm okay," and he held me tighter.

"No, I'm supposed to take care of you. Don't make excuses for my mistakes."

I poked him in the gut. "Hey, everyone makes mistakes sometimes."

Aiden gave a wry grin before he replied. "Yes, ten minutes with me and you almost pass out. I'm clearly not perfect."

I tipped my head up, hoping for a kiss, and stated, "Neither am I, Sir. We can be imperfect together."

When he looked down at me and could tell how serious I was, he claimed what I offered and kissed me softly. What started out as simple exploration turned heated quickly. He tasted like cinnamon, and I brought my arms around his neck to push myself deeper into the kiss. Our tongues dueled and my pussy became wet when his cock hardened under his shorts. He broke off the kiss right as I thought to shift and straddle him so I could grind against him.

"Okay, enough of that. Time to teach you to be a real sub."

He forced me off his lap and slapped my ass when I stood up. His grin and twinkle in his eye told me he enjoyed joking around with me.

I gave him a jaunty, half-mocking, "Yes, Sir," and the grin turned fierce.

"Doll, don't tempt me. You reminded me you're just learning so we're going to take this slow."

My brain buzzed at his words. It tempted me to push him and see what would happen if we sped up the training, but the sane part of me recognized caution was smart. Plus, my wet pussy was down for whatever happened, and as long as today ended with his cock inside of me, I'd be ecstatic.

"So, Doll, kneel for me."

My pulse sped up and I became breathless in a good way while I sank to my knees in front of him and rested my hands lightly on my thighs. I kept my eyes downcast, wishing I had the guts to peek up at him, but I wanted to prove that I was worthy of training.

Aiden moved in front of me. His shorts slid to the floor and he kicked them aside.

He hoarsely stated, "Doll, I want you to show me how well you can suck cock."

I glanced up at his words and he moved forward. His thick, erect cock jutted towards my face. I didn't respond verbally, but opened my mouth to signal my willingness to serve. He slipped the tip of his cock between my lips and I had to open my mouth further when he pushed in. His groans as my lips clamped around his shaft made me wetter. I reached a hand up to help guide his cock and he didn't complain. He let his hands drop from his rod and rest against the sides of his legs while he concentrated on moving his hips to fuck my mouth.

His saltiness on my tongue had me humming around his cock in approval. He was quite the mouthful since he's thicker than Nate, but I could take Aiden in fully. He started out slow, but once he realized I could take his full length, he sped up until he fucked me at a brisk pace.

He moaned every time my lips reached the base of his shaft, and since he didn't tell me to rub my clit, the sense of being used solely for his pleasure was erotic. My inner thigh was damp and my pussy ached for his cock. I hoped he planned to fuck me soon. As I imagined his cock sliding into my wet hole, I became disoriented by the realization that he might come in my mouth without fucking me. It was his choice, not mine. I felt an odd fluttery feeling in my belly and my thoughts went fuzzy. I forgot what I was doing and when he shoved his cock into my mouth again, I made a small choking sound and my gag reflex kicked in.

Fuck. That cleared the fog from my brain, and I concentrated on my task. I'm supposed to prove I can give amazing blowjobs. My slight gagging noise spurred Aiden on to plow into my mouth faster. He moved his hands to the back of my head to force me to hold him deep in my throat for a few seconds before letting me breathe. I stroked him with my hand and played with his balls. When they tightened against my fingers and his member throbbed in my mouth, I knew he was close to his climax. I sucked harder, hoping he'd come and not caring any longer if it meant I didn't get his cock inside me, but he pulled out with a loud groan.

"Good girl," he panted while he patted me on the head. "Now stand up."

I tried to rise gracefully, but stumbled, and Aiden gripped my arm to help me. He put his hand on my elbow and led me towards the hallway to what I assumed was a bedroom.

Halfway down the hall, I heard him mumble, "fuck it," right before he shoved my shoulder blades towards the wall. I caught myself with my hands and leaned in close to the wall. He spread my legs and used his hands to wedge my pussy open as he thrusted his cock inside of me. Once he was fully in, he rammed against me hard, forcing my breasts to squish against the wall. He grabbed both of my wrists, bringing my arms above my head, and secured them both with one hand. The other newly freed hand pressed against my shoulder, pinning me as he fucked me roughly.

"Oh, my god," I moaned out as my body ignited. I panted and started grinding my ass and cunt against him, desperate to feel his shaft as deep as he could go. I was barely coherent, and all I knew was that I needed to come. Every thrust into me sent tingles of delight throughout my entire body.

Aiden's harsh demand cut through the silence as our bodies slapped together. "Do you like it hard like this, slut?"

Oh god, no one has ever called me a slut before in person and it was so goddamn arousing. I moaned out, "Yes, Sir."

Aiden gave several sharp thrusts and replied, "Good, slut."

He hammered into me and groaned while I chanted out, "fuck me" repeatedly.

This was better than I thought it would be. Being shoved up against the wall and used hit a good kink and I could feel my orgasm getting close. As Aiden slammed into me, my nipples scraped against the textured plaster on the wall and the pleasure shot straight to my clit. My body quivered as I spiraled higher and higher.

My moan intensified to a sharp peak as my pussy spasmed and clenched. I trembled and rocked as my entire body shuddered and I came so hard I saw stars. He continued to fuck me, and it seemed like the climax was never-ending as I rode the waves of ecstasy.

As I finally came down from my peak, Aiden growled and load after load of his hot cum spurted inside me, coating the walls of my pussy. He flexed and shuddered before pulling out and leaned against me.

Holy fuck, that was amazing. I wanted to tell him how fabulous it was, but no words formed. Aiden and I stumbled together down the hall and he led me into a bedroom with a king-sized bed and we collapsed on top of the comforter together.

Expecting to be done, I pulled myself up towards the pillows on my stomach and squeaked in surprise when he grabbed my hips and flipped me over.

"I'm not done with you yet, slut." He growled.

My mind was a puddle, but I didn't complain as he pushed open my legs and bent his head down to taste me. His tongue on my sensitive bud made me gasp and arch my back, driving his tongue further between my pussy lips. He continued to lick and suck, swirling his tongue around my clit while I moaned and thrashed under him. When he pressed a finger inside of me, I practically screamed out as I quickly peaked.

"Oh, my god!"

My body spasmed and a splash of wetness leaked from my pussy as Aiden furiously licked to clean me up. As the tension drained from my body, he crawled up the bed and pulled me into his embrace. Before I closed my eyes and fell asleep, he questioned me. "How long before you have to go home?"

Oh fuck. I woke up at the mention of home. "Uh, what time is it?"

When he told me the time, I relaxed again. There was at least another hour before I had to leave. I mumbled how long I had as my eyes drifted shut. I heard him pressing buttons on an alarm clock, and my last thought before I passed out was how nice it was for him to think about that and that it was about time someone licked my pussy.

NATE

I got to Aiden's apartment complex about 10 minutes before Emily did. I drove around the block once, getting the lay of the land before I parked down the street where I could get a clear visual of anyone who walked up to his front door. His unit was conveniently in a secluded part of the complex and I scrunched down in my seat in case Emily passed by the car and noticed me. Luckily, our car is generic and we continually lose it in parking lots because it looked the same as everyone else's.

When Emily arrived, she parked in a visitor parking spot, and I could tell she was nervous when she got out of her car. She glanced around the parking lot and picked at her beautiful pink sundress. God, I always loved that dress on her. It left her shoulders bare and always made me want to kiss her neck and nibble my way down her arm. Why did she have to wear that dress today? I fixated on her choice of clothing for a moment, as if it really mattered. Her wearing my favorite dress somehow compounded the cheating in my mind. It's became even more personal.

She entered the apartment, and I waited in the car for exactly seven minutes before getting out. It was the longest seven minutes of my life. I vacillated between feeling anguished and horny, as I imagined Aiden fucking Emily as soon as she opened the front door. I reminded myself that Aiden wanted her to strip and go to the living room in his message. That would take a few minutes.

When I figured Emily had enough time to go to the living room and get into position, I strolled across the parking lot with a confidence I didn't feel since I didn't want to look suspicious. Instead of walking to his front door, I cut around the building and once I'm out of view from the street, I slowed down and skulked.

I crept up to a window and at first I saw nothing except a plain living room with no people, but then I realized Emily and Aiden were on the couch. She was in his arms being held tenderly while he stroked her arm. *Oh, fuck.* I didn't expect a loving scene.

My throat tightened up, and spots flashed before my eyes as I became dizzy and nauseated. When my lungs constricted and it got harder to breathe, I knew I needed to get out of there immediately. I couldn't risk passing out on his lawn. I stumbled to my car, not caring who saw me this time, and sat in the driver's seat, gripped the wheel and stared out at nothing. My thoughts spun as I totally focused inward, not paying attention to my surroundings.

I had no words to process how I was feeling, and I sat in the car for another ten minutes before I had the mental energy to drive back to work.

What in the hell was I going to do now?

CHAPTER
FOUR

Over the last month of visiting Aiden twice a week, Nate's and my sex life has oddly improved and I can now appreciate Nate's softness. I don't need to be fucked roughly all the time, and Aiden is fulfilling that need. The slow, sensual sex with Nate is great again.

The other change is that Nate wants sex more often, and I haven't figured out why. It's almost like he smells sex on me, despite me taking a shower every time I come home from Aiden's. Invariably, those are the nights he wants sex. The first time I went along with him out of guilt, assuming I wouldn't enjoy it. I had already come super hard earlier with Aiden, so the second powerful orgasm of the day left me speechless for a few minutes.

While I lay there panting and unable to speak, I glanced over at Nate and the smug expression on his face spoke volumes. He was quite pleased with himself. When he approached me again a few days later, I eagerly followed him into the bedroom. I'm not one to turn down multiple orgasms, even if they are several hours apart.

Which brings us to today, another Saturday morning where we wake up, he gets his weekly blowjob, and now he's making me breakfast.

The last few weekends he's made me a special breakfast and last night on the way home from work, he stopped at the store to pick up supplies and told me it was for a surprise.

He makes me sit in the chair with my back towards the kitchen and doesn't let me turn around to watch. My stomach rumbles from the smell of bacon, which tells me breakfast is going to be delicious. I don't care what else he serves, bacon will elevate it to amazing.

I tease him a little. "I know you're making bacon, you can't hide it."

Nate laughs before replying. "Yes, but you don't know what else."

"Does it matter? Let me watch. You know I love watching you cook in your bacon apron."

I gave him an apron as a joke Christmas gift several years ago, along with other nicer presents. It's green and patterned with tiny cartoon strips of bacon, and it ended up being one of his most used gifts. It saved him from many painful chest grease splatters while frying bacon for me while he had no shirt on.

He only replies with an "uh-huh," and I pout for a moment before realizing it's pointless since my back is to him and he can't see me being cute. I tilt my head to the side and slowly attempt to peek over my shoulder at him without him noticing.

"Emily." His low, dominant tone stops me.

"Fine! I'm just curious."

His joking tone returns. "Babe, just sit there and be a good girl."

Obviously my attempts to be adorable and sassy aren't working, but his use of 'good girl' gives me an unexpected flush. Guess Aiden's training also works when other people say it as well. This is the first time Nate has called me a good girl since I started my affair. He only used to do it when he was teasing me, and life hasn't been too merry around our house in a long time. I've been enjoying the return of my happy-go-lucky husband these last few weeks, along with the revitalization of our sex life.

When he sets a plate in front of me with eggs Benedict and bacon, I clap and bounce with giddiness in my chair before leaning in to sniff appreciatively.

"You know the way to my heart." I beam a smile at him as he sits down with his own plate and we both dig in.

I chew in silence as he chatters about his plans for the day. He wants to build me a flower bed for another variety of rose I want, and he's talking about dimensions and other plants to put next to the roses. The contrast between now and a few months ago hits me. This is the man I fell in love with. He has a zest for life and is talkative and planning for the future.

I can't help but wonder if he'd been like this a few months ago, would I have said no to Aiden? I can't wish away everything that has happened with Aiden. It's been an amazing experience and I've grown to love him, but the dual life is taxing. The problem is that I can't stop with him. I'm so addicted to the man it's pathetic and if Nate ever finds out, I don't know what I would do.

Before this, I didn't know it was possible for me to love two people at the same time, but loving both of them somehow makes what I'm doing okay in my mind. I might have had some initial guilt, but once genuine feelings developed with Aiden, the continual tightness in my chest whenever I thought about what I was doing eased. What's that saying? You can't pick who you love? I didn't choose to love two men, though I know I also didn't guard against it.

The main issue is that I didn't understand the connection between a dominant and a submissive back then. Since I was new to BDSM, I'd never experienced such a strong, instantaneous bond with someone. I didn't know it could lead to love. Aiden and I haven't said we loved each other, and the one time I tried to tell him he cut me off and told me not to say what I was about to say yet. He told me that too many times submissives say, "I love you," but don't recognize the difference between love and the dominant and submissive bond because of the intense emotions that come out in play.

I appreciated how he didn't tell me I couldn't love him, but that instead he only wanted me to wait to make sure. By now I'm positive, but I'm following orders to give it more time. Next time I express my feelings, I don't want my Sir to stop me. Saying you love someone should have the proper weight when it's spoken and I'll know when the time is right.

But none of this helps me with Nate, and like this morning, I'm torn by the duality of everything. When I blow out my birthday candles this year, my wish is going to be that I can somehow keep them both.

~

NATE

I need to get over the sense of illicitness whenever I make love with Emily on the days she's been with Aiden. It seems dirty to get aroused and come while watching them fuck, and then not be able to keep my hands off her later that night. Being the one racked with guilt while making love with my adulterous wife is laughable.

What's even more ludicrous is that her cheating revived our relationship. Emily's increased sexual confidence is alluring, and she has an inner glow that was missing for a long time. She's like the cat that ate the canary and is content and happy. She reminds me of the younger Emily who drew me in with her joyous, infectious giggle and sparkling eyes. Emily is an introvert and had zero clue how many guys were interested in her, but I was the lucky one she clicked with.

I want to dote on this new Emily and please her. She mentioned a rose variety called Love & Peace that she admired for its multicolored yellow and pink petals, and my brain immediately started plotting where to put in another flower bed. The last few Saturdays I've started making her special breakfasts, as well. I know part of me probably wants to remind her how wonderful I am, but this urge to satisfy her every desire is hard to ignore.

Today I made her eggs Benedict with a side of bacon, and she's especially adorable as she grins at me while I talk about my Saturday plans. She's mostly silent and at one point seems lost in thought, and I can't help but wonder if she's daydreaming about Aiden. Gazing at a distracted Emily, my head aches and my heart pounds. My eyes grow wet and my throat thickens, but luckily she doesn't notice any of this. I look away and blink rapidly to avoid crying, and realize that I can't continue like this much longer. She's going to need to make a choice.

CHAPTER
FIVE

EMILY

Saturday night, Nate and I snuggle on the couch to watch Deadpool for what's got to be the 11th time when he pauses the movie and studies me. Uh, what's this? When does he interrupt a movie? He's the type who will get up and go to the bathroom and leave a show running, which prompts me to grab the remote and hit pause because I don't want him to miss anything. Though the 11th time through any movie, I'd probably let it run. So him pausing it is even more odd.

Nate is staring at the wall next to the TV and doesn't speak for a moment. I want to ask him what's up, but hold back. If this were Aiden on the couch with me, I wouldn't hesitate to ask what was wrong, but something is off with Nate and I wait for him to speak.

"Emily, we need to talk."

As soon as he speaks, my stomach drops and I have difficulty breathing. *Oh fuck, he knows.* The room spins for a moment and there's a sour taste in my mouth. Maybe I'm wrong and it's something else?

"I know about Aiden."

I close my eyes, flop back on the couch, and an unexpected release of tension washes over me. I don't know how he found out, but I know something is about to change.

"You must decide, Emily. Which one of us do you want?"

Nate's voice is sad when he asks, as if he knows the choice won't be him. His tone, more than anything else, punches me in the gut. What the fuck have I been doing? I love this man deeply, and his obvious hurt devastates me. My hands curl and my fingernails cut into my palms. I want to ball up and cry that it's come to this, but I still can't make a choice. I love them both and want things to stay the same. When I don't immediately respond, Nate tries again.

"Emily, I need to know."

I keep my eyes closed for a moment and rub the middle of my forehead. When I glance at Nate, he's looking at me, and I open my mouth to answer him, but shut it again. I'm at a loss for words. How do you tell your husband that you also love another man?

The sinking feeling in my stomach doesn't go away, and a flood of guilt hits me. I need to tell him the truth, and find out if what I truly want is possible.

"Nate, I can't make a choice. Can I have you both?"

~

NATE

I finally get up the guts to confront Emily and her response sucker punches me in the gut. Can she have us both? My mind races through several scenarios with that idea. I'm uneasy with anything my mind conjures up and flustered at the thought of either decision. If I say no, will she choose him? If she's at the point where she can't decide, haven't I already lost her? I don't know if she'll ever be happy with me again if I say no.

The unbidden thought of the multiple orgasms I've had jerking off to Emily and Aiden together makes my head spin. My cheeks burn and I can't look at Emily. I angle my body away from her as I think. Could an open relationship like this work? Would I even still find it hot if you remove the cheating aspect? There are too many unknown factors, and I don't want to admit how turned on this makes me.

But Emily is expecting an answer. My stomach aches and I'm flushed when I turn to her and respond.

"I'm willing to try."

The End

CONTROLLING EMILY

AN MMF ROMANTIC BDSM EROTICA SERIES

CHAPTER

ONE

EMILY

Last night Nate told me he'll try an open relationship to let me stay with Aiden, and my head is still spinning when I wake up the next morning, but remembering the conversation floods me with warmth and devotion to my husband. God, I really love him and I want to make things right.

We barely talked after the decision and went to bed early, each of us with our own thoughts. I'm not sure how this will work. He didn't say how he found out about Aiden, so he might not know how often I visit him. There are so many details Nate and I need to discuss, but my mind blanked when he agreed. Later, when the shock wore off, tons of questions popped up and sleep eluded me.

When Nate gets up early on Sunday to take his mom to church, I pretend to be asleep. I'm not ready to talk to him yet. I need more time to think about what to say. My stomach is tense when he leaves the bedroom and I'm hoping when we have our discussion later, he'll ask questions I can specifically answer without volunteering too much other information.

A few minutes later, the faint grind of the automatic garage door tells me Nate left. I relax in bed, breathing easier, and pick up my phone, intending to message Aiden to give him the exciting news. I pause before opening the app. Shit, what if Aiden doesn't think this is good? Some guys like to cuckold other men, and I don't know what motivated Aiden to start our relationship. Will he still want me if we're not a secret?

I stew over what to do and the longer I waver between my choices, the worse it gets. My heart races and my palms are sweaty when I decide to go for it. I can't handle worrying about Aiden on top of my upcoming conversation with Nate. Plus, if Aiden breaks it off with me now that he's not cuckolding my husband, it will change everything. I wipe my hands on the sheets and type out my message.

EMILY

Sir, I have something to tell you.

After hitting send, I don't wait for a reply and continue on.

Nate found out about us and agreed I can keep seeing you. Does this change anything?

I squirm after I finish the text and toss my cellphone across the bed like it's a hot potato so I can't stare at the app to see if Aiden is responding. There's no turning back now. A pit in my stomach opens up and I practice deep breathing with my eyes closed to calm myself. I inhale to the count of four, and then exhale for four. I'm about to repeat it, but jolt when a muffled ping indicates I have a text. Oh fuck, that was fast.

I sit up and reach for the phone. Aiden's message pops up when I swipe the screen on.

AIDEN

Well, Doll, this seems like a good deal. Don't you think?

Squealing at his response, I giggle at myself and reply with, "Yes, Sir," while warmth floods my body. I set the phone next to me and flop on my back to stare at the ceiling. My thoughts race and it's all a jumble in my head, but the tingle from my pussy is obvious. Running my hand up under my nightgown, I tease my nipples while contemplating this new reality. How crazy would it be if I could one day openly tell Nate I was in love with both of them and he'd be okay with it?

Oooh, or what if I someday fucked them at the same time? My head whirls faster at the thought of both of them at my breasts. It's only a fantasy, but what woman wouldn't want to be the meat in that sandwich when she loves two men?

Using both hands to pull on my nipples, I imagine my fingers are their mouths. I snake one hand down my stomach, imagining Aiden kissing down the length of me. When I spread my legs and run my fingertips over my pussy, I'm dripping wet. Rubbing soft circles around my clit, my loud moans fill the room and I wish Aiden's tongue was swirling between my folds instead.

I need more, so I reach into my nightstand and pull out my newest vibrator. It's slender with a slight curve that reminds me of Aiden's cock. I press the button on and cycle through the vibration selections until I find my favorite alternating long and short buzz. Sliding it in, I giggle when the tip hits a sensitive part, causing pleasure to rocket through my core—yeah, not the same as any cock.

When my second hand joins the first one between my legs, I spear the vibrating toy in and out of my twat, while using the fingers of the other hand to massage my swollen clit. Playing with myself feels better than usual this morning, and the two-man daydream really revs my engine. When the idea of Aiden's cock in my ass and Nate fucking my pussy pops into my head, I buck against the vibrator to force it further inside. Double stuffing was never a big fantasy of mine. It sounded too complicated and messy. But now that I have two men in my life, the idea of both of them inside me at the same time gives me a naughty zing.

I continue to imagine both of them pressing inside me and the speed of my fingers picks up. I'm furiously rubbing my clit and edging close to my orgasm. It's impossible to think, and all I can do is pump the toy into my pussy and fuck myself hard. I tense up as the ecstasy coils through my body. When the release finally comes, I cry out and convulse while a current of energy emanates from my core all the way to my toes and fingertips. Waves of pleasure wash over me and I ride the vibrator until I come down from the peak and my pussy is too sensitive to continue.

All my tension drains and I pull out the toy and drop it on Nate's side of the bed. My brain is fuzzy from how hard I came, and my shitty night of sleep catches up to me as I yawn and tuck the surrounding covers underneath my sides like a cocoon. I should get up and clean the vibrator and put it away, but my groggy brain decides I'll do it after a catnap.

~

NATE

I'm too distracted this morning to enjoy church. I'm not religious in the slightest, but I normally find peace as I relax and clear my mind. After I explained what I do to get through the service, Emily started to joke and call it my weekly meditation, and she's not wrong. I like singing the hymns, but otherwise I use the time to commune with my inner self instead of God.

Today I can't stop thinking about Emily and wondering how her continuing to fuck Aiden will work. I have some pretty strict requests in mind that I'm not sure she'll like. This won't be an Emily free-for-all sex party with her just coming and going as she pleases. I'm still her husband and I want her dedicated to our marriage and not using this as a slow transition to leave me.

A little devil pops up on my shoulder and whispers in my ear. But what if she likes Aiden better? My stomach clenches and I'm sick at the thought. If that were the case, she wouldn't have asked to have us both, right? I hold firm to my conviction that she would have said she wanted a divorce if she really wanted to be with Aiden, and I brush aside the devil whenever he tries to say otherwise. I wish I could find my normal peace and relaxation. Being in church is only making me think more about the unusual arrangement I agreed to. I can never tell my mother. She'd probably send a clergy member to my house to discuss our life choices.

Halfway through the service, my mom leans over and whispers in my ear.

"Nate, I'm not feeling well. Let's go."

She didn't have to say it twice. I slip our hymnals into the storage pocket on the pew in front of us, and my mother and I slink out of the chapel as quietly as we can. As I drive, my mom rattles on about her indigestion causing her lack of sleep. When we get to her house, I help her inside and see that she's settled into her favorite recliner with a snack and some juice before heading out. She's already nodding off when I close the front door. It hurts to watch her age, but I'm grateful for all this time I've had with her after my dad passed. At some point I'm going to need to look at assisted living facilities for her, but thankfully we're not there yet.

The drive home is a blur as I focus on my problem with Emily. She won't be expecting me back this early and my chest tightens when I realize she could be on the phone making plans with Aiden. My stomach churns the entire drive, and when I pull into the garage, I have to sit in the car for a few minutes because I'm dizzy. I try the deep breathing exercises that Emily taught me to calm myself; Inhaling for the count of four, exhaling for four, and then repeating.

Once I have the spinning under control, I enter the house as quietly as I can. I have an odd desire to catch her in the act of whatever she's doing and hope she didn't hear the garage door open. She's not in the office and when I peek into the bedroom, she's a tight little ball, all snuggly in the comforter, on her side of the bed. The immediate surge of relief makes my knees weak. God, I thought she was rushing off to talk to Aiden and instead she fell back asleep.

As I go to leave, I spot her vibrator on my side. Oh, fuck. Was she having phone sex and fucked herself into a stupor? I stumble into the living room and collapse on the couch. I can't get the picture of her vibrator out of my mind and my cock hardens as I imagine her sliding it into her tight pussy while panting in Aiden's ear. Rubbing myself through my church slacks, I can tell I need more than pressure through cloth.

I'm throbbing as I pull my rod out, and it's already glistening with pre-cum. I use the moisture as lubrication and hum from the pleasure as

I stroke myself. A wave of self-loathing washes over me as I continue to imagine Emily using her toy with Aiden, and instead of turning me off, I rub harder. Fuck, why is thinking of them together so hot?

The image of Aiden's cock pops into my head once again, and I realize I want to watch him press into her pussy in real life. I know exactly how it looks as her cave entrance stretches and molds around the tip of a cock, but I hunger for a closeup view of seeing that from another angle. I want Emily on her hands and knees while Aiden fucks her from behind so I can move in front of her and watch the expressions change on her face while he plows into her. That's a view I've never seen, and imagining her bliss skyrockets me over the edge.

I climax so hard I see stars as cum splatters on my dark blue dress shirt. Tingles of pleasure course through me as I milk the last few drops from my cock. This outfit will need a good washing, so I don't worry about getting stains all over my pants. I'm shivering as I come down from the intense peak and I slip my softening member back into the slacks before stretching out on my side on the cushions. Snagging a blanket from the back of the couch, I lump it up and tuck it under my head as a pillow. I yawn and my eyes drift closed as I think about the upcoming conversation with Emily. I'm sure the talk will go better if I catch a quick catnap.

~

AIDEN

I sit on the sofa in my living room and stare at my phone in shock after Emily's text message that her husband knows, and my chest feels lighter. I'm instantly hard and throbbing. Whenever I chat with Emily, I'm aroused and firm, but this is different. I'm energized, and I pull my cock from my sweatpants so I can rub it slowly while my thoughts race about the future. Emily is an amazing sub, eager to learn and wanting to please, but sneaking around behind her husband's back never felt right. Don't get me wrong, I'm no saint and I've had plenty of one-night stands with married women, but I've never taken on a sub whose spouse didn't agree beforehand.

It's cliche, but there's something about Emily that's unique. I've never fallen this completely for any of my past subs, but she hooked me before she ever called me Sir. The weeks we spent getting to know each other online, I could tell she was smart, funny, thoughtful, and had zero clue she was submissive. My dominant side reacted to her during our first conversation, but I held myself in check. I enjoyed the flirting, and since she was married I expected nothing else. The night her little elf offered herself to me in the online game rocked my world and I gave in to temptation.

Getting to know the real life Emily has been a rollercoaster. She's so sweet and giving, but I have to keep reminding myself she's not mine beyond her submission and our short afternoons together. The day she almost told me she loved me, I felt like I had won the lottery but later that night realized it was a trick prize I can't cash in. I've had to erect an emotional barrier between us because I couldn't be all in while she was sneaking around on her husband. This could end at any moment if he found out, and while Emily is brilliant, I've also noticed she is a little careless and easily distracted. She didn't say how Nate found out, but it wouldn't surprise me if she accidentally left evidence out for him to find.

I continue to rub myself with long caresses, firmly gripping the base and teasing myself all the way to the tip. A tingling pleasure runs through me as I envision it's Emily going down on me instead of my hand. I pause and swirl my fingertips on the underside of the head, as Emily likes to do with her tongue because she knows it drives me wild. Since this is her first BDSM relationship, I'm positive she isn't fully aware of the power she has over me yet, and her willing submission makes me ache. I groan and speed up my stroking as I imagine how she looks on her knees while I use her mouth.

Unbidden, the thought of Nate pops into my head. Emily showed me family photos of them and he's an attractive guy. With one of my past subs, we made videos for her husband, and knowing he was watching me fuck his wife, or her on her knees sucking my cock, gave the encounter an extra zing. I liked to put on a show for him, and I always came harder imagining his reaction.

Would Nate ever want that? I moan as I imagine Nate watching a video of me fucking Emily. I'm spurred to greater heights and I reach down with my other hand and massage my balls while still focusing on my shaft with the first. The pressure mounts and I'm lost in my fantasy of Nate and Emily when I finally erupt. I shudder from the intense bliss as cum spurts onto my shirt. I milk my rod gently and drift in a pleasant sexual daze.

This new development of Nate knowing about us has me excited about the future. So many things could go wrong—I've been down this road before—but I can't stop the blossoming hope that maybe this time everything might be okay.

CHAPTER

TWO

NATE

My nap on the couch was longer than I intended, and I get up, stretch, and tiptoe into the bedroom to change out of my soiled trousers. Thinking Emily might still be asleep, I'm as quiet as possible when I open the door so I don't disturb her. The bed is empty, so I stop being careful and switch on the overhead light. I change out of my dirty church clothes, putting on jeans and a t-shirt, and go search for her. I'm refreshed after masturbating and the nap, and I'm ready to face a conversation with her head on. It's time to explain my requirements and see if she can live with them. But what happens if she refuses?

I assume she's in the office, and I pause in the hallway when I exit the bedroom and rub my forearms. My throat is dry and uncomfortable, and I opt to get some water before confronting her. I'm looking down at the floor as I walk, and already the tension is mounting in my shoulders. My relaxation from the nap was short-lived. God, I hope she agrees to my requests.

I don't notice her sitting at the kitchen table until I open the cupboard for a glass, and jump when she greets me.

"Hey, Nate." Her voice is subdued, and worry lines mar her forehead. I immediately want to rush over to her, engulf her in my arms, and take all her stress away, but we need to have a conversation first.

"Nate, I think we should talk."

Oh, thank God. My breath comes out with a whoosh when I answer. "Yes."

I fill my glass with water, and noticing she doesn't have a beverage, I bring her some as well. I sit down across from her and we sip in silence for a moment while looking at each other.

We finally both speak at the same time.

"I have some demands."

"How's this going to work?"

I laugh, and she does her adorable giggle. I can see the stress on her face drain away when we both start off with a lighthearted attitude from stumbling over each other.

Emily takes on a flirty tone and her eyes twinkle when she says, "Oh, demands?" Her sexy demeanor helps calm me and some of my tension loosens as my shoulders relax. Maybe this won't go badly after all?

I hate disappointing her, and if she reacts negatively once I explain my needs, I don't know what will happen. But I have to say it. I take a deep breath and press on.

"Yes, demands. I want to know every time you go over to his house. If I'm at work, text me."

Emily smiles and replies, "Okay."

"And I want you back by the time I get home. I want us to still have dinner together."

"Okay."

"And no weekend visits."

"Yep, understood." She grins after that one.

"And no bringing him to our house."

"Okay."

"And you're married to me, not him. I want to come first."

She nods eagerly, while saying, "Of course."

Emily's pleasant manner seems suspicious. Why is she happy-go-lucky and easily agreeing to everything? I pause while I mull over her attitude and she presses me.

"You have more?"

She's so damn cute sitting there, smiling, and waiting for me to give her more rules, but I've been avoiding the big one.

"And I want to meet him."

Her eyes widen, and she hesitates briefly before she responds. "You do?"

My heart pounds and a fluttery emptiness yawns in my stomach. I realize I shouldn't have prohibited them meeting here, or on the weekends. I WANT to see them together. I've been secretly watching them for weeks and I don't want to stop.

I grow hard at the thought of watching them fucking in person, and I'm glad the table hides my jeans. My reaction makes me meaner than I intend.

"Yes, I want to meet the man you've been cheating on me with."

Emily jerks as if I smacked her and the smile fades. Her voice is soft when she answers. "Okay—yes."

Wanting to soften the blow and bring back the happy Emily, I continue on.

"But I've changed my mind about no weekends and will allow him to come here. After I meet him, I think it'll be fine."

"Oh." She doesn't seem to know what to say, and I can't handle the distance between us anymore. I push my chair away from the table without standing up.

I'm gentle when I say, "Emily, come over here and get in my lap."

Whenever she's upset, she likes to sit on me and cuddle. She jumps up quickly and climbs into my lap, leaning her shoulder against my chest. She presses her butt against my hard-on, and her legs dangle to the side. She wiggles a little as she settles in and I almost groan. I'm pretty sure she knows exactly what she's doing. I bring my arms around her and she sighs.

She's quiet for a few minutes and I relax with her, trying to ignore how good her ass feels. When she sniffles, I realize she's crying.

"Nate, I'm so sorry. I didn't mean for any of this to happen. I love you so much."

Pulling her closer to me, I rock her gently, and give her little kisses on her head. I wasn't expecting an apology today, and now that I have one, I'm conflicted. I want to accept that she's sorry and move on, but I'm still unsettled and can't.

"I know, Emily. But it's going to take time."

I don't clarify, and she kisses my neck.

"I'll talk to Aiden. I'm sure he'll agree to meet."

I want to tell her that if he doesn't, I won't allow the arrangement, but I bite my tongue and stay silent. I'll cross that bridge if he declines the invite. When the conversation started, I wanted to make love to happy and teasing Emily, but vulnerable and loving Emily intensifies the urge. When she shifts in my lap again, this time I'm not able to hold back a tiny growl and I wonder if she ever sits in Aiden's lap and does this to him.

~

EMILY

When I climbed into Nate's lap, his erection surprised me. What was he thinking about that caused it? His listing of the rules made me wet, and I'm sure he didn't notice he was turning me on. He could have bent over me over the table and had his way with me by the time he finished, but he's clueless. I'm wearing sweatpants and an oversized t-shirt, and I can feel his hardness through the fleece. I wiggle against him to tempt him, but he doesn't take the bait. He's being so loving and as soon as I relax, I'm overwhelmed by what I've done to him.

I don't know what the fuck I was thinking when I started up with Aiden. Looking back on it, it seems like temporary insanity. But it's too late now since my feelings for him have deepened and I can't wish any of this away. I just hope we can somehow make it work. I'm amazingly lucky that Nate is letting me explore this with Aiden, and I vow to myself that I'll follow Nate's rules and pay attention to his emotional needs and communicate better.

Thinking about the hurt I'm causing Nate makes me cry, and I can't hold back my sniffles. I try to apologize, knowing that whatever I say will never be enough. I'm going to have to just show him in little ways every day how much he still means to me.

His cock feels so good against my ass, and I'm an odd mixture of horny and upset. I want Nate to fuck me to prove that he still wants me, but that isn't his way. I shift against him again, yearning for the closeness that comes with him buried inside me. When he growls, I smile against his chest.

I kiss his neck some more and nibble on his earlobe, my breath tickling him, and whisper, "Take me to the bedroom."

He lowers his head and brushes his lips against mine before giving me a teasing, "Maybe."

I shift my butt against him, making me needier, and kiss him hard. "You sure about that maybe?"

Nate bucks up and forces me to stand, and I giggle, assuming I am about to get what I want. He stands up too, but instead of grabbing my hand to lead me out of the kitchen, he pushes me against the counter, bends me over it, and dry humps me. Well now... this is a delightful surprise. I whimper and press back against him, wishing the barrier of clothing would magically poof into nothingness.

He doesn't spend too long tormenting me before he stops. "Yes, let's go to the bedroom."

My heart skips a beat, and I smile at him and lead the way. I'm a quivering bundle of desire by the time we get in the room, and I pull off my shirt and turn towards him, pressing my breasts together and playing with my nipples while he strips. When he's naked, he pushes me back onto the bed and I laugh when I bounce a little. I hadn't removed my sweatpants yet, and I intend to do so and then crawl up to the pillows, but he hooks his fingers in the waistband and pulls them off, taking my panties down at the same time.

I've still got my socks on, and today I wore a brand new black and white striped pair that has a panda face on the toes. He hasn't seen them before and he lifts up one foot to examine it closer and I wiggle my toes at him. He laughs as he removes them. When he tries to tickle both my bare feet at the same time, I squeal and move them away from his hand, which conveniently spreads my legs for him.

He curves his hands behind my knees and drags me towards the end of the bed until my ass is at the edge, and I gasp when he presses my thighs open as far as they will go. Holy shit, this is hot. It's been a while since he fucked me like this, and as I glance up at the overhead light, I realize it's on and I'm spread out in all my glory. I flush at how wanton I probably look, and close my eyes in embarrassment.

Nate fingers me, and I sigh as he glides around my clit in soft circles. *Fuuuuck, this is perfect.* I'm still tender from coming earlier when I played hard with my sex toy and Nate's softness is a welcome relief. Since my eyes are closed, I don't realize that Nate dropped to his knees until his breath is on my inner thigh. *Oh fuck. Is he really doing this?* Last time I thought he was going to, he didn't, so I tell myself to calm down. When he spreads my pussy lips and dips his head forward, I gasp out, "Oh, god Nate, please."

He gives me his corny, favorite line from *The Princess Bride*, "As you wish," and I don't have time to laugh like I normally do because I'm too busy gasping from his tongue flicking against my clit. When he increases pressure and does a few long licks up my entire slit, I writhe and toss my head. Shit, I've missed this. Caressing my breasts while he licks my pussy, I gently tweak my nipples and press my snatch up towards his face, trying to grind against him.

I squeal out when he presses a few fingers inside me and continues to flick at my pearl with his tongue. My legs quiver and the mounting ecstasy from my core tells me I'm going to come soon.

I'm breathing harshly and when he stops and pulls away, I cry out. "Oh, god, don't stop."

Nate only laughs softly as he grabs under my thighs to hold my legs up and fits the tip of his cock against my slippery entrance. He almost purrs as he presses in.

"Oooh!" I'm very vocal as my pussy stretches and molds against him and I chant for him to fuck me. He pauses at my words and I realize that is something I'm more likely to say to Aiden, but I'm beyond caring. When Nate speeds up and pounds into me roughly, I know my request for him to fuck me worked, and I'm edging closer to my orgasm with every thrust.

I try to open my eyes and the harsh light glares at me, so I squeeze them closed as pleasure washes over me. Nate presses my knees up towards my chest, and the sensation of his cock rubbing deep inside me at a different angle forces my climax.

I buck and cry out as I splinter and waves of rapture wash over me. I'm barely coherent as Nate jackhammers into me and roars with his own release. My brain is mush and I'm shuddering with aftershocks as he pulls out of me and gently lets my legs down so my feet are on the floor.

He shuts off the overhead light before climbing on the bed. "Come up here, Emily."

I grumble and roll over so I can crawl up beside him. He's on his back and I collapse next to him, face down, with my head on his chest and one of his arms underneath me and wrapped around me. He smells like sex, a comforting combo of my scent and his, and I nuzzle against him and slide an arm across his stomach, feeling protected and safe as he rubs my back.

I was wide awake before sex, but I think he fucked me senseless because all I want to do now is nap. I yawn and murmur, "I love you," and he replies, "I love you too," and hugs me.

My last thought as I drift off to sleep is, "Yeah, this is the good stuff."

CHAPTER
THREE

When I messaged Aiden to tell him that Nate wants to meet him, Aiden's reply was enthusiastic and encouraging. He seemed all on board with helping Nate become comfortable with us together, which makes me appreciate Aiden even more. We agreed on a coffee date the following Saturday. I didn't want to press my luck with Nate, so Aiden and I agreed to wait to see each other again until after Saturday.

This is the first time we've skipped an entire week, and I'm antsy and missing the stress relief from clearing my mind while Aiden controls me. We try to do a few things over text, but it's not the same anymore. Now that I've tasted the thrill I get in real life, anything online pales in comparison.

I'm still confused over what got Nate so hot when we discussed the rules, but he's preoccupied this week and I don't work up the guts to question him about it until Thursday night after dinner. We're cleaning up the kitchen when I finally broach the subject. It's super awkward to figure out how to word what I want to ask, so I just blurt it out.

"Nate, last Sunday when we talked and I sat in your lap, you were... uh...turned on...."

I trail off and hope he'll get the gist of where I'm going with this. He pauses while rinsing a plate at the sink, replies, "Yeah, I was," and continues cleaning dishes. Dammit, he's not making this easy for me.

"Um, Nate? What was that about?"

Nate mumbles, but the running faucet garbles his words. All I heard was "hot" and "watching."

Uh, watching what is hot? I need clarification and I'm trying to be gentle and not get annoyed that he's being unclear.

"Nate, can you turn that off and look at me?"

He switches the water off and turns around, leaning against the counter. Staring towards the bottom of the stove across the room, he won't look me in the eye as he fidgets and his face flushes. *Is he embarrassed?*

I'm getting concerned by his behavior because it's so unlike him. "Hon, what is going on?"

He shuffles his feet before answering. "I was thinking about watching you and Aiden together."

His answer is not what I expected and it stuns me silent for a moment.

"Like in the same room while we're fucking?" I'm intentionally crude because I need him to be honest.

He finally looks up at me. "Yes."

"Oh, okay. That seems fine."

I have no idea how to respond to him, and I'm sure I just fucked it up.

He turns back around and starts rinsing more dishes and I help finish cleaning the kitchen while my brain whirs. *Fuck, that's hot.* I don't want to admit to Nate how on board I am with this idea since he and Aiden haven't met yet, but suddenly my double-stuffed fantasy seems a lot closer to reality than I thought possible.

My stomach churns as I think about the upcoming coffee date. I already was a tad nervous, but Nate's reveal just upped the ante. Shit, this meetup needs to go well.

~

NATE

When Saturday rolls around, I feel sick from the stress and I'm afraid I'm going to throw up on the drive to the cafe. I know what Aiden looks like, but I need to pretend I know nothing about him. Emily didn't ask how I found out about them, and I never volunteered the information. If she doesn't care, I'm not going to admit I was going through her computer. Emily is silent, but she's twisting her hands in her lap so I can tell she's anxious too.

The coffee shop is in a busy part of town, but we get lucky and a close parking spot opens up right as we pull into the lot. I turn the car off and we both stare at the building. It's a beautiful day and the outdoor patio seating area is open, and Aiden sits at a table in the shade, waiting for us.

Emily's voice is soft when she speaks. "That older guy with the grey hair and the dark blue shirt is Aiden."

Time to play dumb. "Oh. How old is he?"

"I'm not sure, but I think in his early 50s."

I don't ask anything else but we still don't move.

"Nate, this won't get any easier the longer we sit here."

Snorting, I unbuckle my seatbelt. "You're right. Let's go."

As we approach Aiden, I can tell the moment he sees us. He sits up straighter and a wary expression crosses his face as we approach the table. Is he expecting me to blow up at him, or is this how he acts around other guys? I've spied on Emily and him through his apartment windows for weeks, so I know he's kind and gentle, though a strict dom, which seems to thrill her.

He and I shake hands and introduce ourselves and my palm tingles as he brushes mine. *Uh, what was that?* I don't want to think about what just happened, so I shove it to the back of my mind. I'll evaluate it another day. Aiden already has coffee but Emily offers to get a drink for me, and I assume it's an excuse to leave us guys alone for a few minutes. I request a peppermint latte and she scurries off with a relieved look on her face. When I sit down, Aiden and I stare at each other for a few moments.

It wasn't until I was facing him that I realized I had questions.

"Did you know she was married?"

Aiden is direct with his answer. "Yes."

"Did it matter?"

This question makes Aiden pause. "Yes."

Huh, not what I was expecting. "But you still slept with her."

"Yes."

Aiden idly moves his hand up and down his paper mug, as if he's lost in thought, and suddenly I imagine his fingers stroking his cock. When a tiny thrill shoots to my groin and I feel myself stiffen, I'm uneasy. *Uh, what the fuck is going on?* There is no doubt that Aiden is a handsome guy. I knew that from his pictures and from seeing him from afar with Emily. But I wasn't expecting any reaction to him in person. That dimple in his chin is sexy and I understand why Emily finds him attractive.

Once my body responds to him, I flush and it's hard to meet his gaze. I stare at the table and rub the back of my neck. Emily needs to get back so she can chat and give me a chance to recover.

Aiden finally speaks more than one word to me. "Not that this probably matters, but I wouldn't have done anything with her if I had known you guys lived in my state. I'm not comfortable having an in-person sub when the husband doesn't know."

That makes me glance up at him, but he's gazing into the cafe, as if he's searching for something—probably Emily.

"Then why didn't you break it off when you found out we were close?"

He turns to me. "It was too late at that point. She has a way of getting under your skin without you realizing it."

I snort, yeah he's right. I'm so devoted to Emily, I'm sitting here having coffee with the guy she cheated with and I'm going to let them fuck in my our house. What does this say about me?

My cock hardens painfully at the thought of them screwing in our bed, and I think there has to be something wrong with me. I hate that I find this hot.

Aiden still strokes his cup and he notices me tracking his hand. I dart my eyes away, as if he caught me doing something I shouldn't and I spot Emily weaving around tables inside and heading our way.

Aiden's voice is commanding but quiet. "Nate, we could always make the best of this situation and let everyone have some fun."

I glance at him sharply right when Emily gets to the table, and he's looking at me with a twinkle in his eye and a slight smile. My heartbeat speeds up and a sudden flush of warmth spreads from my groin. Did he just proposition me?

Emily shoves my drink in front of me. "Here you go."

I take it and she sits down, intentionally scooting her chair a little closer to mine than Aiden's, and I briefly wonder if she's doing it to pander to me, but I'm too distracted by Aiden to give it much thought. I don't know what I want anymore, but Aiden's comment gives me hope that he would be open to me being in the room when they're together, and I have the sudden resolve to ask Emily to see if he's willing.

My head spins while Aiden and Emily chat and make small talk. I respond when appropriate, and the longer we're at the cafe, the happier Emily becomes: she's animated, bubbly, and in her element. Every time I peek at Aiden, he's staring at me intensely and I want to squirm and blush. I'm not normally a shy guy, and rarely blush, so I don't know why Aiden is bringing this out, but I'm uncomfortable and wish we could leave. I've met him and he seems fine. Emily is obviously elated, so I consider this day a success.

AIDEN

Nate is not what I expected at all, and when my dom side reacts to him, I'm surprised. That blush of his is so fucking adorable and he's got an innocent air about him that makes me itch to corrupt him. When they announce it's time for them to leave, I say goodbye but stay at the cafe. As they head to their car, hand in hand, I can't help but wonder if I just met my kryptonite couple.

I've never responded to both a husband and a wife and I thought I had a handle on my relationship with Emily. Nate just threw a wrench into the entire plan. I sit back in my chair and drain the last of my drink.

Intrigued and energized, I contemplate the future. I never considered Nate being a part of anything I do with Emily other than maybe making him some videos, but now I imagine them both on their knees with their mouths open, waiting for me.

Oh yeah, life just got a hell of a lot more interesting.

CHAPTER

FOUR

AIDEN

Emily and I make plans to see each other on Monday. It's been too long since we were together and the week reinforced that I'm addicted to her. I was tense, jumpy, and craving her attention for the first half of the week. The D/s bond can be powerful with the right sub, and the few times I've had a strong connection with one, I end up feeling this way. I've reached that point with Emily, and seeing her on Saturday partly calmed me, but my reaction to Nate counteracted any sense of well-being I got from being around her.

On Monday when Emily arrives, I pounce on her as soon as she walks in. I swing the door shut and press her up against the wall. She drops her purse and moans as I ravish her lips, and I run my hands up her short pink skirt. I told her two weeks ago to stop wearing panties whenever she's around me, and I'm pleased to find she obeyed me. She spreads her legs as my fingers slip between her pussy lips, and she's wet and ready.

Emily has a kink about being used, and I make sure I don't take advantage of it. She's told me before that I can use her more often than I do, but I love making her gasp and pant as she climaxes. But right now, I need her too much and she might not come. She normally has to ask before she hits her peak, but today the rules are different.

"Emily, I'm going to fuck you right here. If you get close, you have permission to come without asking, but don't wait because I'm going to use you hard and I won't last long."

She peeps out a tiny, "Oh," as I unzip my jeans, pull out my throbbing cock, and ram it into her wet cunt. I hold on to her legs as I pound into her furiously and knock her against the wall. She wraps her arms around my neck and her eyes glaze over while she whimpers, "Oh, my god," repeatedly. I don't slow down, and for a few minutes the only sound is a wet slap with each thrust and her vocal cries.

I'm lost in the bliss of her silky folds caressing me. The pressure mounts and I'm about to explode when she cries out my name and comes all over my cock. Her entire body quivers and her cave walls clench around me as I grunt and come so hard my head spins. *Holy shit, that was good.* I jerk against her a few times, emptying myself fully, as she goes limp in my arms.

I'm not sure I can make it to the living room while carrying her, so I turn us around and gently lower us to the floor, pulling her into my lap. Her cellphone in her purse gives a muffled ping that she received a text message, but she only murmurs nonsense in response. I'm assuming she's saying she'll check it in a bit when she can think again. I relax fully, not caring how uncomfortable the floor is, and she melts into me with a soft murmur of contentment.

I'm not sure how long we lie there, but eventually Emily stirs and gets playful. She brings one of my hands to her mouth and nibbles on my fingers. When I bop her on the nose, she giggles.

I kiss the top of her head and ask, "Hey, you want a cinnamon roll? I made some this morning."

She's super cute when she replies sweetly, "Mmmm. Yes, please!"

We climb up from the floor and while I'm getting plates out and reheating the cinnamon rolls in the microwave, Emily checks her text message.

"Oh, it's from Nate. He's at home for lunch."

She perches on the edge of a barstool at the kitchen counter and stares at her phone intently.

"You told him you were coming over, right?"

Last week Emily explained his conditions for her to continue seeing me, so she better have messaged him. I make a mental note to double check every time she comes over. She doesn't answer me, preoccupied with her phone.

"Emily?" I give her my stern voice to get her attention.

"Hmmm?" She glances up at me. "Oh, yes. I told him."

I set the plate with a cinnamon roll down on the counter in front of her and put a fork next to it. I lean against the counter and dig into my roll. *Goddam, I really know how to make delicious desserts.* I take a few bites and realize she's on her phone again and not touching her roll. It might be time to remind her who is dom here.

"Emily, put your phone down, now."

She drops her phone quickly and it clatters on the counter. "Yes, Sir."

"Good girl. Now eat your cinnamon roll."

She takes a sample and groans around the fork while satisfaction pings my brain. I might have a slight kink about making people dessert and watching them enjoy it, but I'm not sure I'll ever tell Emily. I might just keep baking desserts and gauge her reactions to figure out her favorites. The cinnamon rolls seem to be a hit.

"Sir?"

I get the familiar buzz whenever she calls me Sir. "Yes, Doll?"

"Um, Nate has a question for us."

She pauses and takes another bite and I study her while she chews, trying to decide if she's meaning to be a brat by not saying the entire thought at once. When I raise an eyebrow at her and set my fork down purposefully, her eyes flash with alarm and excitement and she rushes her words.

"Uh, Sir—Nate wants to know if he can watch us fuck in our bed at home."

Well, now. That's interesting. My cock stirs to life, even though it was just satisfied. "He said just watch?"

"Yes, he said watch."

I slowly finish my cinnamon roll and don't respond to Emily. Now I'll make HER wait.

NATE

Emily doesn't reply for an agonizing 33 minutes while I sit on the couch and keep checking for messages on my phone. Knowing that she's probably not answering because Aiden is fucking her brains out doesn't help. My stomach is in knots and my palms are sweaty. I just need to know!

My lunch break is only an hour and I'm going to be late back to work at this rate, but I can't stop watching my phone. The text finally comes and since I'm already looking at my screen I see the answer immediately from the preview that pops up.

EMILY

He says yes. How does next Saturday sound?

My heart catches in my throat and my entire body tingles with excitement. Shit, this needs to go well.

The End

OWNING EMILY

AN MMF ROMANTIC BDSM EROTICA SERIES

CHAPTER
ONE

EMILY

"Emily, are you going to show Nate that you're a good girl and will do as you're told?"

I'm naked and on all fours at the end of the bed, as Aiden commanded, and he's standing behind me. I can only moan in response to his question as his cock slides into my pussy and my cave walls stretch and mold around his thick shaft. I'm overwhelmed by the pleasure and my eyelids flicker, and I fight to keep them open as I gaze straight at Nate. He's sitting on the bed, leaning against the headboard, watching us. He sat down shortly before Aiden pushed his rod inside me.

As soon as the sexy fun started, Aiden turned into a director as if he were putting on a show for Nate. At first, Nate moved around the room, watching us from different vantage points, but he settled in front of me on the bed once Aiden demanded I get on my knees at the edge.

At first, I'm concerned because Nate isn't talking or making any noise. If he were in Aiden's spot he would tell me how much he loves me or moaning how amazing I feel. So having a sexual experience with him in the room, but silent, worried me. But I can see his rock solid bulge in his shorts and I noticed him stroke himself through the fabric a couple of times. He's clearly enjoying the Aiden and Emily show, so I stop worrying about him and focus on doing as I'm told.

"Emily—Doll, when I ask a question, I expect a response. Are you going to show your husband that you are a good girl and do exactly as I say?"

Aiden is fucking me slow and steady and my brain is fuzzy. He hits a delightful spot deep inside my pussy, sending ripples of pleasure through my body. I'm breathless as I answer. "Yes, Sir."

"Good girl." Aiden ends the affirmation with a hard slam against my ass, and I squeal out from the shock of his roughness and lock eyes with Nate.

Nate's eyes widen as Aiden fucks me hard, and his hand drifts down to his crotch as he rubs himself, without caring that I can see. He's got a lust haze in his eyes that makes me think he's beyond noticing that he's stroking himself. Having Nate in the room escalates my pleasure. I didn't know him being here with us would be this hot. I desperately want him to pull down his shorts and free his shaft, but I don't say it because I can't form complete sentences. All I can do is hang onto the comforter and groan as Aiden uses me.

I'm spiraling towards an orgasm and Aiden knows me well enough by now that he can tell. His voice is harsh when he pants out, "Doll, you better ask permission before you come."

Shit, I always forget. I never know how he's going to respond, and it seems about 50/50 on whether he says yes. I gasp out, "Sir, can I come? Please?"

Aiden jackhammers into me and I almost come before he answers. "No, Doll. I haven't decided if you're coming today. I *might* use every hole and if you please me well enough, I *might* say yes."

Ooooh, fuck. His filthy words shock me. Nate and I didn't talk about whether it was okay if I had anal sex with Aiden or not. It's something Nate and I do on rare occasions and more of a treat. I should have talked to him about it before now. My eyes roll into the back of my head as my body starts quivering, on the brink of my orgasm.

Aiden pulls out, announces, "Oh, no you don't," and slaps my ass sharply. The sting stops me from coming and I mewl out in frustration.

I love being used and whenever Aiden doesn't let me come, it's exquisite torture, but I never considered he would deny me in front of Nate.

I glance at Nate again, trying to gauge his reaction to all of this. He isn't stroking any longer, and his hands are on the bed beside him. A soft smile plays at his lips, making me wonder what he's thinking.

∼

AIDEN

Having Nate in the room makes me want to mentally fuck Emily up more than ever before. I want her to be a drooling mess when I'm done with her, and I want him to think about what I could do to him if he let me. Emily doesn't know it, but I'm going to let her come. She's going to have to beg and plead first, and hopefully I can watch Nate as she does it.

My instinct at the coffee shop was correct. Nate is responding to my control over Emily. She probably assumes he's finding this hot because he's watching her get fucked, and that is part of it. But whenever I command Emily to do something, Nate gets a look in his eyes—a yearning. I need to make this a show he's going to be fantasizing about for days.

Emily is panting on all fours in front of me and my cock aches for me to ram it back into her, but I want Nate to participate more than he's done so far.

"Nate." My voice is sharp and commanding, and his eyes fly up to meet mine.

"Yes?" He's hesitant, as if he's unsure why I'm talking to him suddenly, and I hope that's true. I want him on an emotional roller-coaster of neediness and desire.

"Do you think I should let this little fucktoy come?"

Nate hesitates before he answers. "Yes?"

"Oh, I don't know. You seem uncertain about that."

I yank on Emily's hair, forcing her head up. "Fucktoy, did that sound like he thought I should allow you to come?"

"No…" Emily's reply is almost a sob.

"Okay. Let's try this again then, shall we?" I let go of Emily's hair and her head hangs down towards the bed. "Nate, do you think this fucktoy deserves to come? Your answer determines her fate."

Nate drops his gaze from mine and almost whispers, "No."

Emily's head whips up as if she's surprised, and I laugh and slap her ass, causing her to jump. "Well, now, guess your husband doesn't think you deserve an orgasm. Let's see what other hole I want to use before I ask him again."

Emily groans and lowers her upper body towards the bed, forcing her ass cheeks to spread open wider, tempting me. But I have other plans for her.

"Doll, get on your knees on the floor. It's time for you to show your husband how deep you can take my cock."

I watch Nate as Emily crawls off the bed and kneels before me. She's flushed and her skin glows in the soft light. One of my favorite things about her is how she's soft and squishy in all the right places, and I could lose myself in her breasts. I'm not sure she realizes how fabulous her tits are. I could devour those firm, soft globes and I have future plans for pushing them together and rubbing my shaft between them until I splash on her face. But that isn't for today.

Nate shifts closer to the end of the bed as if seeking a better view, and I fight the urge to call him a good boy. Nate surprised me when he said 'no' to Emily coming. I enjoy that type of power play with two subs, and if Nate embraces what he and I both already know he's feeling deep down, this could be a really fun dynamic.

When Emily opens her mouth and sticks out her tongue, I almost groan. My desire to control them both intoxicates me, and I might not last as long as I hoped, but I want to get Nate stroking again at least one more time.

I glance down at my eager submissive and the thirst in her eyes decides how I want this to end. She won't have to beg after all if she's a good girl. "Doll, I'm going to use your mouth until I come. If you swallow every single drop without losing any of it, I will let you come afterwards. Deal?"

She nods, keeping her tongue out.

I turn my head towards Nate. "Do you think that seems fair? Fuck-toys deserve a chance to orgasm, right?"

He squeaks out a, "Yes," and I grin at him, grab the base of my shaft, and bring the tip towards Emily's waiting mouth.

~

NATE

As Aiden's thick rod presses into Emily's mouth, I'm shocked at how turned on I am. I assumed I'd be a casual observer, like watching porn, but Aiden talking to me and making me a part of the process thrills me unexpectedly. What neither of them knows is that I've already seen how deep Emily can take his cock, but having a close-up view is more arousing than peeping through a window.

Aiden slips his cock all the way down Emily's throat until her nose is in his pubic hair and I see her throat working before he withdraws and she gasps for breath. The room spins as a punch of longing hits my gut. I don't know what I'm even longing for, but seeing my wife suck another man's cock is amazingly hot.

Aiden fucks Emily's mouth with long, slow movements. He doesn't force himself down her throat as far as he did with that first thrust, but since he's so thick, she has to work to take most of him in. I've been rock hard this entire time and my cock twitches in my shorts. I can't resist the urge and I reach down to stroke myself.

With my first rub, Aiden moans loudly and I realize he's staring at me and not Emily. He and I lock eyes as I rub, and he speeds up the fucking of Emily's mouth while she gurgles happily around his cock. When he slowly runs his hands over his chest and arms, I get the mental image of me doing that to him instead and I fight the urge to reach out.

I thought I should imagine myself in Aiden's place, but a vision of me on my knees with Aiden fucking my face pops into my head and I flush. I wish I dared take my cock out of my shorts and stroke until I come at the same time he does. We didn't discuss that beforehand, and I have the urge to ask for permission, which is odd. I don't want to do anything to ruin what's happening, so I stay silent.

Aiden closes his eyes, puts his hands in Emily's hair, forcing her to hold still as he presses harshly against her mouth. He groans out loudly as he comes, and his buttocks flex as he twitches against her lips. Emily is making excited noises around his cock, and I can tell she's loving the rough treatment. When Aiden finishes unloading down Emily's throat, he opens his eyes and looks at me again. He's still inside her mouth and I can tell she's swirling her tongue around him and I see her throat swallowing.

"Did my little fucktoy lose any of my cum?"

I glance at Emily's mouth and down her chest before answering. "No, she swallowed it all."

"Good girls deserve a treat."

Aiden brushes the side of Emily's cheek softly with his fingers as he pulls out from her mouth. "Lie on your back and spread your legs, Doll."

Emily doesn't waste any time and climbs on the bed, as eager as she was to get on her knees before. When she spreads her legs, her swollen pussy is on full display and it makes me want to taste her instead of Aiden. But again, I stay silent.

She is back far enough that her head is on a pillow and Aiden has to crawl on the bed to get to her pussy. She moans out as he leans in and uses his hands to spread her folds so he can get to her clit. I can't see what's happening because Aiden's head is in the way, but I can tell when he finds the hard nub based on her loud gasp and the way her hips buck against him.

He's not hesitant as he eats her out, licking and savoring her. He's a noisy eater and the slurping noises and her little murmurs of delight make my head swim. As Emily gets louder and thrashes about, Aiden inserts two fingers inside of her and continues to suck on her clit while finger fucking.

I need to come just as badly as she does and suddenly I get the terrible realization that I'm not comfortable coming while this is going on because I don't feel like I have permission. My choices are to stroke and just do it, ask if I can, or to not touch myself at all. I can't bring myself to do it without asking, but I'm frozen and can't ask. I ache as Emily tips over the edge and screams out as she comes. The bed vibrates as she violently shakes from the force of her orgasm, and knowing it was a strong one makes my neediness worse.

Aiden crawls up onto the bed beside her and flops on his side facing me, pulling her to him and spooning her. I'm in shock and don't know what to do, but the intimacy of them spooning makes me stand up.

My voice is hoarse when I speak. "Thank you for letting me watch."

Emily murmurs, "I love you," towards me, but she's too far gone to say much else.

Aiden smiles, his face shiny with my wife's juices, and he winks at me. "You're welcome."

I want to flee the room, but I force myself to walk slowly so it doesn't appear that I'm running away. I forgo the master bathroom and take the stairs up to the mother-in-law apartment and sit on the closed toilet lid in the bathroom there. My heart is beating fast and I'm breathless. I need to come.

I pull my cock out of my shorts, pull a couple of tissues from a box on the counter, and picture Aiden's face as he fucked Emily's mouth. Within a few strokes, I groan and come so hard into the tissues that I almost black out. I grip the edge of the vanity next to me, reeling. Holy fuck.

I'm not sure how long I sit there, but eventually my heart rate slows down. I'm not ready to leave the bathroom yet, and my thoughts swirl. I toss the tissues in the trash, knowing that Emily is the one who empties it. A part of me wants her to know how affected I was. I'm half ashamed at how hard I came thinking of Aiden, and half wanting more. What is happening to me?

CHAPTER

TWO

EMILY

The next day, after Nate got back from church on Sunday, we ended up in bed. He was an enthusiastic lover, so I know everything is fine between us. I was afraid he'd regret what happened or be upset. But he acted like his normal self all day and I have no reason to suspect he's harboring issues.

On Monday morning, I'm cranky as soon as I roll out of bed and I don't know why. After such a great weekend, I should be on cloud nine. I cuss under my breath as I climb the stairs as annoyance washes over me. Even though I work part time and could clean most any day, I try to keep myself to a chore chart so I don't slack off. Every other Monday I go to the top floor and clean the mother-in-law apartment. I like to keep it dusted and ready for company for the rare times we have any. It takes less than a half an hour to spruce it up, and I open the windows while I'm tidying up to let in the fresh air so the room doesn't get stale.

When I go into the bathroom to wipe down the counters, the trash has two pieces of tissue in it and a flash of anger hits me—now I have to empty this trash!! But then I pause. Wait, when and why was Nate up here using this bathroom? We don't have ghosts—that I know of—so it had to be Nate.

I'm pondering that mystery when I realize I forgot to open the windows. Shit! I hurry over to the windows and crack them open to let the warm breeze blow in, and I try some deep breaths to ease my irritation at life. Sitting down on the bed, I close my eyes and try to clear my mind of everything that's bugging me.

I can't figure out what my problem is. Saturday was a smashing success and Nate is good. He didn't say anything about watching Aiden fuck me, but it was clear he found the afternoon arousing. I was out of it after my orgasm, so I barely remember Nate leaving the room, but he must have come up here and jerked off in place of our normal Saturday night sex.

My crankiness drains away and a thrill runs down my spine when I picture Nate up here jerking off, daydreaming about Aiden using me. Shit, that's hot. I still wish I could have seen him come, but maybe if there IS a next time, he'll do it in front of me.

I can't shake the idea that Nate was up here wanking, and I lie back on the bed and slip a hand down the front of my sweatpants and underneath my panties. I moan out softly as I press a finger between my soft folds and caress circles around my clit. Since I want to air out the room for a bit, I have some time to kill up here. I keep myself busy, using my fingers to drain away every ounce of stress.

～

NATE

It's hard to concentrate at work on Monday. I just keep replaying the visual of Aiden and Emily on Saturday in my head and I'm sporting a hard-on that I've been trying to hide behind my desk all morning. Luckily, I don't have any meetings today so I can hide out in my office.

When Emily and I ended up in the bedroom on Sunday, I tried to imagine I was Aiden fucking her, and it worked well enough that I came super hard. The problem is that I might want more. I would have liked to have been free enough on Saturday to pull my rod out and stroke it.

There were moments that Emily could have sucked on my cock while Aiden fucked her, but isn't that a threesome at that point? Do I even want that—does Emily want that?

I'm a ball of nerves and I keep making careless mistakes as I enter numbers into the database at work. At one point I wonder if I'm going to need to double check all this work again tomorrow. My head better be on straight by tomorrow, but it's possible I'll be mulling this over all week.

I usually go home for lunch, but I don't want to today because I'm so turned on, I might bend Emily over an armchair and rail her until she's seeing stars. She'd love that, but then she'd have questions about what got into me and I'm not ready to talk about my thoughts yet. I know I'll have to come to terms with everything and talk to her soon, but I need more time to digest what I want to say since I don't even know what I want. I'm conflicted, confused, and needy for something that I don't understand.

Opting to eat my lunch in the car, I drive around to a secluded section of the parking lot where no one will see me. I take a few bites of a sandwich I bought out of the vending machine in the break room but then set it down on the dashboard. I'm too worked up to eat, and I need to do something about my horniness. Not wanting to spend the rest of the workday turned on, I unzip my trousers and ease my twitching cock out. Trying to stroke slowly, I envision Emily's lips around Aiden's shaft and I can't hold back. I grab some tissues from a travel pack. I don't want my work clothes to get messy.

My heart rate speeds up as I rub my member, caressing all the way from the tip to the base. My balls tighten and ripples of pleasure spasm through me as I moan loudly and grip the base of my shaft tightly for a moment before letting go and furiously pulling and yanking on my cock in a frenzy. I imagine a naked Emily kneeling on the floor, eyes sparkling with excitement, with her mouth open, waiting for Aiden to milk out his cum onto her waiting tongue. My dream Emily slips a hand between her legs and plays with a nipple with the other hand. I groan as I explode and convulse while my orgasm rips through me. Shocks of pleasure wash over me, and I close my eyes and let myself drift in a sexual haze before cleaning up and heading back into work.

~

AIDEN

I'm a little unsettled on Monday and unsure what to do about Nate. In the past, whenever I was in a relationship that turned into a threesome with the husband and wife, the husband was very much a willing participant and vocal about wanting to take part. Nate running off on Saturday right after Emily's orgasm, and his hesitancy with stroking himself in front of me, makes me think he might take a step back if I try to force him to embrace this before he's ready.

If I push Nate too hard, it will fuck up what I've got going on with Emily. But I also know that he won't be able to make the first move. This is a unique situation for me, and I have to tread carefully because I don't want to scare him off. Every submissive is different and I have to figure out the right approach, but getting involved with a guy who is only just learning he's submissive isn't something I've done before.

I'm looking forward to my next encounter with him. Nate's a riddle I'm excited to solve.

CHAPTER
THREE

EMILY

Before Nate leaves for work on Wednesday, I let him know that Aiden is coming over shortly. He gives me an odd look and I can't decipher what it means. But when he kisses me goodbye like usual and tells me to have a fun time, I don't dwell on trying to figure him out. Aiden only has a couple of free hours before an appointment, so he won't still be at the house when Nate comes home for lunch. Someday I hope it won't matter what time Aiden leaves, but I'm hesitant to have him stay long until Nate and I discuss what happened on Saturday.

I'm so turned on picturing Aiden here at the house, my pussy practically drips. The newness of the dynamic turns me on more than I imagined it would, and I can't believe how fucking lucky I am that Nate is letting me have both of them. My heart warms and I vow once more to make sure Nate knows how much I love and appreciate him. It's a rare husband who would be okay with his wife having another man come to their house to fuck her.

I need to get dressed, and knowing Aiden doesn't want me to wear panties, I slip on a light blue sundress with nothing on underneath, choosing to go braless as well. Trying to keep my mind occupied, I wander into the living room and sit on the couch. I add a few rows to a blanket I'm crocheting, but my trembling hands make it difficult. I've almost given up when the doorbell rings.

He's here! My heart rate increases as the chime echoes through the house. When I jump up from the couch, I almost trip over my feet in my rush to get to the door. Aiden is on the stoop, grinning at me when I yank open the door. That adorable dimple in his chin makes me want to gobble him up, and I fight the urge to pull him inside and throw myself on him. I don't know what he plans for today, but I need something inside me as soon as possible.

"Hi, Doll. Nice dress."

I flush at the compliment, but don't have time to respond. He strides in, kicks the door closed behind him, and crushes me against the closest wall. A surge of lust blasts from my pussy as he ravages my mouth, forcing my lips to part. I wrap my arms around his neck as our tongues duel, and moan when his hand skims up the back of my leg underneath my dress to grip my bare ass.

He breaks off the kiss, nibbles down the front of my neck, and murmurs "Good girl," at me. I assume it's because I'm not wearing panties, but if I'm honest with myself, it doesn't matter why he said it. Every time I hear it now, a soft tingle runs through my body and I'm immediately wet.

He squeezes my breasts and teases my nipples through my thin dress. I was expecting sex, but I assumed we'd exchange small talk before he manhandled me. It amplified the difference between Nate and Aiden since I couldn't imagine Nate ever being commanding and taking what he wanted as soon as he walked in.

I gasp when he pinches my nipples hard. I arch my back, press against him, and ache for him to slide his cock inside me. My body is on fire and I quiver in anticipation of what's coming next, moaning out, "I need you, Sir," as he continues to play with my breasts.

Aiden stops tweaking my nipples and pulls my sundress off over my head. His smoldering gaze sweeps the length of my body and I shiver.

"Let's go to the bedroom. I have a mind to fuck you in your bed while your husband isn't here."

Oh fuck, that's hot. My mind short circuits, and I'm unable to respond. He grabs my hand, walking fast and dragging me towards the bedroom. I do a little half skip to catch up so I don't fall flat on my face.

When we enter the bedroom, he pushes me onto the bed. I lie on my back, propping myself up on my elbows to get a better view while he strips. A gush of wetness leaks from my pussy as he disrobes, and I imagine caressing his chest. His cock is hard and thick, and in the dim lighting I can tell it's shiny with pre-cum already.

I lick my lips and bite the lower one, hoping he tells me to suck his cock. But it doesn't seem like that's going to happen as he climbs up on the bed between my legs, forcing them open. He hooks his hands underneath my thighs and drags me towards him. I throw my arms above my head and leave them there as I gasp from the unexpected movement that brings my pussy close enough to him that he's able to let go of my legs, grab his shaft, and trace the head up and down my slit. I keep my knees bent, and my feet flat against the bed, knowing I can press against him easier this way.

"Oooooh." I moan out long and loud when he finally presses his cock inside me. He pauses once he's fully sheathed, letting my body adjust. I buck my hips, trying to get him to move and he fucks me slowly to start. I close my eyes, lightheaded, as ecstasy washes over me.

"We have some rules today, Doll."

What's this? Aiden sounds entirely too unaffected, as if he's sitting down and casually talking to friends.

I open my eyes to look at him, and stammer out, "Rules, Sir?" trying to not sound breathless.

He grins at me, the dimple on his chin deepening. "Yes, Doll. If you say 'oh, my god,' more than ten times, you aren't allowed to come today."

He gives a hard, deep whack against my pussy after his announcement and I moan out, "Oh, my god," without thinking. Aiden chuckles at me.

"One."

What the fuck sort of game is this? It's not like I have to be quiet. No one's home. Aiden plows into me faster, and my toes curl from the intense spikes of bliss. He shifts positions, pushing one of my knees up to my chest and letting my calf rest on his shoulder, and I gasp out another "Oh, my god."

"Two."

Shiiit. I'm not sure I can stop myself from saying it. If I don't come fast today, I'll ruin my chance to come at all.

"Why, Sir?" I whimper out, trying to clear my head enough so I don't involuntarily keep spewing out the words I shouldn't.

Aiden slows down his thrusts again, and I want to weep from the exquisite torture, but I'm not able to lose myself for fear of what will happen.

"Why?" Speeding up, he jackhammers into my pussy and I hold my breath, trying to not moan. "Because I can."

Knowing he's just toying with me for no good reason and just doing it for control makes my head swim. My brain lets go of the struggle. My mind clears of all thoughts while my eyelids flutter. Relaxation slips over my body and it feels like I'm floating.

"Yes, Sir," I mumble, not caring anymore. He can do whatever he wants to me since every movement and touch is amazing.

Aiden pulls my other leg up towards my chest and his cock thrusts in at a new angle and the pleasure makes me moan out, "Oh, my god," twice in a row.

"That's four." Aiden's voice finally sounds strained and not as relaxed.

When he adjusts his position again and hits the magical spot deep inside my pussy, I give a tiny squeal. He groans in response, which makes me moan out the fifth, "Oh, my god."

Aiden doesn't count this one down and rams against me roughly, grinding so hard with each inward thrust, it feels as if he's trying to force his balls into my cunt along with his shaft. I'm beyond knowing what I'm doing and from a distance I hear him count.

"That's seven...that's eight."

I don't remember hearing him say six. Pressure mounts in my belly, and the muscles of my cave walls quiver as I edge towards my orgasm. He lowers my legs, and I spread them as wide as I can with my knees bent outward while he leans into me and kisses me deeply. I moan into his mouth as our tongues entwine and each flick of his tongue shoots tingles straight to my pussy.

He nibbles on my neck and playfully bites his way down to my breast, sucking a plump nipple into his mouth. He flicks at the stiff peak with his tongue and I groan out what I hoped was nonsense.

"That's nine, Doll. Seems like someone doesn't want to come tonight."

Aiden's voice has a playful lilt, but I know he's not joking. He's toyed with me and orgasm control in the past, and if he says he's not letting me come, he sticks to it. Knowing I'm so close to being denied almost tips me over the edge. My toes curl again and I clench the bedsheets in desperate claws.

He stops moving inside me. "Maybe I should stop now?"

What? "No, please—no," I gasp out and thrash against him.

"Emily, look at me," he commands harshly.

His use of my first name in a stern tone forces me to meet his eyes, but it's hard to focus. I need to come.

"Beg."

Fuuuuck. He knows I can barely think when he's screwing me, and begging is ten times harder when you can't form complete thoughts. But I have to try.

"Please, sir. Can I please come? Oh, god, please?"

Too late, I realize that I might have said something too close to the forbidden words and hold my breath, waiting for his reply.

He grins and laughs indulgently. "Not good enough. Try again."

I rock against him, hoping he'll just start fucking me, but he's immobile and it's like pressing against a mountain. I get slight relief from forcing his shaft to rub against my inner walls, but it barely scratches the itch. Losing all inhibitions in my need to come, I gush out a tumble of words.

"Please, oh god. If you let me come, I won't wear panties for a week and send you pictures of my pussy every day and I'll get a Brazilian wax. I'll dress up in a maid's outfit and clean your apartment, or come over in a sexy schoolgirl outfit and you can spank me with a ruler for being naughty. I'll come over every morning for a week, give you a blowjob, and then leave. Just please, please, please, please, please, let me come!"

At the end of my pleas, Aiden pumps his hips against me a few times and I moan out, thinking he's going to let me come. Until he pauses again.

"The blowjob offer is quite nice."

He gives a few experimental thrusts, as if he's considering what he wants to do.

"And I do have a thing for women dressed as naughty schoolgirls."

He rams against me harder.

"One last question, Doll. If you answer it correctly, you can come."

Before he asks, he fucks me hard and fast with an audible wet slapping noise each time he bangs against my pussy. My core quivers with pulses of electricity. I tip my head back and flex my hips, meeting him thrust for thrust.

"Emily, who owns you?"

My breath catches and I can't answer and can only groan. Aiden tries again.

"Tell me who owns you, Emily—NOW."

My head clears for a brief moment and I lock eyes with him. He looks feral and wild, and the truth settles over me.

"You do," I whisper.

Aiden closes his eyes, growls out, and savagely plunges as deep as he can, repeatedly knocking against me so hard my breasts jiggle and bounce. The pleasure-pain of his thrusts sweeps me over the peak. I chant out, "Oh, my god," as I explode with a spine-tingling scream. The waves of pleasure wash over me and I continue to cry out in a crescendo, and Aiden's roar joins me as he explodes.

His hot cum coats my tunnel as he continues to fuck it back up into me as my walls clench and milk his cock for every drop. He shivers, and I moan softly as he slows down until he eventually stops. He slumps against me with his cock still buried inside me, twitching.

I'm still floating in a happy and relaxed place when he rolls off me. The cool air hits my sweat-dampened skin and the temperature difference pushes me slightly back towards consciousness.

"Holy fuck, Aiden."

He's on his side next to me and I turn towards him. He looks exhausted, but he's grinning at me and snuggles close to kiss my nose.

From the pile of clothes by the bed, his phone chirps at him, and he groans.

"I've got to get cleaned up and go, Doll. I'm glad I set an alarm."

He climbs off the bed, and I direct him to where the towels are in the bathroom in case he wants to shower. I hear the water running a few moments later and knowing there is a guy in my shower who just fucked me in my bed—and it's not my husband—is surreal.

I drift between awake and asleep, but Aiden coming back in to get dressed wakes me up fully. He comes to the side of the bed and I flip over so he can lean down and kiss me goodbye. When he straightens up, he smiles at me with a wicked glint in his eyes.

"What time are you coming over tomorrow for that blowjob?"

Oooh, shit. My eyes widen and I stare at him.

He laughs at me. "I'll text you later and ask again. Bye, Doll!"

When he leaves the room, I close my eyes. What the fuck did I just agree to, and how am I going to explain it to Nate?

NATE

Double checking the numbers I just typed into the database at work, I sigh when I have to correct a couple of mistakes. I don't know how to make myself less distracted when I know Aiden and Emily are together, but I can't keep doing this. One of these days, I'm going to fuck up royally. I love my job and I can't risk losing it. I need to focus on work and not think about Aiden bending Emily over the couch. Not that I have any idea what they are doing. That's what's killing me.

My stomach muscles tense and my chest burns the more I think about them together, and I force myself to unclench my jaw. I keep repeating to myself that it doesn't matter and I agreed to this, but somehow watching them together in our house made everything worse.

The real fucked up part is that I don't want them to stop. I just want to be there right now with them, watching, or—I don't know what else I want, but the desire to be at home and a part of whatever is going on is driving me nuts. This is for Emily and I can't keep butting in...can I?

Aiden works at night. If I said they could only play when I was there, that would limit their time to weekends only unless he had the night off. That doesn't sit right with me either. Shit, I don't know what I want, but I'm not ready to face Emily at lunch and see her freshly fucked and relaxed after a romp with Aiden. I text her that I'm working through lunch and all I get in response is an "oh, okay" back. I imagine her half passed out and floating in subspace when she responds and my gut clenches again.

Work is a blur, and I'm an odd mix of horny and angry all day. I want to go home and make love to Emily with long, deep strokes until she cries out my name instead of Aiden's. On the drive home, I calm myself down by singing along to some Ed Sheeran songs. I don't remember loading them into my music player, so it must have been Emily's doing, but the songs are catchy and they help ease my anxiety.

When I get home, the house smells like lasagna. If Emily took the time to make lasagna, she must have a guilty conscience. She only makes it as an apology meal. I eye her suspiciously as I enter the kitchen, but she appears to be in a good mood and is smiling. Her eyes light up when she approaches me and gives me a kiss.

"Hey, love. I had free time today since I don't work today, so I made your favorite."

I mumble that it smells good while I unpack my lunch supplies and shrug out of my jacket. She fondles my ass as she walks past me and the sexual zing puts my cock at half mast. Dammit, I had just gotten my cock and head calmed down on the drive, but her sexiness and playful mood gets me considering my original plan of fucking her thoroughly until her head spins.

Emily's cutesy voice breaks my train of thought. "Do you want to watch a show with dinner, or should we eat in the dining room?"

"Oh, uh..." Food was the last thing on my mind, so I can't decide.

"Oooh, maybe we should eat by candlelight tonight at the dining table?"

Now I really am suspicious. Cute and romantic Emily? Something is going on. But I'll play along with the game until she reveals her hand.

"Sure, Doll. Let me go get out of these work clothes."

I take two steps and freeze. *Did I just call her Doll?* I pivot and look at Emily and she's standing still, looking at me with wide eyes.

I blush and fumble on my words while a sinking feeling settles in my lower half. "Uh, shit—sorry."

It only takes a few seconds for Emily to recover and she giggles. "Fuck, that works when you say it, too."

"Oh, huh." I don't know how else to respond, so I beeline out of the kitchen before I stick my foot further into my mouth.

I change out of my work clothes and my shaft is now standing at attention and ready for action after calling her Aiden's pet name. Everything about this situation seems so wrong to my brain, but my cock doesn't care. Is this what being a cuckold is? One time I overheard locker room jokes at the local gym about some guy named Brent who enjoyed being cucked. Brent was one of the guys in the group and he joined in with the fun and teased himself as well, but I always felt bad for him. I'd never want my friends to know that I get uncontrollably turned on when my wife fucks a guy behind my back. All those weeks of wanking it in the bushes outside Aiden's apartment or in the car after watching them fills me with self loathing and I try to not think about it.

But being at work today while Emily and Aiden played without me? I couldn't concentrate on anything else. Ugh, I know I need to talk to Emily about this. I sigh, resolved, and head to the dining room. While I changed, she'd dimmed the lights, lit some candles, and turned on some relaxing instrumental music.

I've been on such a rollercoaster of emotions all day, so I can't imagine any of this means anything good. She wouldn't go to all this trouble unless she was trying to break something to me gently. The crazy thought enters my head that maybe she wants a divorce, but I shake it away. She wouldn't be in such a good mood if she was about to spring that on me—would she?

Emily enters the room from the kitchen and has two plates of lasagna in her hands. She smiles when she sees me.

"Good timing. The food is ready."

I'm quiet as I sit down, and she sets a plate in front of me and takes the seat next to me. She gives my thigh a squeeze under the table, and my cock jerks a little to remind me he's still there, like I could forget. I take a few bites, chewing methodically, but the food is sawdust in my mouth. I have to talk to her.

Setting the fork down, I look at her. "Did Aiden come over today?"

She hesitates briefly with her filled fork in the air, but recovers quickly, saying, "Yes," before sticking the tines between her lips. I stare at her, not speaking, until she's done chewing.

She shifts in her chair, as if she's trying to get comfortable, and chirps out a defensive, "What?"

It's now or never. My stomach is in knots, but we promised to communicate.

My voice is soft when I tell her, "I didn't like it."

"What?" This time she's startled, and her shoulders droop as if she had worked herself up for some big fight and I took the wind out of her sails. Her voice is tiny and hesitant. "You want me to stop seeing Aiden?"

Oh, fuck. I am going about this all wrong. "No, love. That's not what I'm saying. I didn't like it because I had to work."

It's lame, but I can't bring myself to say exactly what I mean. I'm hoping she reads between the lines. She sets her fork down, and I can tell she's mulling over what I said.

"You wanted to watch again?"

My breath whooshes out and I didn't realize I had been holding it in. "Yes. I was a little jealous."

There. I said it.

I wait for her to make the next move. I can see her brain churning for a moment, and then she gets out of her chair and moves to stand next to me. She pushes my dinner plate towards the middle of the table so she can lean her ass on the edge in front of me. I scoot my chair back so she has more room.

"I love you, Nate. I can talk to Aiden and find out if he enjoyed you watching and would want to do it again. Okay?"

She gives me a deep, sensual kiss until I'm weak in the knees. I don't tell her what I already know. Aiden enjoyed me watching and he'll want to do it again.

The longer the kiss lasts, the more I need Emily. She's wearing a long, soft skirt, and I run my hands underneath it. Her tiny moans drive me wild and when I stand up and push her legs open, her gasp makes my cock throb.

Suddenly she's frantic, pawing at the zipper of my trousers. Our lips lock together harshly and the kiss turns into both of us fighting to claim the other's mouth. She finally reaches the prize as she pushes my trousers and boxers down just far enough for my shaft to spring free.

"Oh, god, fuck me, Nate," she pants as she rubs me and I fight the urge to come immediately. I've been so turned on all day and knowing I might get to see her and Aiden fuck again is more than my poor cock can handle.

I push her back on the table and pull her skirt up, fingering the fabric of her wet panties. I make the split second decision to not waste my time removing them, and I pull the fabric to the side so I can guide my cock to her tight, wet entrance.

I groan as I press inside her, the pleasure almost more than I can take, and my heart hammers as I force myself to thrust slowly, despite the frantic tone we started out with. Enjoying every inch of her cave massaging my shaft, her squeals tell me she's loving it. I don't speed up and keep the same pace until she's writhing and bucking underneath me with her climax, which forces my own. I come so hard I see stars as I unload a massive amount of cum and release all the tension I've been holding in all day.

When my cock stops jerking, I collapse into my chair and pull Emily into my lap. I cuddle her against me, and she lays her head on my shoulder.

Her contented sigh warms my heart, just as much as her soft "I love you," does. Kissing the top of her head, I pull her closer to me and whisper in her ear that I love her, too. All of my earlier issues about Emily and Aiden seem inconsequential in this moment, and I hope I can stay in this happy bubble for a long time.

∼

AIDEN

The morning after Emily promised me a daily blow job, I decide to text her and have some fun with it. I don't really expect her to come over every day, but this is too good of an opportunity for teasing to pass up. I keep my first message short and simple.

AIDEN

> Doll, what time can I expect you over for my morning blow job?

I smile to myself as I imagine her reading the message and freaking out. I don't have to wait long for her reply.

EMILY

> Sorry, Sir. Too busy this morning.
> Raincheck?

I laugh aloud at the text and decide to skip the typing and just call her. She picks up on the first ring.

"Emily, we need to talk about this."

She pauses on the line, and I smirk again until she continues and her voice shakes, sounding like she's scared.

"Uh, yeah, so I didn't talk to Nate about it."

The light and fun feeling drops away. I don't want her to be worried about pissing me off since I didn't intend to enforce it.

"Oh, Doll. I was just teasing. Don't worry about it. When you see me on Thursday, you'll be getting a nice face fucking to make up for it."

Her tiny "oh" is so Emily and makes me smile again. Whenever I say something that thrills her, all she can reply with is an "oh." It's one of her tells, and it's how I know when I've hit my mark. I start stroking my cock, thinking about how rough I'm going to fuck her face and wishing it was Thursday already.

"Sir?"

"Yes?" I try to keep my breath even.

"Um, Nate wasn't too happy about yesterday."

I stop rubbing myself and sit up straighter. What's this?

"How do you mean?"

She sounds uncertain when she replies. "Um, I think he was jealous."

I almost laugh at that. Oh, you bet your ass he was jealous. Nate was so turned on watching me with Emily, I figured it was only a matter of time before he asked again.

Curious about what Emily thinks, I question her. "Nate seemed like he wanted more. Do you think he does?"

Emily pauses before answering. "More than watching?"

"Yes."

I let Emily sit with that thought for a moment and I stroke again, imagining both of them on their knees in front of me. Maybe Emily won't want to share. That would be amusing.

"Sir, I don't know about more, but he wants to watch again. Can he?"

"Doll, do you want him to watch us again?"

My cock quivers in anticipation while we wait for her answer. We both hope she says yes.

She stumbles over her words, changing what she was saying mid thought. "I wouldn't—yes."

"Good girl."

I stroke a little faster and struggle to not moan into the phone. Emily drives me wild on a normal day, and knowing I'm going to have Nate in the room again really revs my engine.

"So Saturday again, Sir?"

I'm almost lost in the sensation of my hand on my cock, thinking about Nate and Emily taking turns sucking on me.

"Sir?"

Oh, right. She asked a question.

"Yes. Saturday is fine, Doll."

Her sigh of relief speaks volumes about how worked up she was over the conversation.

"Doll, I've got to go, but we can do the same time on Saturday. Okay?"

"Yes, sir. Thank you."

Polite Emily pleases me, and her obedient nature pushes me closer to the brink.

"Oh, one more thing, Doll. Don't forget, I'm coming over on Thursday for that face fucking. It's time you learned that mouth of yours is just a hole for me to use."

Her tiny gasp and small, "oh," really makes me smile this time, and I hang up without saying anything else.

Emily's open mouth is what I think of as I speed up my stroking. It doesn't take long before I'm jerking and spurting cum all over my jeans. Oh yeah, Thursday is going to be fun.

CHAPTER
FOUR

When Emily tells me that Aiden is coming over on Thursday, I tell her to invite him for lunch on Wednesday if he's free, so we can talk. I'm don't know what I want to accomplish, but the hope is that I can get comfortable with Aiden and maybe I can work peacefully on Thursday without thinking about them in our bed fucking like wild animals.

Emily said Aiden was fine with me watching again on Saturday, but what if I wanted to do more than watch? If I have a moment to bring it up during lunch, I think talking to them both at the same time would be best. Making Emily the go-between with Aiden won't work long term, so I need to establish a friendship with him.

I wish I knew what I wanted. Whenever I think about Aiden and Emily, my stomach churns. I'm not sure what would satisfy me. Do I want them to play without me or do I want to make that off limits? Why does being around Aiden make my mouth go dry? I'm sure another meeting won't clarify everything, but it will be a step in the right direction.

Aiden works ten-hour shifts and he has a rotating day off every week. He said he could do dinner instead since Wednesday was his night off this week. I don't believe in divine beings, but Emily seemed tickled that the universe knew he needed the night off. I don't want to be a downer since she seems so happy, but every time she says it's fate, I want to argue with her that there's no such thing. Since I don't want to fight with her over something stupid, I bite my tongue and wish the dinner was over so that my anxiety would lessen.

For dinner that night, Emily makes salmon and wild rice because it's easy to make but looks impressive. I'm sick to my stomach by the time Aiden gets to the house, and I'm not sure how much I can eat. Emily asks me to get the door when the doorbell rings, and I want to tell her no. But of course I don't.

Aiden smiles at me when I open the door and my heart drops. Oh fuck, he's handsome. I'm reminded of it every time I see him by the fluttery sensation in my gut. It's uncommon for me to be this sexually attracted to a man. It's happened before, but rarely and never when anything might come of it. I stare at him, tongue-tied.

After what seems like an eternity, Aiden asks, "Nate, can I come in?"

I feel my face flush and I hope my tan hides it. "Oh, yeah, of course, please do."

I step back so he can walk past me, and the spice of his cologne hits me and makes me want to move closer to him and inhale the scent fully. I want to know how much is him and how much is cologne. He pauses when he's next to me and doesn't move. I have a hard time looking him in the eyes, but when I do, he's studying me. He opens his mouth to say something, but Emily calls from the kitchen.

"Hey guys, the food is ready."

He grins instead and heads towards the kitchen while I follow him. *What was he going to say to me?*

Emily is all smiles and giggles, clearly enjoying having both her men with her. I keep catching Aiden watching me out of the corner of his eyes and I'm sensing a tension in the air between us. He's not angry at me, so I don't know how to interpret what I'm feeling. Emily seems oblivious to it, and just being her normal adorable self. She's extra handsy with us both and whenever she passes by one of us, she drags her hand along in a soft caress – sometimes across his shoulder, sometimes down my back, but always touching whoever she's near.

We help dish up our plates and all go to the dining room. She lowered the lights and lit candles again, and suddenly it feels like I'm on a date with two people. Well, this dinner just got awkward as all fuck. I can't bring up doing more in the bedroom with them now since she set this up as some romantic dinner threesome.

I try to avoid both their eyes as I sit down, wishing the floor would open up and swallow me whole. This was a horrible idea, and I consider pleading sick right when Emily's cell phone rings.

"Fuck, it's work. I need to take this."

Emily takes the phone into the kitchen, which makes everything worse since now I'm alone with Aiden. We take a few bites in silence, but I keep expecting him to say something to me. I feel like he wants to, and the anticipation of waiting for him to say whatever it is makes it so I can't relax.

Emily's voice rings out clearly from the kitchen.

"Joel can't come in? I have company over."

Oh fuck, her work is calling her in? She's a key holder for the store, and they always need to have one person there at all times who is a designated key holder. She gets called into work for an emergency sometimes, but rarely.

Emily pokes her head into the dining room. "Fuck, guys, I have to go to work for a couple of hours. Cameron fell down the stairs and broke his arm, and I'm their only option."

I don't like her leaving, but Cameron is one of her favorite coworkers. I've met the guy several times and he's always friendly and helpful.

"Is he going to be okay?" I ask as she's cleaning up her side of the table.

"Yeah, I think so. But he's in a lot of pain right now and the pain meds make it so he can't work."

I don't ask her what Joel was doing where he couldn't come in instead of her. I'll find out later since I'm sure Aiden has no desire to hear about her coworkers.

"Are you guys going to be okay finishing dinner without me? I'll heat my salmon up when I get home." She's putting on her coat as she talks.

Do we have any choice? I can't be rude and kick him out.

I try to reassure her. "Yes, we'll be fine. Don't worry."

She comes over to me and presses a kiss to my forehead. "I'll see you after closing."

She turns to Aiden and I wonder how she's going to say goodbye to him. I'm half hoping she kisses him, but she didn't kiss me on the lips, so the other half of me doesn't want her to show him more affection than she did to me.

"Emily." Aiden's voice is firm.

"Yes, Sir?"

"I want you to find time to kneel somewhere for three minutes when you are on a break and take a picture. Send it to both me and Nate."

I stop mid-chew on a piece of salmon and my cock stiffens. *Okay, that's hot.* Getting turned on throws me into a tailspin and I'm dizzy and taking small breaths.

Emily bends down and kisses Aiden on the forehead and whispers, "Yes, Sir."

She gives us both a jaunty wave as she heads out, and when the door closes behind her, the house is too quiet. Feeling like I'm short of breath, I take a sip of water to see if it calms me. I don't know what's causing this reaction. I'm afraid of what Aiden is going to do now that Emily left, and yet I'm still expecting something and almost longing for whatever it is. The breathless feeling turns to panic, and I'm afraid I'm going to pass out. I can't seem to take a deep breath.

"Nate, look at me."

Aiden's commanding tone breaks through the alarm, and I meet his eyes.

"I'm going to count down from ten, and you are going to relax. Okay?"

I can only nod my head.

"Ten. You feel your chest loosening."

No, no, it's not. I think to myself that this won't work.

"Nine. You take one deep breath."

My lungs expand, and I can take a deep breath.

"Eight. You feel your butt touching your chair, centering you."

I notice the chair underneath me. *Oh, he's sort of good at this.*

"Seven. You feel your body relaxing."

When I do feel a slight relaxation, I almost laugh.

"Six. You take another deep breath."

I inhale again.

"Five. Your thoughts are calm."

Peacefulness washes over me.

"Four. You feel your neck and shoulders relaxing."

The tension in my shoulders eases and I relax them down, elongating my neck.

"Three. You can breathe normally now. Nothing is stressing you."

He's right. I am breathing normally. About that stress though...

"Two. You are happy, relaxed, and ready to enjoy your evening."

Dang, I need him around whenever I'm anxious. His countdown worked wonders.

"One. You say, Thank you, Aiden."

Oh. I freeze for a moment and my brain has a slight buzz. I hear my response as if from far away.

"Thank you, Sir."

~

AIDEN

When Nate calls me Sir, I get an intense high immediately and I have to fight the urge to call him a good boy. I'm not even sure Nate realizes what he said. He's relaxed now, and I watch him pick up his fork and start eating again, as if nothing happened. The need to dominate him and give him orders is hard to resist, but I am not the type of guy who would ever start commanding someone without a discussion first, especially since Nate seems unaware of what he did.

I don't know where to go from here. Tonight just took a turn down an unexpected path and I'm at a loss for how to correct our course. Talking about Emily seems to be the safe route while I gather my thoughts.

"Emily said you wanted to watch on Saturday."

Nate swallows before he responds. "Yes, if that's okay with you."

I'm assuming that Emily already told him I said it was fine, so him asking if it's okay with me pings my dom side again. If he had tagged on a 'Sir' at the end of his comment, it would have been exactly what I expected my submissive to say.

"Yes, that's fine."

Suddenly, I'm not too certain I want to be around Nate without an agreement with him of some sort. He's triggering me too much and I don't want to be fighting to control my impulses towards him while I'm mentally compromised from fucking his wife. It's time to be blunt.

"Nate, do you want more?"

His eyes widen, and he stumbles over his words. "Mo-more?"

Nate lays his fork down on the table and he looks flushed. He glances away from me, not able to maintain eye contact. His reaction solidifies a plan in my head. I lean back in my chair and smile indulgently at him while he studies his fork and fiddles with it.

"Nate."

He glances up at me again.

"I know you've been thinking about me."

His sharp inhale tells me all I need to know.

"I know I've been making you restless, and making you want more."

Nate swears softly, "Oh, fuck." I stop talking and gaze at him silently for a moment, holding his eyes captive until he visibly trembles.

"Do you want me to continue?"

He's quiet for a second before replying.

"Yes, Sir."

The End

MASTERING NATE

AN MMF ROMANTIC BDSM EROTICA SERIES

CHAPTER
ONE

EMILY

"No."

A wave of fury washes over me and I stare Nate down. "Just—no." I can't believe he even asked me this. I get home, all happy that Nate and Aiden were bonding over dinner and now Nate wants to be Aiden's submissive too?

Nate turns to me, incredulous. "Can you say no?"

I want to snap at him, "Of course I can motherfucking say no, this wasn't part of the agreement," but I hold my tongue. My chest tightens and my mind races, searching for answers. I don't understand what the fuck could have happened while I was gone, but all I can think is that Aiden is MY dom. Do I have to share everything with Nate? Can't I have this one thing of my own? Fuck, everything was going so well. Last Saturday was fun, and Nate asked to do it again so he obviously enjoyed himself.

I'd barely walked in the door from work when Nate rushed towards me, vibrating with excitement—or what seemed like it, but now I'm wondering if it was just him being all horny for Aiden. We came out to the living room to talk, and as soon as I sat down on the couch, nausea rolled over me. Fuckity, fuck, fuck, fuck.

Work sucked, and I wanted to be home having dinner with my men. If I had been there, this wouldn't have happened. I'm confused at how they got to this point, but Nate is pacing around the living room, getting more worked up by the minute.

"Nate, we need to talk about this. You don't realize what you're asking."

I try to keep my voice soothing because he really doesn't. He can't know what it's like to be a sub for Aiden. Is my wonderful husband even submissive? The tightness in my chest travels upwards and the dull throb in my head tells me a nasty headache is coming on. After the research I'd done, I understand there are all kinds of dom-sub relationships, but I can only imagine Aiden would want sexual control with Nate. Does he grasp what that entails...wait, is my husband bisexual?

Nate continues his circles around the living room and huffs at me, "Emily, I know more about BDSM than you did when you cheated with him."

I flinch at his comment and spots flash in front of my eyes. Is he going to bring that up every time we argue? It's true, I fucked up big time, but we were working past that and moving in the right direction. He's fighting dirty, and it pisses me off.

I snap at him, "Nate, you don't understand the first thing about being a submissive. There is so much you don't know."

That gets him to stop pacing, and his reply is snide. "Yeah, well, guess what? Aiden seems to be an excellent teacher. Don't you think so?"

The throb in my head intensifies and I'm done with this conversation. I can't think clearly with a pounding headache and Nate is so angry I don't see how anything we say is going to be constructive.

I sigh loudly. "Nate, I can't do this tonight. I'm exhausted. I'm going to sleep in the spare room and we can talk more tomorrow."

"Fine."

Nate's sullen tone doesn't make me feel any better, and when I walk past him, he looks miserable. My heart aches and I want to wrap my arms around him and tell him we'll work this out. But I don't see a way through right now, and I need to lie down.

I take nothing upstairs with me other than my cell phone, and I strip down to just my panties before sliding into bed. The moonlight shines through a crack in the curtains, creating a glow on the ceiling, and I stare at it. Deep down I recognize I'm being selfish, but his request surprised me and I blew up. I close my eyes, hoping that a good sleep will fix everything.

~

NATE

When Emily goes upstairs, I stare at her retreating back, dumbfounded. I never expected her reaction. She should be the first person who would understand the need to submit to someone and feel their control. And dismissing my wants without a discussion and just saying no...my shoulders drop and I'm dizzy so I sit down on the couch. If this is the way she's going to be, this might be the end of our marriage. Everything can't always be about Emily. She has to understand I have desires and needs too. Sighing, I get ready to sleep alone in our bed and hope she's more open to the idea in the morning.

I don't sleep well and I'm still resentful when I wake up and grumble to myself in the shower. If she won't let me explore this part of me, do I even want to do couples counseling with her? The fact that I can't answer the question scares me. Emily is the love of my life and we've been through a lot together in the last couple of months, but that might not be enough.

When I get out of the shower, Emily is in the bedroom waiting for her turn. Why does she need to be clean this early? Is she seeing Aiden today? My pulse speeds up and I glare at her when she walks past me. I bet she's planning on seeing Aiden because what Emily wants, Emily gets.

As I dress for work I notice her phone laying on the bed. I can still hear the water running so I feel like I have a second, and I irrationally snatch her phone and try to turn the screen on. It asks for a four-digit code and with only a moment's hesitation, I type in the same numbers she seems to use for everything and snort when it works. I look at her contact history and pull Aiden's name up and dig my phone out of my trousers so I can put his number into it. I make sure her phone is back exactly where it was and finish getting ready for work.

Not waiting around to say goodbye, I rush out the door and sit in the parking lot at work when I'm ten minutes early. My hands shake as I pick up my phone and message Aiden.

NATE

This is Nate. Emily came home last night and said I couldn't be your sub.

I don't know what I expect from Aiden, but I have to tell him what is going on before Emily sees him today. When he replies immediately, my pulse speeds up as I read it.

AIDEN

I'll talk to her today. Don't text me again until I tell you it's okay to.

Uh...is he angry at me? I want to ask him if he is, but that seems needy and he just told me not to text him. I'm disturbed as I walk into work and when a coworker has to say hello twice before I respond, I can tell this is going to be a long day.

AIDEN

I set the phone down after telling Nate not to text me. Jesus Christ. Emily blurts out whatever pops into her head sometimes, but I'm curious about what happened last night between them. Texting Emily, I tell her I'm coming over today and emphasize that it's just to talk. She replies with, "Yes, Sir," and I wonder if she knows Nate messaged me.

This wondering-what-they-are-saying-to-each-other crap annoys me and I stomp around my apartment while I get ready to leave. Recalling the day when I first met Nate at the cafe and how I wondered if I had just met my kryptonite couple...it's possible I really did. This is exactly why I don't get involved with couples that often. The open communication needed for a BDSM relationship to work smoothly isn't easy, and it sounds like Emily and Nate need to sit down and talk.

On the drive to their house, I contemplate breaking it off with both of them. I don't need this shit in my life. But I realize I actually half WANT this shit in my life. Last Saturday was fabulous. Am I willing to give that up? I'm so close to having them both on their knees for me and the rush I get around Emily is addictive so it would be difficult to break it off. I can easily see the same thing happening with Nate, and I crave it. My cock stiffens at the fantasy of commanding both of them to play together, and I smirk and tell my junk to relax because he's not getting that today.

But one thing I won't do is talk to them behind each other's backs. They have to communicate with each other, or this won't work and I'll have to move on, no matter how much it hurts.

CHAPTER

TWO

EMILY

When Aiden gets to the house and is barely through the door when he tells me that Nate texted him this morning, I'm cranky all over again. I felt a bit better today, but not now. Heat flashes through my body and my jaw clenches. It's a good thing Nate is at work. It wouldn't be pretty if he was in the same room as me. I bring Aiden into the kitchen and we sit down to talk. He's watching me, so I take a few deep breaths to calm down a little.

When he asks me, "Did you guys fight?" I want to snicker, but hold it in.

"Yeah, we did."

I don't elaborate, but as the scene from last night replays in my head, I keep going back to how forlorn Nate was as I left the room. I scrub a hand over my face and pinch the bridge of my nose as a knot forms in my stomach. Shit, I was such a bitch last night.

Nate stayed with me after I blatantly cheated on him, and he's been trying to give me the freedom to express myself. So why wouldn't I do the same for him? But does Aiden even want this?

"Um...Sir?"

Aiden's lip twitches when I call him Sir, and the knot in my stomach eases as a tingle of desire spreads through me. Does he have to be so dang sexy? Even when I'm angry and had a horrible night, I still hunger for him.

"Yes, Doll?"

"Would you even want us both as your sub?"

There, I said it. I'm uncertain what I wish to happen, but if he has no interest, there is no point in worrying about it.

Aiden takes a moment to reply and I can tell he's considering it. "It's tough to suppress desires. If he needs this, do you really want to say no?"

He's right. Once I realized I was submissive, I wouldn't have been able to lock it away again. It would have led to Nate and me splitting up. I can't expect him to either. But Aiden didn't answer my question. I open my mouth to point that out, but he continues.

"I'd like to see if we could make this work instead of you guys fighting."

"Yeah..." There's nothing else to say to him because trying would be better than arguing about it for days or weeks, and ultimately I just want Nate to be happy. But I'm still torn.

Exhaling loudly, I tell him, "I need to think about it."

Aiden stands up and I'm surprised. He hasn't been here that long. "Talk to Nate and let me know how it goes. I don't want to come over again until you have things settled with him."

Oh fuck, now I don't get to see him until Nate and I figure this out? A part of me was hoping we would talk and then he would fuck me hard so I could forget all my troubles.

When he kisses my forehead, and says, "I'll talk to you later, Doll," I sigh unhappily.

I walk him to the door and wave goodbye to him from the porch before he drives off. After I go back into the house, I lean against the closed door and hold in my tears. Ugh, this sucks.

I work a mid-shift today and decide, "fuck 'em," and call in sick. Telling myself I need a mental health day, I try to not feel guilty. Since I'm not the closer, they don't need me there as a keyholder and they'll be fine without me tonight. I yawn and decide I deserve a nap.

~

AIDEN

Turning on my favorite 80s music station, I tap my fingers on the steering wheel to "Don't Stop Believin'" by Journey and smile. I really hope Emily considers Nate's needs before she says no. Singing, I try to avoid ruminating over worst-case scenarios. I need to believe she's going to do the right thing since I'm not ready to make a choice if she refuses to let him explore his submissive side.

~

NATE

When I get home, I'm surprised to see Emily's car in the garage. She's supposed to be working for another hour. I find her in the office playing a computer game.

"What are you doing at home?" My tone is accusatory to my ears. Shit, I didn't mean to sound that way.

She glances up at me with unreadable eyes. "I took a mental health day."

I turn and leave the room without speaking to her. Sure would be nice if I could just call in sick whenever I wanted as well. I recognize I'm being petty, but I'm hungry and tired, which is a bad combo. I pull lasagna from the freezer and, as I pop it into the oven, I'm cranky again. How hard is it to put a frozen meal in the oven? She could at least make dinner if she was staying home.

Knowing the lasagna is going to take an hour to bake, I change out of my work clothes, set an alarm, and snuggle into bed for a nap. When the buzzer goes off, I'm groggy and blink. Is it morning already?

It takes a few moments for my brain to warm up, but when it does, I remember I put lasagna in. I find Emily out in the kitchen dishing us both a plate.

"Oh, hi," I blurt out and stare at the floor, not wanting to meet her eyes. If she's still angry, I'll take my plate to the living room and eat alone and watch a show.

Her voice is soft when she replies, "Hi," in response.

Since she doesn't sound irritated, that gives me the courage to glance at her. She's studying me and I can't tell if that's good or bad.

She asks, "Do you want to eat in the dining room?"

"Oh, sure."

Does she want to talk to me? My muscles tense and my pulse speeds up. I don't want to fight again tonight, but we need to discuss what happened and where to go from here.

We settle in at the table and eat in silence for a bit and I relax, half relieved, and yet knowing it would be better to get the conversation over with. We're almost finished with dinner when I get the guts to bring it up.

"Emily, we really should talk."

She mutters under her breath, "Yeah, I know."

I wanted to pick my words carefully, but now that the moment is here, I can't remember anything I wanted to say and burst out with, "You can't just say no to me."

She studies me, pensively. "So you're saying I have no choice and you're going to do whatever you want?"

Fuck, that's not what I'm saying. "No..."

"Nate, that isn't how this works. You can ask for something and I might not want it."

I want to tell her that the street runs both ways, but the difference is that I said yes when she asked if she could have us both when I didn't have to. It probably would have ruined us if I hadn't, but I made the choice. Is she TRYING to ruin us?

"Nate." Her voice is sharp. "Look at me."

A punch of desire hits me and I almost laugh at myself. Now is not supposed to be a funny moment but my immediate response to her command is telling. I lift my eyes to hers. Her face is strained, and I can tell she's getting worked up again. Fuck, we're going to end up fighting. I say nothing and wait for her to speak again.

"Nate, you don't know what you're asking for."

I tap my foot and narrow my eyes at her. She keeps repeating the same argument and I'm getting sick of going in circles. I'm not a fucking child.

I don't hide my annoyance. "How do you know?"

Her eyes widen with a hard glint, and her voice is steely. "So you think you understand what it is to be a submissive?"

My cock stiffens from her tone, and my stomach flutters. *Uh, what's happening here?*

I lower my eyes and reply in a low voice. "Not fully, but I want it."

She laughs harshly. "You want to suck his cock?"

A neediness spreads through me. "Yes, I do."

"What if he wants to fuck you in the ass? Are you going to say, 'Yes, Sir' and bend over?"

She's being deliberately crude and she's trying to turn me off, but it's doing the opposite. My cock pulses and instead of imagining Aiden fucking my ass, I picture Emily with a strap-on.

"Yes, I would."

I dare to peek at her again. She's sitting straight up in her chair, flushed, and her eyes are blazing. She looks like an angry goddess and I want to worship her.

She pushes back her chair, and when she rises, she seems taller than usual. I tilt my head way back to meet her gaze, and she radiates an aura of power.

My mind buzzes, and the room spins. My cock throbs and I want whatever is about to happen.

"Nate, stand up and strip."

The command in her voice has me immediately obeying. I get out of my chair and remove my clothes as fast as I can. My cock stands to attention, and I'm willing to do whatever Emily wants.

She steps forward and grasps my shaft, squeezing painfully. I wince, but a thrill runs through me at the same time.

"You're going to be my fucktoy tonight and we'll see if you really want this."

A rush of pleasure ripples through me and my cock pulses in her hand.

I don't know where submissive Emily went, but I'm 100 percent down for the change.

I moan out, "Yes, Mistress," as she jerks my shaft.

"Mmm, then you're coming with me."

She keeps a firm grip on my cock and leads me towards the bedroom.

CHAPTER

THREE

EMILY

As soon as we get into the bedroom, I drop my hand from his cock and pull off my clothes. I want him to know what he's getting into and he's going to do exactly what I tell him to, or else he's going to get punished. I've never felt this whirring in my brain before, like a soft static. It's making me want to fuck around with Nate and see exactly how far he'll take this.

Nate appears dazed and a warmth of love for him floods me while my fingers tingle with the need to stroke his cock and see if I can make him mindless like Aiden so masterfully does to me. I don't know what I'm doing, but I desperately want to hear him beg. When he called me Mistress, it felt right. Tonight, I AM his Mistress and he's going to see exactly what serving ME would be like.

"Nate, my pet?" I purposely keep my voice light and airy.

"Yes?" he stammers out.

Oh no, that won't do at all. Thinking back on my training with Aiden, I almost smile, but I'm able to contain it.

"No, that isn't how you address me. You will say, 'Yes, Mistress.' Got it?"

He only hesitates for a moment before replying, "Yes, Mistress."

I walk over to him and lovingly cup his chin, forcing him to look directly at me when I say, "Good boy."

His eyes widen slightly and a thrill of power engulfs me. It's pretty fucking amazing to know he's standing there waiting for me to tell him what to do, and that if I trained him, eventually he'd do anything to hear me call him a Good boy.

And I know exactly what I'm going to do and my wet pussy approves.

I slink onto the center of the bed, roll onto my back, and tuck a pillow under my head. When I'm comfortable, I draw my knees up, placing my feet flat on the mattress and spread my legs. Nate is at the end of the bed with a very graphic view, and my wetness drips down my crack. I slide a hand between my legs, moaning softly as my fingers slip between my soft folds to caress my clit.

I'm already more turned on than usual and I close my eyes, lost in the inferno of need my fingers create as they glide across my sensitive bundle of nerves. A slight shuffling sound at the end of the bed makes me open my eyes. Nate has moved a foot closer to the bed until he's touching the mattress and he's rubbing his cock. I allow myself to grin this time. Oh, this is going to be fun.

"Nate." My voice is pointed, and he pauses mid stroke. "Did I say you could touch yourself?"

He's tentative with his reply. "No..."

I sigh dramatically, more elated by his response than anything else.

"No...what? Say it the correct way, or I'm going to have to punish you."

I hear the intake of breath when I mention punishment, and the buzz in my head gets louder. Oh, it seems like someone likes the idea of discipline. Maybe my pet wants to edge tonight and not come? When Aiden was training me to edge, it was rough at first, but I've grown to enjoy it. I don't think I've ever purposely had sex with Nate with the intention of not letting him come, but that might be just the thing he needs to find out if he really wants to be a submissive to Aiden. You can bet your ass that Aiden will enjoy making Nate a drooling pile of need and forcing him to continually stroke for hours without coming.

When Nate whispers, "No, Mistress," I'm so engrossed in my fantasy of denial that I almost forget what he was responding to. Oh yeah, my plan.

Brazenly, I tell him, "Stop touching yourself and crawl between my legs. Your days of not licking my pussy are over."

He doesn't protest and climbs onto the bed, straight for my pussy. I play with his hair and when he latches his lips onto my clit, I arch up against him, pressing his face against my pussy, and gasp. *God, now this is more like it.* Tendrils of bliss zing from my core as he laves my swollen bean. When he slides two fingers inside me, I moan and buck against his mouth.

He speeds up his movements, and since he's only gone down on me once in the last three years, I forgot how fantastic he is at it. I momentarily wonder why I didn't ask him to go down on me all these years. Looks like now I have a way to make it happen. I chuckle softly, but it turns into a groan when he curls his fingers and massages my cave wall.

I'm hyper focused on his every moment as he strokes deep inside me while he licks my clit. I clench my fists into the bedsheets and writhe against his face as the pleasure builds. When I finally tip over the abyss, I cry out as the waves of rapture crash into me. He doesn't stop his attention on my pussy and the orgasm seems never ending.

When I finally come down from the peak, I nudge his head away. He grins up at me, his face glistening with my juices.

"Good boy," I murmur and I can tell he wants the praise when he beams at me.

Now that I've come, I'm feeling less inclined to edge him tonight. If he becomes Aiden's submissive, there will be enough of that in his future. But that doesn't mean tonight won't be about MY pleasure.

I purr at him, "Nate, come up here and suck on my nipples."

"Yes, Mistress," he chips happily and climbs out from between my legs.

When he immediately scoots up next to me and takes a nipple in his mouth, I want to giggle at how he reminds me of a trained puppy, all eager to please. I run my fingers through his hair and moan as he swirls his tongue around the tip. He uses a hand to play with the other nipple, and my pussy throbs from pleasure.

Deciding it's time for my second orgasm, I push him away from me and onto his back. Mounting him, I put a hand on his chest and guide his cock to my wet entrance. I consider teasing him, but I'm too impatient. Pressing down with one swift motion, we both groan out as he stretches and fills me.

I grab his hands and place them on my hips as I rotate and grind against his shaft. I'm making a mess of him, and the sound of our wet bodies slapping together fills the room. God, this is so fucking amazing and my mind races with all the things I could make him do. The idea of spending hours toying with him and making him pleasure me with my favorite vibrator, and then his cock again when he's able, appeals in a way it never has before. The intense rush of being in control is euphoric. When I look deep into Nate's eyes and they shine with lust and adoration, I feel like a goddess. I bounce against him as the rapture mounts and I can tell I'm going to come quickly.

Just when I'm about to tip over the edge, Nate groans out, "Oh, god, I'm going to come!"

I snap to attention. "You better not. You didn't ask for permission."

Nate whimpers, "I can't hold back," and when he doesn't call me Mistress and thinks he's going to come without asking, the pleasure in my core turns to anger.

When his cock pulses inside of me and he groans, I know I need to stop him from coming or I won't get my second orgasm while riding him. I lash out at him, "Oh, no, you don't," and smack him hard across his cheek.

Oh fuck, what did I just do? Our eyes latch on to each other and grow round.

My mind blanks and I pound against him in a frenzy, seeking release. When Nate closes his eyes and erupts, he jerks underneath me, unloading his hot, sticky cum deep inside my pussy. The room spins and stars explode behind my eyes as I peak again and cry out with the force of my orgasm. Waves of delight wash over me and I ride Nate as my pussy clenches and milks every last drop from him.

As I come down, I wince because my twice-orgasmed bits are too sensitive now and I roll over next to him onto my back. The sound of heavy panting from both of us as we try to catch our breath causes reality to come crashing down on me. I don't know what happened. I've never hit him before, or even wanted to. What am I going to say to him? "Sorry" seems pathetic, and he's going to hate me.

My stomach clenches in disgust at myself and I want to pull the covers over my head and hide, but I need to apologize. I turn on my side and cautiously raise my eyes to his face. Nate has a soft smile and appears blissed out. He looks more content than I've seen him in a long time.

Holy shit, he liked that? What do I do now?

NATE

I'm floating in a warm, comfortable bubble and roll over towards Emily. I'm not sure I've ever loved her more than I do in this moment. She's not a violent person, so for her to give me the roughness I didn't even know I needed was amazing. She's staring up at the ceiling and I have an overwhelming desire to hear her say she loves me. I cuddle up against her and drape my arm across her waist. She shifts and pulls her arm out from between us so I can rest my head against her breast while she rubs my back. I'm completely spent and happy.

I kiss the side of her breast and my voice is rough when I whisper, "I love you, Emily."

When she kisses the top of my head and croons that she loves me too, my heart skips a beat and I can't help but wonder if this will change her mind about me being Aiden's sub.

FOUR

AIDEN

It's barely 8 a.m. when my phone chirps at me with a text message. This is usually the time I'm just rolling out of bed, but I overdid it playing basketball yesterday and woke up with a horrible leg cramp. When I had to get up and walk it off and realized my alarm would go off in 30 minutes, I said fuck it, and stayed up. I usually play basketball weekly with the same group of friends, but the closer I get to 50, the more I seem to have assorted aches and pains after a game. Getting old sucks and yet I'm happier at this age than I was in my 30s.

I smile when I see the message is from Emily, but her words quickly twist it into a frown.

EMILY

Sir, I fucked up and I need to talk to you.

Huh. I scratch my chin. I'm curious, but I figure this is about her and Nate fighting. Do I want to get into this so early in the morning, or should I have some coffee first? I head to the kitchen and start my coffee brewing, but I'm too intrigued not to find out what's going on, so I reply to her.

I'm a little busy right now, Doll. Give me a hint, what's up?

I'm not really busy, but I want to see what she'll say. This really better not be about them fighting. They need to work out their issues together.

I went domme and slapped Nate.

What's this? Maybe she slapped him without going domme. I think everyone has the potential to be a switch. I hadn't felt it from Emily yet, but it's always possible. Rolling my shoulders in the hopes of loosening the tight muscles, I think about Emily's journey. She and I have been so focused on her training, she might not have had the freedom to explore that side of herself yet. I decide to respond to her now instead of making her wait.

How do you know you went domme? What did it feel like?

My coffee finishes before her next reply comes in and I sit down at my kitchen table and sip while I read her long block of text.

I don't know. It was strange. I had a rush of power and I wanted to play and tease him all night. I was super focused on him, but I wanted to control what he did and said. He called me Mistress, so I made him continue with that and I wanted to edge him, but I ended up not. Then I forced him to eat my pussy, and then rode him. He was going to come without permission, so I smacked him. Then we both came.

My cock springs to life when she said she forced him to eat her pussy. Well, well, well, now isn't that interesting? Everything she described sounds like she went domme—controlling him, making him do what she said, and the night getting out of hand for an inexperienced domme. It looks like I have a switch on my hands. I text her and tell her to not stress about it and just make sure Nate is okay with what happened. I sip my coffee and contemplate this new discovery. There are so many fun things I could do with her and Nate, and my cock throbs at the thought of making her command him. Oh, yeah, this is going to be interesting.

When my phone rings I grin when I see it's Emily.

"Yes, Emily?"

"Uh Sir, sorry to call you but I'm freaking out a little here. He seemed to like it."

She seems confused, and I'm careful not to sound amused by her plight. Years of experience makes this seem like no big deal to me, but I know things are scary when you're new to them.

"Have you guys talked about any of this?"

Her voice is contrite. "No, we tried to talk and then he pissed me off and I went domme."

I could just imagine angry Emily, and she's making it difficult not to laugh. I bet Nate loved every minute of it.

"Sir..." She pauses before continuing. "I think I want to try this."

A strong pulse runs through my cock at her words and I'm ecstatic she came to this decision on her own without me pressing for it. This was the outcome I wanted, but it needed to be her choice.

"Why don't I come over on Saturday and we can talk about it together?"

Her breath blows out into the phone like she was holding it in. "Oh, please? That would help."

"I'll come over at 10, but you have to talk to him and tell him you want to try this, okay?"

She rushes out eagerly, "Yes. Yes, of course. I'll talk to him."

I say goodbye to her and reiterate I'll be there at 10 on Saturday but think of one last thing.

"Oh, and Doll?"

"Yes?"

"Tell Nate to think of a safe word."

When she peeps out a small, "Oh," I disconnect the call with a smile.

~

NATE

The day after Emily fucked me senseless, I'm happy and beaming at work. So much so that a close friend jokes that I must have gotten laid the night before. I wiggle my brows at him and smile secretively, which makes him laugh. I get a nice illicit zing from knowing we had kinkier than our standard vanilla sex. No one I know would ever guess that I crave being dominated in the bedroom. I'm eager to get home tonight to Emily and I check our joint calendar to see what shift she works. Excited butterflies swirl in my stomach when it says she only has four hours on mid-shift, so she'll be home around 6 p.m.

The day drags by and I keep watching the clock. When it's finally quitting time, I stop at the store to buy some chicken and corn chowder for dinner. I swing through the bakery aisle to nab a loaf of Emily's favorite French bread to go with it and select a bottle of Merlot from the liquor department.

When Emily gets home, the soup is ready and I'm pouring her a glass of wine.

As she comes into the kitchen and sees the spread, she exclaims, "Wow, hi!" and kisses me on the cheek she slapped last night.

I feel myself blushing when I remember how hard I came from her slap. Why was that so hot? I've tried to not focus on that aspect too much today and just let myself enjoy the overall naughtiness of the experience. But liking it when she struck me seems wrong. When my cock hardens, I focus on Emily and ask her how her day was to divert my attention elsewhere.

She shrugs. "Eh, it was stock day, and you know that always sucks."

I've heard her grumble about everything she has to do when new product comes in, but even knowing she might be tired and grumpy doesn't make my cock less interested. Distracting him didn't work. He's now fully hard in my jeans from being close to her.

Emily selects a thick slice of buttered bread and leans against the counter, munching on it. "Want to watch a show tonight while we eat?"

She sounds hopeful and I imagine kneeling on the floor between her legs, kissing up her inside thigh while she runs her hands through my hair and keeps her eyes focused on the TV.

My vivid fantasy has me tripping over my tongue. "Uh, ye—yes, sure."

"God, that sounds good. I'm going to change and then we can eat."

When she leaves the kitchen, I tell myself to get a grip. She's grumpy tonight so she probably isn't in the mood.

She comes back in soft cotton shorts and an adorable t-shirt with a panda on the front. I can tell she isn't wearing a bra underneath, and I have to hold back a groan.

She seems oblivious to my desire, and we carry the soup and bread out to the living room. She sets up our TV trays while I go back to the kitchen for the wine. It doesn't take long and we're snug on the couch, eating and picking a show to stream since we recently finished the series we were watching together.

As I play with the streaming app and list our choices, she's quiet and doesn't respond. I glance at her, assuming she doesn't like any of the series I mentioned.

"No? Not that one? We have more options."

I fiddle with the remote some more and pull up another page of shows we bookmarked for later.

"No, it's not that."

"Oh?" I peek back over at her. "What's wrong?"

She reaches over and slides her hand into the one of mine closest to her, which luckily wasn't the one holding the remote. The warmth of her palm makes my cock twitch, as if he's reminding me he's still there.

"Nate?"

Her voice sounds serious, which confuses me. "Yes?"

"Let's try what you want with Aiden."

I wasn't expecting that, and time slows to a standstill. The room becomes silent for a moment and I'm stunned.

Suddenly, all my senses switch on and everything crashes back into me with a whoosh. The furnace blows louder through the register and the aroma of the chowder is distinctive, which makes my stomach growl in response.

I don't know what to say, but there's a lightness in my chest and I want to scoop her up into a big hug. Instead, I beam at her and bring the back of her hand to my mouth and kiss it.

"Thank you, my love."

~

EMILY

Nate is all in a dither on Saturday morning before Aiden comes over and it's cute. Last night when I told him he needed to pick a safe word, he quickly spat out the word 'pineapple,' and I laughed. With how fast he came up with it, I suspected he'd been thinking about needing one. We should have had one the other day, but we weren't prepared for what happened the night I slapped him.

We're in the living room when the doorbell rings, and Nate jumps up off the couch.

"I'll get it."

I smile indulgently at his retreating backside. Ever since I went domme the other night, I've had the same feeling lurking in the back of my consciousness around Nate. I'm assuming if Aiden makes me his mindless fucktoy, I'll flip back to my normal subby self.

Nate and Aiden come into the living room together and Nate sits on the couch next to me while Aiden takes the rocking chair across from us.

Aiden immediately speaks. "We need to discuss how this will work."

Oh shit, he's not wasting any time. Nate and I both nod our heads at him, and my pussy clenches as a gush of wetness hits my panties. The immediate ache between my legs has me thinking about my double stuff fantasy and imagining both of them fucking me. Now isn't the time for my slutty self to be daydreaming. Tilting my head, I stretch my neck, trying to clear the sexual fantasy and pay attention.

"When you are with me, you are both my submissives and I'm in control. What you do in your free time is your own business, okay?"

I quietly say, "Yes, Sir," and Nate echoes me.

I squirm a little on the couch, trying to ease the itch from my pussy. I think he just gave me permission to domme Nate. When I peek over at Nate, he's got a soft smile on his face. Yeah, he's enjoying this.

Aiden looks at Nate. "Did you choose a safe word?"

"It's pineapple."

Aiden nods, all business, and I wish I was sitting in his lap, rubbing against his cock through his jeans. I didn't expect to get this turned on by watching Nate be submissive to Aiden, but it's hot with both of us under Aiden's control and my response removes any lingering doubts about whether I will like this.

"We're going to take this slow and see how it goes. If anyone is uncomfortable, we need to communicate and talk it through. I don't want my phone blowing up every night because we're not being open with each other."

I catch Nate flinching out of the corner of my eye. Yeah, he's the guilty party on that one.

"Do you both agree?"

When we nod, Aiden smiles. "No, I want to hear you say it."

Nate blurts out a, "Yes," while I calmly say, "Yes, Sir."

Knowing what is about to happen, I school my face to not show my glee.

Aiden's voice is patient when he instructs Nate. "Nate, you chose to call me Sir, so I want you to use it when we're together."

Nate peeps out a small, "Oh...yes, Sir." I almost giggle at how much he's mimicking my submissive side. It's charming to see him like this.

"Well, now...you two ready to begin?"

Nate and I glance at each other, wide eyed. Are we ready for this? My pussy thrums again and the flush on Nate's face can't hide his excitement.

"I'm ready, Sir," I call out in a clear voice.

Aiden leans back in the rocking chair. "Emily, I want you to strip and show Nate the display pose for inspection."

I jump up, eager to do his bidding. Shedding my clothes as quickly as I can, I toss them into a pile on the floor and stand with my back to the couch.

"Good, girl." Aiden stands up and circles me. "Emily, I want you to command Nate to do the same thing."

Huh, what's this? Nate's sharp inhale of breath makes me wish I was facing him so I could see his expression, but I hold my position steady.

"Uh, Nate. Stand up and do this pose."

It seems stupid to be directing Nate while Aiden is right here to do it himself, but when the sound of clothing rustles behind me and I know that he's removing them because I told him to, a tiny flicker of power wells up inside me. Nate brushes my elbow as he moves next to me, and with a side eye, I can see him getting into the correct stance.

Aiden circles us both. "Good girl...Good boy."

I get the familiar ping of pleasure to my brain, knowing that I satisfied him. I'm needy with desire and moisture runs down my inner thigh. Aiden never said what he was planning, but I hope it includes me having an orgasm. A tiny part of me doesn't care if Nate gets one. I'd find it amusing if his edging training starts today, but Aiden said we're taking things slow, so I doubt he'd do that.

Aiden sits down in the rocking chair again and folds his hands on his stomach. "Emily, make Nate sit on the couch so you can kneel between his knees and suck his cock. I want to enjoy watching my subs play together."

When I turn towards Nate and drop my hands from my head, Nate's eyes glaze with lust as he meets my mine. I almost feel sorry for him. He's getting a double dose of control for his first session with Aiden. But then I realize the rush I'm getting from doing what Aiden wants is intoxicating for me as well. I'm Aiden's puppet, and he's toying with both of us.

The need to do well and receive a "Good girl" again makes my voice firm. "Nate, sit on the couch and spread your knees."

He plunks down without hesitation. If Aiden wants a show, I can give him one. Lowering myself to all fours, I wiggle my ass towards Aiden and crawl between Nate's spread legs. I'm rewarded with the "Good girl" I hoped to hear, and I smile as I prop myself on Nate's thighs with my forearms and grip his cock between both hands.

His shaft pulses against my palms and when I peer up at his face, I want to call him a 'Good boy' myself, but I'm not sure if that's allowed. I gather a pool of saliva against my tongue and open my mouth over the tip of his cock, letting the wetness drip down onto him.

As I work the moisture into his shaft, he moans and twitches. Knowing that Aiden is watching heightens all my senses and my nipples harden and my breath puffs in excited gasps. When I lower my mouth to the head of his cock, I take in just enough to swirl my tongue around it, slowly stroking the base. Nate's thigh muscles flex, and I can tell he's more worked up than usual. A quick look up tells me he's focused on Aiden. Desire and longing infuse his face and my stomach flutters.

Fuck, that's hot.

More wetness leaks from my pussy and I imagine Aiden behind me while I suck on Nate. I wiggle my ass towards Aiden some more, in case he notices, and I throw myself into the blowjob. With a firm grip at the base of his shaft, I engulf the entire length of him, sucking and swirling my tongue as I bob my head. Nate's hands are on the couch next to him and he tries to bring them up to my head. When I pause, about to remove his cock from my mouth and tell him to stop, he drops them back onto the cushion, so I continue with my task.

The room fills with the sound of his groans and the wet sucking of my mouth, so I don't hear Aiden get out of his chair. I moan loudly when I feel his warmth press against me from behind and the tip of his cock prodding the entrance of my pussy. The brush of his bare skin against my ass tells me he removed his clothes and I didn't notice. He grabs my hips and slams into me, shoving Nate's cock further down my throat as Aiden's thick shaft tunnels its way to my core, stretching me gloriously.

Ooooh, fuck. I gurgle around Nate's cock, unable to vocalize the moans as Aiden pummels into my sodden hole. This might not be my double stuff fantasy, but it's fucking amazing and knowing I'm giving pleasure to both men at once is almost more than I can take. The room spirals and a sharp smack to my ass has me crying out. Each deep thrust continues to push Nate's shaft deeper and deeper down my throat.

Nate's moans intensify and when his cock pulses, I know he's close to coming. Aiden grabs a fistful of my hair, pulling my head back and forcing me to release Nate from my mouth.

Aiden pants out, "Tell Nate to come on your face."

He continues to keep his grasp on my hair and I'm looking straight at my wonderful husband, whose pained expression tells me he's trying to hold back his orgasm.

"Nate, stroke yourself and coat my face with your cum."

I can't believe how slutty this is, having one man plowing me from behind while making my husband blow his load on me. Hot waves build in my core and move outwards to my fingers and toes. A few well-timed spanks from Aiden have me groaning and getting closer and closer to my climax.

Nate tries to stroke himself slowly at first, but within seconds he's yanking his cock furiously and shuddering. I close my eyes just in time as he moans loudly and splatters my face with his sticky cum. Some lands on my forehead and I don't want to open my eyes, and it tickles as it slides down my face and nose.

Aiden hammers against me, and each whack against my pussy elicits a nice pleasure-pain zing. When Aiden groans out that we're such a good girl and boy, I can't take anymore and erupt.

I cry out, "Oooooh, my god," as waves of pleasure wash over me and I buck and shudder against Aiden.

Aiden comes with a roar, and he yanks my hair back harder, causing my scalp to tingle, but it also intensifies my continued orgasm. Spikes of rapture rush up and down my body and I milk Aiden's cock as he fucks his cum back up inside me.

When Aiden finally slows his thrusts, I'm quivering and my mind is fuzzy. He pulls me down to the floor on my side so he can spoon me. The cum has either dripped off my face or it's drying, so I'm able to open my eyes.

Aiden holds his hand out towards Nate, and Nate slides off the couch, takes his hand and joins us on the floor. Both men cuddle up close to me, Nate in front and Aiden behind, and wrap their arms around me so that they can also embrace each other. I try to catch my breath, but the room keeps spinning and my body occasionally spasms with aftershocks of pleasure.

Nate's eyes are closed, but he has the contented look of a man well satisfied. When I glance down and see the men have their hands entwined together, I'm bathed in a warm glow. This really is going to work.

The End

AIDEN'S CONTROL

AN MMF ROMANTIC BDSM EROTICA SERIES

CHAPTER
ONE

AIDEN

As I walk into work on Monday, I wave hello to the bartender and head to the back office. It's going to be difficult to concentrate today. Since I left their house on Saturday, all I've been thinking about has been Emily and Nate. I haven't had two subs in several years, and I've only played with a wife and husband duo twice. I'm intoxicated by the thought of having them both on their knees for me soon, but this isn't just about them pleasing me. It's important to make this a positive experience for everyone, and hopefully now with their improved communication, it will bring them closer as a couple.

I love Emily, more than I thought possible in the brief time I've known her, but I won't let myself get carried away since she ultimately belongs with Nate. Now about Nate...

I sigh as I take off my leather jacket and hang it on the hook behind my office door, along with my motorcycle helmet. It's a nice day out, so I rode my bike to work. Switching my computer on, I scan my emails for anything important—mainly looking for emails from Zane, my boss and best friend.

I'm the manager of a small, successful bar; I met the owner, Zane, in college when I went back to school as a non-traditional student in my late 30s to get a business degree. It's an unlikely friendship with Zane because he's younger than I am. He was this punk-ass kid straight out of high school who didn't know jack shit about himself or understand his darker desires. He reminded me of myself at his age and I could tell he was going to get into trouble and possibly hurt someone. I took him under my wing and helped him understand he could control his sadistic side.

After he graduated, his grandmother passed away and left him enough money to follow his dream of owning a bar. He hired me as the manager since I'd been a bartender most of my adult life, and then he opened a second bar that he manages himself. I'm more than an employee, and I've been working with Zane for about eight years now. My job is stressful sometimes, but one bartender manages three nights a week, including weekends, so I have Friday and Saturday nights free, plus a rotating day during the week. I occasionally have to work weekends if it's a major drinking holiday, or we have a big event planned, but I love this schedule. I enjoy working four tens, and not having to manage on the busiest nights of the week. It pays to be Zane's best friend. I could ask for anything and I think he'd make it happen.

Rubbing the back of my neck, I delete a few emails before my thoughts drift back to Nate. What am I going to do with him? He's barely tapped into his submissive side, but at least he's admitting to it now. Directing them both on Saturday was erotic as all fuck and every time I reminisce about Emily on all fours sucking on Nate's cock, I get hard and want to stroke. I long to dominate Nate, but I'm also uncertain of the best path to take with him.

The high I got from controlling them both had me close to losing my restraint, though it's not something I'd admit to them. I told them we'd take it slow last Saturday, but I wanted to edge them both for hours until they were a quivering mess. I hungered for total submission, and it was difficult to stay levelheaded and make sure this first time was all fun and games.

Knowing that Nate enjoyed being slapped adds another layer to my confusion. Emily doesn't enjoy much pain, but Nate might ask for it someday and I'll have to know what I'm willing to do to help him explore that side of himself. I can give more, but would Emily be able to handle seeing it? This is all the stuff we must work out together.

Whatever happens, those two have to keep the lines of communication open and discuss their problems. No matter how well Saturday went, I can't have a married couple as my subs if it's going to destroy their marriage. I didn't guard my heart against Emily, and my attraction to Nate could prove difficult as well if shit blows up between them.

Realizing I'm chewing on the end of my pen, I smile ruefully and get back to scanning my emails. I have over nine hours left of this shift and somehow I'm going to have to focus. I wonder what Emily and Nate are doing right now.

NATE

When I get home from work on Monday, Emily has dinner almost ready and we exchange a brief kiss in greeting. Does she work anymore? It's beginning to feel like she's home more often than not. As I put my lunch containers in the sink, I turn and watch her test the doneness of the chicken breasts she's baking. She has to bend over slightly to remove the dish from the oven, and I admire the stretch of her yoga pants across her curvy ass. Her panty lines are visible through the fabric and my fingers itch to rub her pussy and see if I can get her so wet it seeps through the two thin layers. It's probably not the best idea while she's working around a hot stove and trying to cook.

Sighing, I lean against the counter and adjust my stiffening junk. All I can think about is sinking into her wet folds and the cute little moans she makes whenever I hit just the right spot. I need something to distract me.

I almost groan, but cover it up with a cough before speaking. "You didn't work tonight?"

She's holding a spatula and her back is towards me. She pauses with the utensil in the air as if she's thinking about how to respond. "Work changed my hours."

Hmm...did work change them, or did she? "What shift do you have now?"

She's efficient as she portions out the chicken onto plates and gives each one a scoop of steamed broccoli from a pot on the stovetop. I grin at her, even though she can't see it, when she takes the time to arrange the florets in an attractive pile next to the chicken before answering. "They want me to work two eight-hour shifts per week."

Sixteen hours is less than what she was working before, but she only does it to feed her crafting addiction and get the discount on supplies. "Will that be enough money for you?"

She turns, holding both plates, and her eyes glimmer. "I'm not exactly crafting as much anymore. It'll be more than enough."

Heat radiates through my chest and the mental image of her and Aiden, naked and sweaty with their limbs tangled up. I spied on them fucking often enough to know exactly how that looks.

Keeping my tone light, I razz her. "No, you're got more fulfilling duties."

Her silvery laugh rings out. "After dinner, I might need another *hard* task to work on. Do you have anything *hard* enough to keep me entertained?"

She raises an eyebrow and glances at the bulge in my trousers before turning and heading into the dining room. She sways her hips purposefully, and a warmth rushes through me. There's no doubting what she means. Oh, I've got something hard for her all right.

"How fast can you eat dinner?" I joke loudly.

A hint of amusement is in her voice when she calls from the dining room. "Bring us some water and get your ass out here. If you're a good boy, I'll let you have me for dessert."

My pulse speeds up. I'll be the best boy there is. I'm desperate to plunge into her tightness and hear her moans as I fill her up. How did I not realize I craved submission? It's crystal clear to me now, but I should have known before my mid-40s. Her happiness has always been my top priority throughout our marriage, and I'd do whatever she asked of me sexually.

I get extreme satisfaction from pleasing her, even though she recently accused me of not going down on her for years. I thought she didn't like it, but watching Aiden lick her pussy was an eye-opening experience. She was moaning louder than she ever did for me, so he might be more adept at it than I ever was. Fuck, I've got to stop thinking about sex or I'm going to be begging before we're done with dinner.

I fill two glasses of water and join her at the table. Her chicken is already missing a sizable chunk and she's chewing faster than normal.

"Sit." She waves her fork with a piece of chicken on it. "Eat."

I put the glasses down and slide into my chair, fighting the urge to say, 'Yes, Mistress.'

Aiden said we could do whatever we want on our own time, but this is uncharted territory and I plan to follow her lead. Which right now includes me eating, since it seems like Impatient Emily is driving the bus.

I grab my fork and knife and I'm about to hack my chicken to bits so I can eat it fast, and pause.

Wait...

Using extreme care, I slowly cut a piece of chicken and avoid her gaze. I bring it to my mouth and close my eyes while chewing thoroughly.

"Mmm," I moan in exaggeration. "This is delicious. I'm going to savor every single bite."

When her silverware hits the plate, I peek at her. She's flushed, and her eyes glint with determination. She's so freaking beautiful. My cock pulses from a shiver of lust. The first time she went domme we were also eating dinner and Emily was magnificent that night. It is one of my top sexual experiences and it brought us to where we are now with Aiden.

I'm not sure I've ever felt contentment like I did on Saturday when Aiden instructed Emily to command me to do things. I've had this hidden submissive side of me and I'm finally free, so if domme Emily comes out more often, I'll be a happy man.

I meticulously cut another piece of chicken and lower my eyes to hide their shine. I want to grin but it will ruin the effect. My cock strains against my trousers from a flood of desire. I'm practically vibrating and desperate to rub against her to ease the ache growing between my legs. My movements are steady as I chew and swallow deliberately before taking a long sip of water.

"Nate," Emily snaps, and I bite down on my smile. Raising my eyes to her, I try not to squirm in my seat as I blink at her. "Yes, Emily?"

If I'm innocent and cute, will she go hard or soft on me? Her lips part and she's breathing heavily, but she doesn't speak for a moment. A fluttering sensation builds in my chest the longer I wait.

She leans back in her chair, gives me a coy smile, and slides her knees apart. My mouth goes dry as I watch one of her hands slide inside the front of her yoga pants. I can tell when she reaches her clit because she moans softly, and my cock jerks in response. Oh fuck.

I reach for my glass, and drain it in one huge gulp. The table is in the way of seeing everything she's doing, but her forearm rotates while she caresses herself. I'm mesmerized and can't look away.

Licking her lips, she purrs at me. "So Nate...are you finished eating and ready to fuck me, or shall I come without you tonight?"

I pointedly place my fork and knife next to each other on the right of my plate to show I'm done, and raise an eyebrow in challenge. The next move is hers.

~

EMILY

I hold in a laugh as Nate puts his silverware down. Early in our marriage we had an argument on proper table etiquette because he was doing it wrong and claimed he wasn't. It turned into one of those stupid things that become a bigger debate than it should, and I got way too much satisfaction from being correct after he did an online search. Now he does it occasionally to make me laugh, knowing that I'll notice. Not that I care about etiquette–it was more about being right, so he heckles me and calls me uncivilized when I don't place my silverware correctly when I'm finished.

Nate's little game has my brain whirring with confusion, and the back of my neck prickles. He's willfully baiting me, and I'm not sure I enjoy being manipulated. Part of me wants to deny him satisfaction, but the need for his cock is winning out. Pressing a finger inside my pussy, I finger fuck myself for a moment while a low simmer of lust burns in my core. His shaft would do a far superior job of bringing me to orgasm than my hand. I'm going to take what I want tonight, even though it rewards his naughty behavior. I'll figure out what to do about my bad boy after I use him. He better hope I let him come once I do.

Pulling my hand out, I stand up and give him my best no-nonsense voice. "Go take off your trousers and sit on the couch. I'll be there in a minute to ride you, so be ready for me."

I don't wait for him to move, and head into our bedroom. It only takes a few seconds to strip off my clothes, but I pause and count to 10. The entire point of coming in here was to make him feel controlled and wonder what I'm doing.

Is this why Aiden leaves me alone in a room and doesn't say when he's returning? I never considered it from the dom's side, and when he tells me to kneel and wait for him, it turns me into a quivering mess. The longer he takes, the deeper into submission I get. It's quite effective.

Hmm...I perch on the edge of the bed, getting more turned on as I imagine Nate waiting for me. Shit, I should have told him he can't touch himself. Jumping up, I rush out of the bedroom, but slow my walk right before he can see me.

Nate is sitting calmly on the couch with his palms on either side of his thighs, flat against the cushions. My desire to fuck him rises a notch, and my pussy floods with eagerness. He says nothing, but his glazed expression speaks for him. Oh, yeah, he's mentally fucked already.

The best thing about him being all subby is that he did it to himself. Being domme is incredibly enlightening on how Aiden controls me. Nate wants to be dominated, so I barely have to do anything and he's halfway in subspace already. Fuck, does he even know what subspace is? I need to talk to Aiden about training Nate, but theoretically if I treat Nate like Aiden did to me when I started out, it should be fine...right?

I stride towards the couch and stand in front of Nate. He's naked, but I didn't tell him to remove all his clothes. Is he trying to piss me off? Wetness drips down my leg and I quickly sift through my options. He deserves a spanking, but I really want to fuck him and get my orgasm. A buzz in my brain reminds me I'm in charge. He's not the one who decides what happens.

"Put your hands straight up in the air," I command, and get a nice thrill when he obeys.

A sense of freedom wells up inside me and I want to laugh at the sheer joy. He's so fucked now that I understand my power. I could keep him submissive for an entire week and make him eat my pussy daily without touching himself, and he'd probably thank me every time. We should have explored this in the bedroom before now, but I was too busy wishing he would dominate me to consider that I might enjoy being the one in control.

I straddle him and use my hand to guide his cock to my eager pussy. As I press down, I groan in pleasure, and he shudders when my silky cave walls massage his full length. His hands are still in the air. If I never told him to put them down, would he do it on his own?

I don't know my limits yet, and I'm struggling to find the balance between fun and harsh domme. It doesn't help that every time I give him a command, something pings my brain and I want to dominate him even more. I shouldn't leave his hands in the air, though.

"Hold on to my waist, and don't you dare come before me."

"No, Mistress," he whispers and grasps me firmly as I roll my hips.

Pleasure surges through my core. Ohhh, god, this really won't take much time. I bounce erratically and smile when he moans. My breasts sway with my movement, and remind me to demand attention.

"Nate, suck my nipple. If you please me, I'll let you come."

A burst of lust zips through me as his tongue swirls around my nipple. I grope my other breast and pull at the stiff peak as I grind against his cock. The closer I get to my orgasm, the less inclined I am to care about whether he comes.

"Nate...my toy..."

He mumbles around my nipple. "Hmm?"

"Look at me."

He doesn't remove his mouth, but tips his head up so he gazes upwards while still sucking on my breast. Shit, that's hot. I shimmy my hips faster as his eyes cloud with lust.

"Nate, you're going to have to beg if you want to come."

"Now?" I can barely understand him since his mouth is full of my tit.

Pleasure ripples through my pussy and I gasp out, "No, after I come."

He closes his eyes and says something that sounds like, "Whatever you want."

I want to agree with him and tell him that tonight it IS whatever I want, but I stay silent since I'm uncertain how far to push him. If I keep going domme around him, I'm going to require more training. Is that even what I want? This is all too new for me to know and I lose control too easily. The fact I slapped him in the face last time proves it.

When he switches his mouth to my other nipple, my brain finally switches off and I ride him faster, as pings of delight zip through me. With each bounce against him, I moan as his cock brushes against the magical spot deep inside me. My body tightens and I'm inching closer towards my orgasm.

I'm desperate to come, and I shove a hand between us so I can fondle my clit. My fingers brush my swollen bundle of nerves right when he uses his teeth lightly on my nipple. My orgasm rips through me, and I convulse around him while I scream out from the force of the climax.

He stops sucking on my nipple and my tits bounce as I ride him aggressively. The waves of pleasure wash over me, and I'm spaced out from bliss. Nate comes with a groan and unloads his hot seed deep in my pussy, and I rotate my hips, trying to force it all out of him. He's panting and shuddering, and the impulse to claim him hits me.

Leaning forward, I whisper in his ear, "Mine," and he murmurs, "Yes."

Slowing my movement, I rest my forehead against his. Our chests heave and we're both sweaty. The room smells of sex, and god knows what condition the couch will be in when we get up, but a deep contentment stirs with me. I might not know what I'm doing, but I'm more fulfilled than usual. I move off him and drag him down onto the couch cushions to spoon me and snuggle.

He slides his hands around my waist and I lift one up to my mouth and kiss it. "I love you, Nate."

His lips brush against my shoulder. "I love you too."

Drifting in a sea of satisfaction, I grin when his breathing evens out. I'll nap here for a few minutes before taking a shower.

My eyes close for a moment before snapping open. Wait, he came without begging!

I fight the urge to jostle him awake and demand an apology. Ugh. I stew for a minute until I giggle and force myself to relax again. Closing my eyes, I sink further into the cushions. I think I'll let it slide...this once.

CHAPTER
TWO

AIDEN

I've barely opened my eyes on Tuesday and I already have a text from Emily. My heart gives a happy burst before I even read it. Whenever she sends me messages in the morning, it always brightens my day because that means she's thinking of me.

EMILY

Sir, I went domme again last night. I think he was a brat on purpose, hoping to trigger me to punish him.

I laugh aloud as I type back to her. She's so adorably innocent sometimes. Nate's just starting to explore this side of himself, so he probably did try to trigger her. She yearns to be my fucktoy, so she should understand.

AIDEN

Are you okay with that?

I should get out of bed, but I don't move and wait for her to type back.

Sighing, I consider what to tell her. Those two really should talk about this, because if my suspicions are correct and Nate likes roughness, she might be worrying for no reason. But they should figure out their boundaries, and if she doesn't want to do that, she has to learn to rein in her impulses.

Rolling on my side, I contemplate my life. How did I get here? The online game Emily and I met in was one I played off and on for years, and I took it up again shortly before joining the guild Emily was in. And now a few short months later, I've got a mostly trained sub who is a budding switch and needs help learning what this means for her, and another sub to train.

I'm turning 54 this year, and when I was younger I always assumed I'd be married with several kids by now, but my life didn't exactly go as I planned. I've had several serious relationships, but I didn't find the women through the BDSM community and my desires to have a submissive caused problems. The first time, I told myself I could do vanilla with only occasionally tying up my girlfriend and thrilling her. But the longer we were together, the more I struggled. We eventually broke up and I thought I had learned my lesson.

My next relationship was an open one and I had a submissive as well, but that eventually caused issues and ended us. The last woman didn't understand that even though I'm bisexual, it doesn't mean I would cheat on her to be with another man. She's a good person and I don't judge her for feeling that way. I've learned that bisexuality confuses plenty of people. We're still friends, but we weren't right for each other. I can't live my life apologizing because I also find men sexually attractive, nor do I want to lie about that side of myself. I'm too damn old for games.

Realizing it's been awhile since I last messaged Emily and she hasn't responded, I pick up my phone to ask if she's okay right when it dings with a text from her.

EMILY

Thank you, Sir. When do I get to see you again?

God, I love it when she asks to see me.

AIDEN

I'm off work tomorrow, but I have plans in the morning. Are you free in the afternoon?

She responds quickly this time.

EMILY

No, fucking work changed my schedule. Maybe you and Nate should get together tomorrow evening and talk.

A rush of lust heads straight to my cock at the thought of being alone with Nate. The next time I see him, I'm not sure how much talking I'm going to want to do.

AIDEN

Doll, we should discuss this. He needs training.

I'm uncertain how she's going to react, and a ball of dread lodges in my stomach.

EMILY

I understand, Sir. It would be good for him to be on his knees for you.

Damn, Emily really has taken well to her training, but it's more than her being a good sub. I love that she's willing to embrace this for Nate, despite her misgivings. She doesn't understand how rare of a woman she is, but I also haven't told her I loved her. She doesn't know she owns the heart of two men.

I daydream about Nate on his knees for a few minutes, and it triggers my dom side. A rush of power fills me, and I'm eager to start his training. I hope he's free tomorrow night.

Wishing Emily a good morning, I force myself out of bed so I can shower and start my day. I'll wait until I know it's close to Nate's lunchtime before I text him. I don't want to distract him too much from work, but if he has difficulty concentrating this afternoon, I'll be pleased.

NATE

Shortly before lunch, I get a text from Aiden.

AIDEN

> Are you free tomorrow night for training at my house?

My mouth goes dry and my hands shake as I type.

NATE

> Yes.

Holy fuck, what is he planning? I already know Emily works tomorrow night, but I message her to make sure she's fine with me going over there, and she replies with a winking emoji and tells me to be a good boy for our dom. I'm not sure which message fucked me up more; Aiden wanting to train me, or Emily calling him our dom.

Aiden further compounds my mental confusion with his next message.

AIDEN

> Good boy. I expect you at 6:30.

When he gives me his address, I wince and tug at my collar. I swear the temperature in my office rose a few degrees, but I'm sure it's only me and it didn't really get warmer. Fuck, I should tell Aiden and Emily I know where he lives, and how I felt when I watched them.

Tapping my pen on my desk, I rub the back of my neck with my other hand. I'm not ready to admit how turned on I got by her cheating. I've barely come to terms with my submissive side and everything is going so great right now. What if they get pissed at me for keeping it a secret?

I'm in a dither the rest of the afternoon and I'm glad it's a light work day. We wrapped up a massive project last Friday, and everyone is acting like we're on vacation. My boss told me to expect news next week about an extensive project and I really hope it doesn't require me to travel. It's been a while since they've sent me to another site, so I know it's coming soon. I can't complain since this is my job and why they pay me the big bucks. With Aiden starting my training, exciting things are happening at home, and everything I wished for is coming true, so I don't want to leave now. I sigh, knowing if my boss asks me to go, I'll have to.

Shit, I've got to concentrate. There's a report that has to be finished for a meeting tomorrow so I pull it up and try to focus....Is my training going to be like Emily's? I'm turned on already, and thinking about all the filthy things Aiden might make me do isn't helping. Emily better be ready for a horny husband tonight.

～

EMILY

Work is chaotic on Wednesday. Somehow the inventory didn't get cataloged properly, and I really don't even know how that happened. We have scanners that practically do it for us, so how did everything get so messed up? I have to hand-count stock on the floor to check it against inventory numbers, almost like a mini audit. I want to blame our backup system for the failure because I can't imagine everyone wasn't scanning in codes for an entire day. But it's upper management's problem to figure out what happened. I only have to help clean up the resulting issues. We're a small craft store using old equipment, and maybe this will finally get the owners to spring for the upgrades we've been asking for.

I barely got any sleep last night and I'm so damn tired, it's difficult to see straight. Nate pounced on me as soon as he got home from work, and knowing that the thought of training turned him on revved my engine as well. He didn't even try to make me lead, and he enthusiastically fucked me on various surfaces around the house. We took breaks, but I think I had five orgasms last night...I don't even remember. He kept going down on me, like he was in a pussy-eating competition.

So I might be exhausted, but I'm not complaining. Whatever prompted last night, I wish it would happen more often. It's possible he's taking it to heart that I was angry about the lack of him dining at the Y. If so, good, though I also know I could have communicated to him three years ago about how I wanted it. I mean, clearly he doesn't hate it like I thought he did. My sore pussy today is proof. Between the orgasms and the pounding I got, I'm glad I'm not seeing Aiden today. A day of rest will do me good.

The inventory mess has me cranky, and being tired is a bad combo. As the clock creeps closer to Nate's scheduled training, the more mixed emotions crop up. I keep pushing aside a tiny part of my brain that complains that Aiden is my dom. Nate wants to explore this, and I agreed to it. I'm sure once I get a good night's sleep, my disposition will improve. Sighing, I check the clock again. Ugh, there's still four more hours of this shit.

CHAPTER

THREE

AIDEN

I'm turned on and aching for Nate when he knocks on the door. I considered texting him and telling him to come in and strip like I did for Emily that first day she came over, but I sense Nate needs more time before I toss him into the deep end. Plus, that day didn't go too well for Emily at first, so my methods aren't always the best.

Some doms have a difficult time admitting they make mistakes, but over the years I've learned it's best to be honest. No one is perfect, which is why safewords are so important. Nate already picked out 'pineapple' as his, but part of his training today will be discussing why he should freely use it. One of my male subs in the past had a difficult time using his because he wanted to be a strong man who could take whatever I dished out. That kind of shit thinking can get people hurt in BDSM play, and I don't know Nate well enough yet to say how he's going to react in the moment.

When I open the door, Nate's flushed and already has a slightly dazed, excited look, and my body reacts to him. I want to tell him to kneel in the entryway, but I hold myself in check.

"Good evening, Nate."

There's a hint of steel in my voice and his eyes widen at my powerful tone. He's adorable and on a normal day, his reaction would make me smile. But today, my need to turn him into a puddle of desire overrides any soft side of my personality.

"Follow me."

I don't wait to make sure he follows, and head towards the living room. His soft, "Yes, Sir," from behind me makes me smile, and I'm glad he can't see it. Each time he calls me Sir, he is transferring power to me, and the trust in me isn't something I take lightly. I want him to go home tonight blissed out of his mind with zero doubt that he wants to be my sub.

When we get into my sparsely furnished living room, I turn to him. "Nate, I want you to do something for me."

He stops a few feet away, and gazes at me with a lustful longing. I've seen this face of his before on the day he watched me fucking Emily and forcing her to her knees. I knew he was reacting to my domination over her, as he's reacting to mine over him now, desperate to be told what to do.

"Stand in front of me."

He moves forward as if in a trance. He's not quite in subspace, but close. I want him under my control, but I don't want him completely zoned out...at least not yet. He's still very much a newcomer to BDSM, no matter how much he's read about it. I have to be cautious with him.

Reaching out, I pick up his hand and place it against the bulge in my basketball shorts. He can easily feel my hardness, and I'm curious what he'll do. Is he going to ask for permission or will he stroke without asking?

When he explores the length of me through the thin fabric, I hold in a groan. Fuck, I really need him on his knees, but I want him to under-stand this isn't all about my pleasure and he can expect some as well.

He's wearing jeans, and as I trace the outline of his cock, squeezing lightly, he moans. He's rock hard for me already.

I'm done waiting. "Nate, get down on your knees."

Yearning flashes in his eyes as he sinks down quickly, whispering, "Yes, Sir."

I ruffle his hair and rub his neck, while I hold back from saying,

"Good boy." He seems like he will respond to praise, but I want to save that till after he really pleases me. If I teach him and condition him properly, he'll grow desperate to hear it. Based on his reaction to me every time we're together, I can tell he's going to be an excellent student.

My voice is firm. "Why are you on your knees, Nate?"

He lowers his gaze, as if he's unable to look at me as he admits the reason. "Because you told me to, Sir. I think you're going to use my mouth."

The movement of his hand on his jeans pings my brain with a delicious sense of power because I don't think he even realizes he's rubbing himself. Normally I wouldn't let a sub get away with that without asking for permission, but he's so far gone already and I relax my impulse to decide every movement he makes tonight.

"Do you want my cock in your mouth?"

This time he peers up, locking eyes with mine, and his utter submission is unmistakable. "Yes, Sir."

My cock throbs at the lust emanating from him. He may not know exactly what he's offering, but he is doing it willingly and he'll learn what it means to serve me.

As I pull down my shorts, they fall to the floor, and my cock bounces in front of his face. I'm going to keep him in his clothes today so that when he goes home, he understands I'm the one in command. As I wrap my fingers around my shaft and stroke, his eyes focus. He zeros in on my hand and follows my every movement. A thrill runs through me, knowing he's waiting for me to fuck his throat.

"When did you first see my cock?" I ask him, even though I know the answer.

He hesitates for a split second. "The day I watched you fucking Emily."

Making him talk is a way for me to test how far gone he is. Even though it took him a moment to think of the words, he can still speak. I also want him thinking about Emily and that day when she didn't spill a single drop of my cum. She swallowed it down like a good girl. Every sub is different, but I'll use Emily to help teach Nate how a good sub reacts around their Dom.

I study him for a moment, gauging if he's ready for the next step.

When his mouth falls open halfway without me telling him to, I know it's time.

"Nate, open your mouth."

He opens his mouth wider and sticks his tongue out, surprising me. Has he ever done this before, or is he mimicking Emily? Receiving a blowjob from a man is always an interesting experience. Maybe it's because the guy knows what it feels like; what you can and can't take. It's easier for me to be rough with a guy.

Slapping my cock against his tongue, I angle it and slide it between his greedy lips. As his mouth closes around me, he hums and sucks like I gave him his favorite candy. The wetness of his mouth is heavenly and I don't even try to hold in my moans as I sink deeper into his throat. Sometimes a new sub is hesitant, but either he's got experience with sucking cocks or he's been thinking about this for a while because he throws himself onto my dick with enthusiasm. He seems to know exactly what he wants to do to please me.

My hands drop to my sides while he works over my cock. He's not as gentle as Emily, gobbling at me and trying to get me off as quickly as possible and I consider telling him to slow down and enjoy the experience. When a tremor of bliss runs through me, all thoughts of prolonging the blowjob leaves my head.

"That's good, Nate. Take your Sir deep in your mouth."

Emily hasn't seen Nate suck cock before, and his devotion to his task is commendable. I'm going to have fun getting them both on their knees while I take turns using their mouths. I'll make it a competition to see who can get me off the fastest.

Nate chooses that moment to increase his slurping and suction on my shaft, and I shiver from the pleasure. Slipping my hand around the back of his neck, I press down gently. It's enough to make his lips sink to the bottom of my shaft, and he makes a happy little gurgle. His tight throat is making my cock pulsate and I almost lose myself in the euphoria until I realize he hasn't come back up and still has his lips locked around the base.

"Nate, breathe."

His head pops back up and my cock springs free, spraying his face with pre-cum.

He murmurs, "Want more, want to make Sir come."

The glazed look in his eyes tells me he's reached the point in submission I wanted him to get to today. He really is a good boy, but I've been imagining this moment since that first day I thought about him on his knees. I refuse to let his eagerness derail me, no matter how amazing his lips feel around on my cock.

I thrust back into his mouth, harsher this time, and he grabs my legs to steady himself. His moans vibrate against my shaft, sending waves of pleasure through me.

"Mmmm...that's it, Nate. You're doing so well."

He almost purrs at the praise and my cock throbs even harder. He's thirsty for me to fill his throat full of cum.

I can't help teasing him. "Maybe next time I'll let you come."

He's totally in submission and I don't think he even thought about coming as he fixated on pleasing me. I'm going to send him home with instructions to stroke himself while thinking about sucking my thick cock. He'll get an earth-shattering orgasm from remembering everything he did tonight.

He pulls away a little, enough that he can grab my cock and stroke while he sucks on the tip. My legs tremble and if he keeps doing that, I'm going to blow my load in his throat...but I have other plans.

I withdraw my cock from him, and he sways forward, desperate to get me back into his mouth so he can please me.

I order, "Lean back, eyes closed, mouth open," in a steely voice.

He obeys, because that's all he can do now. I can tell he's in subspace and surrendered to me, waiting to do whatever I tell him.

I want to claim him and make him mine. Fucking his mouth won't be enough. My fingers stroke the length of my cock, and I tense up as the pleasure builds.

Groaning, I explode, spraying cum all over his face. He doesn't flinch or move, and gives me a dopey, charming smile as I milk every last drop of cum over his lips and cheeks. He wanted his Sir to come, and he got it in the most sub way possible.

"Who owns you?" I ask, shivering slightly at the aftershock of the orgasm.

"You, Sir."

I pat his head and guide his mouth back over my cock so that he can lick it clean.

"Good boy," I say at last, giving him the praise he hungers for.

NATE

Aiden's "Good boy" echoes in my head, but I'm in a bubble of fuzzy contentment. My cock aches and the rational part of my brain understands he's not going to let me come, but I don't care. I've been fantasizing about sucking him off for weeks and it finally happened. Will Emily want to hear about what we did tonight? I'd like to share it with her, so I hope she does.

Aiden puts his shorts back on and helps me up to the couch. He has me stretch out on cushions with my head in his lap. As he strokes my hair, it reminds me of Emily and how she sometimes does this, and I'm soothed by his fingers on my scalp. He calls me a good boy again and it makes my head spin. Closing my eyes, I drift for a bit, enjoying how safe I feel with him.

I'm not sure how much time passes. My eyes are still closed, and when I hear him on the phone, it sounds far away, despite my head still being in his lap.

"Hey Doll, I don't think Nate should drive home tonight. Do you want to come over and spend the night with us?"

Oh, hey, he's inviting Emily. I give a dopey grin at no one, as a flame of excitement sputters to life in my stomach. A part of me knows I'm pretty mentally zoned out, and the other part of my brain finds it hilarious. Will I always react this way? I'm happy with no cares in the world, so I'm fine if every session with Aiden ends like this.

Something tickles my face, and I brush it off and stare at my hand for a moment before realizing it's cum. Oh yeah, he came on my face. I lick my fingers clean, and Aiden watches me while he wraps up his conversation with Emily. Some of the cum is crusted and I don't bother with it. Oh, well, I'll wash my face later.

"We'll see you soon. I'll unlock the front door for you."

Aiden disconnects the call and affectionately ruffles my hair as he sighs, "What am I going to do with you? You're in no shape for the safeword talk I wanted to have."

Why does he need to talk to me about safewords? I already have one...my mind blanks. Wait, what is it? My chest tingles and my heart palpitates. Am I going crazy? I'm about to ask Aiden what my safeword is, but 'pineapple' pops into my head. Ohhhh, right...pineapple. Okay, everything is going to be fine.

Breathing out, my chest loosens and giddiness washes over me. I get an inappropriate urge to laugh at myself, but hold it in. This is so stupid. I feel as if I'm drunk, or is this what they call slaphappy? My anxiety about tonight had my stomach tied up in knots all day. I didn't know what to expect, but it was more fun than I imagined it would be.

I drift some more and when Aiden lifts my head, I mewl out in complaint. He's gentle as he eases out from under me. "Sorry, Nate. I'm going to get us water and a snack. Stay here."

I give him a soft, "Okay, Sir," and float in my happy place until he tucks a bottle of water and a travel pack of almonds under my arm.

"Drink...eat," he commands.

He already thoughtfully loosened the cap for me, and I sit up and take a swig while he settles onto the couch again. I try to open the packet of almonds, and when he sees me struggle, he takes them from me and rips the bag open before handing it back. Tossing some almonds in my mouth, I chew mechanically and take more sips from my bottle. The food and water refreshes me and my brain kicks in a little more and I think about the blowjob. Was I any good?

Damn, I was enjoying not thinking and being happy and fuzzy, but now I keep evaluating my technique. What if he didn't like it? It's been years since the night with my guy friend from high school, and sucking one cock doesn't exactly give someone master-level skill.

I peek at him and he's studying me intently. He's probably trying to decide how fucked up he made me. I give him a tiny smile. "Thank you, Sir. The water helps."

His expression relaxes. "Good."

"So Emily is coming over and we're sleeping here?"

He takes a sip of his water and rolls his neck, as if he's trying to work out a kink. "Yes. You shouldn't drive tonight, so this seems easiest. She'll be here shortly."

My stomach flutters and I'm disoriented. We live 30 minutes away, did I blank out for a while? It hasn't been that long since he came all over my face, right? My heart rate increases and I tense. I hope I don't throw up.

"Nate. Look at me."

Aiden's dominating tone pierces my panic, and I raise my eyes to his.

"You're going to be fine. Tonight was great. You were a good boy, and I came hard. Are you okay?"

Am I fine? My anxiety eases a little, and I nod at him.

He looks me over for a moment before continuing. "I want you to relax. Do you need me to do a countdown again?"

Ohhh, that countdown he did for me the night I panicked at dinner was nice, but I am feeling better. "No, I'm good."

He surprises me when he leans over and gently brushes his lips against mine. A tingle runs straight to my cock and I feel myself stiffening again. Hell, I didn't even notice when I stopped being hard.

Aiden's eyes sparkle. "Yeah, you're good."

My reaction to him flusters me. My throat is dry again, and I take a gulp of water. I want to ask him if it really was good for him, but a sudden shyness overwhelms me. I bite the inside of my cheek and look down at the carpet.

Aiden covers my hand with his, squeezes, and doesn't move his hand away. "What do you want to say?"

I shift against the cushions. Why can't Emily get here and distract him?

"Say it, Nate." Aiden's voice lost the dominant tone it usually has, and he sounds like a normal guy wanting a normal conversation. I'm not sure I've ever heard him talk like this.

Shit, I might as well say it. I swallow and go for it. "Was I any good?"

He stills, as if I surprised him and he answers after a brief hesitation in the same light voice. "You were wonderful."

A brightness enters my chest, and I raise my eyes from the floor to look at him.

He grins, and looks like he's about to say something, but a change comes over him and his face hardens.

When he speaks, his dom voice is back. "Did you hear that, Doll? Your husband is amazing at sucking cock. Should we have a competition?"

Oh, fuck. I swing my head towards the entryway to the living room where Emily stands, holding an overnight bag. Her eyes are wide and she obviously heard part of the conversation. How long has she been here?

~

EMILY

I'm not exactly sure why I snuck up on the guys, but I wanted to see what they were doing when they thought they were alone. I didn't expect an intimate scene that almost seemed...loving? What the hell is going on?

I flush when Aiden jokes about wanting a cock-sucking competition, but when neither of them laugh a rock forms in my stomach. Shit, I think he meant it. Aiden stands up and moves to the center of the room. He's wearing the shorts I love on him because their soft texture is nice to rub against, and they're easy to pull down. I have the urge to grumble because he's MY dom and he's wearing those shorts, but this is stupid.

"Emily, get on your knees in front of me," Aiden commands, but I hold my ground as my body thrums with rebellion.

I'm not having a competition with my husband, but the urge to obey him is hard to resist. Fuck, I want him to call me a good girl.

"Emily, don't make me say it again."

Nate's head tilts to the side as he watches me, and there are splatters of something all over his face. It only takes me a moment to figure out what it is. A sudden flush of warmth spreads from my pussy outwards, and my heart pounds. Jesus Christ, that's hot. I can't believe Aiden blew his load all over Nate, but I can picture it clearly in my mind. My panties become wet, and my pussy throbs.

I glance towards Aiden and he's emanating an aura of power. My refusal to obey his first command obviously amped up his dom side. I get lost in his gaze and drop the overnight bag to the floor as I walk forward and sink to my knees in front of him. I wore my favorite yoga pants and tank top, knowing that I was probably going to end up on my knees, and I wanted to be comfortable.

He caresses my cheek. "Good girl. Don't you feel better obeying your Sir?"

"Yes, Sir." I expel my words with a throaty whisper as I sink into submission.

It doesn't matter if he turns this into a competition as long as we please him. It would amuse me if he comes all over Nate again, but he'd probably make me lick it off. An intense desire to do exactly that hits me. I've learned I have a degradation kink and licking my Dom's cum off my husband's face after we both suck him off is pretty damn filthy.

"Nate, kneel next to Emily."

When Nate immediately does his bidding, I squirm, embarrassed that I showed Nate I wasn't always a good sub. I'm probably 95% submissive, but I occasionally balk at what Aiden wants. He never asks me to do anything I won't do, and whenever I'm being bad, it's usually me goading him to punish me. I love it when Aiden gets growly and harsh with me, and it usually ends in a gloriously rough fucking. So, yeah...I might have incentive to not be a good girl ALL the time.

"Open your mouths and stick out your tongues. Whoever makes me come gets a reward."

Ohhh, I like his rewards. They're always sexual, and some of my best orgasms were treats he offered like this. Nate and I both do as Aiden requests while Aiden removes his shorts. He drops them on the floor and pushes them to the side with his foot and stands in front of me, aiming the tip of his cock towards my mouth.

"Okay, Doll. Show your dear husband the best you can do."

Nate's already watched Aiden fuck my throat, but I toss myself onto his cock and wrap my lips around his thickness, and suck. He moans as soon as I take him in fully.

"Hands behind your back," he barks when I make a move to touch him.

I clasp my hands behind me and bob on his shaft. Aiden seems to appreciate sloppy blowjobs, so I make sure my mouth is nice and wet as I swirl my tongue along the underside. Hollowing my cheeks, I try to create as much suction as I can, while still taking him in deep. He groans loudly, and my pussy tingles in response.

When Aiden moves his hands to the back of my head and presses gently, I relax so he can deepthroat me easier, forcing the head of his cock down as far as he can go. My vision films with lust and a deluge of wetness hits my panties. Fuuuuck, this is so hot. He knows how much I can take, and I trust him not to hurt me. I want him to use me until he blows his load, and not let Nate get another taste of him. Saliva drips down my chin onto my tank top and I hum around his shaft. If I suck vigorously enough, he'll stay buried.

"Such a good girl," Aiden croons at me, and it makes me want to please him even more.

He slides his fingers in my hair, grasping my head and holding me still so he can fuck my mouth faster. I don't have time to swallow between each thrust, so my tank top sticks to my skin as saliva streams out all over me and drips onto the carpet. I glance out of the corner of my eye at Nate and he's staring hungrily at Aiden's shiny cock.

I'm too focused on Nate, and Aiden easily pulls out of my mouth. Shit, I wasn't sucking strong enough. I know it doesn't actually work that way, but subby me always thinks I can make it so he can't pull out if I create enough force with my suction.

I watch, fascinated, as Aiden eases into Nate's mouth. My clit throbs and I wish I could rub myself while watching my men together. I didn't expect to be so turned on by my husband sucking someone's cock, but this isn't just anybody. Loving them both changes things.

Aiden picks up speed and groans when Nate works his shaft with his tongue and shakes his head to create sideways friction. Aiden isn't being gentle and I can't pull my eyes away. When Aiden closes his eyes, I can tell he's getting close to coming. I want to grumble that I warmed him up and deserve his cum, but when Aiden slides his hands around Nate's head and drills into his mouth, I decide to stay quiet. Nate can take this one.

Nate's clearly relishing every second as Aiden fucks his mouth harder than he's ever fucked mine. I watch my husband close his eyes in bliss, totally surrendering to Aiden's facefucking. Since the guys are too busy to pay attention to me, I slide my hand down the front of my yoga pants and panties and rub my clit. I gasp at the contact and it alerts Aiden to what I'm doing. He yanks himself out of Nate's mouth audibly, and Nate whimpers like someone took away his toy.

"Emily, stop." This time I obey him without question.

I'm vibrating with lust, as Aiden sits on the couch and spreads his legs. He pats the cushion next to him. "Doll, crawl to me and get up on the couch. Do you want a throat full of cum?"

He doesn't have to tell me twice and with an eager, "Yes, Sir," I crawl to him and climb up. Lying on my side, I put my mouth over his cock and he holds himself steady by the base as I slide my lips down the length of him. Mmmm, this is what I wanted, and he said I'm the one who gets his cum.

"Nate, now you crawl over here and lick my balls."

What's this? I pause my sucking and turn my head to watch Nate on all fours. Aiden presses gently on the back of my head and I give his cock all my attention again while Nate moves between his legs and laps at his balls. Every time I press down to the base of his shaft, I almost touch Nate's face and my long, loose hair gets in Nate's way.

Aiden notices what's going on and he gathers my hair in a ponytail in his fist, allowing him to control my movement with it. I can see what Nate is doing, and I'm surprised when he gently sucks Aiden's balls all the way into his mouth. Jesus Christ this is crazy hot, and my pussy clenches, reminding me she wants attention.

Aiden groans, and his thigh muscles quiver. "You two are such a good cocksucking team."

I thrill from the praise, and when Nate hums with Aiden's balls still in his mouth, Aiden moans loudly and cries out as the first splash of his cum hits the back of my throat. I slurp enthusiastically and press my mouth down to his base as his cock pulsates as he unloads everything he's got.

I keep licking and sucking, cleaning him until he growls, "That's enough."

He releases my hair and I ease off while Nate sits back onto his heels. I'm in a warm, fuzzy subspace and I'll do whatever Aiden wants. The faraway look in Nate's eyes makes me think he's feeling the same way, and an unexpected rush of kinship for my husband slips over me. I understand how he's feeling, and we both want to make Aiden happy.

Aiden strokes my head and smiles at us both. "It's time to move to the bedroom and I'll let my pets play together."

A spike of pleasure zips through me. I hope this involves Nate's cock inside of me.

CHAPTER
FOUR

Emily perks up and her eyes sparkle when I mention the bedroom, and it makes me want to laugh. Those two gave me a wonderful orgasm, so it's time to reward them. Standing up, I help Nate to his feet while Emily climbs off the couch. I hold out a hand to each of them, and when they slide their palms into mine, I lead them to the bedroom. The hallway isn't wide enough for all three of us, so Nate trails behind, still holding my hand.

When we get into the bedroom, I become the director of the show. "I want you to remove each other's clothes, and make it good. You're allowed to stroke and kiss."

I keep a wooden chair in my bedroom so when my back is bugging me I have the option of sitting to tie my shoes. Dragging it to the center of the room, I sit down as Emily and Nate paw at each other. I had envisioned a sensual striptease, and they're going faster than I would like, but they're eager to get their pleasure so I don't tell them to slow down. My two good little subs deserve an orgasm.

They're kissing each other's exposed skin and running their hands up and down each other's bodies. Emily occasionally giggles when Nate touches a ticklish spot, and they both are enjoying themselves which makes my heart sing with happiness. I wanted this to bring them closer together, and it seems to be working.

When they're naked, they turn towards me and I admire them as a pair. Emily's soft curves and lush womanly figure always makes my mouth water. I love the softness of her belly, and I hope she isn't self-conscious about it like so many other women in their 30s.

Nate's cock juts straight out, and he's obviously ready for action. He's lean, and has nice muscle definition, probably from all the land-scaping he does around their house. Their yard is impressive, and Emily mentioned Nate is the one who cares for it.

Emily's chest heaves, and I'm distracted by her rosy nipples for a moment. I'd love to suck on them, but she's getting a desperate look so I decide to put her out of her misery.

"Emily, lie down in the center of the bed on your back. It's time for Nate to fuck you."

She grins, "Yes, Sir," and climbs onto the bed, rolling onto her back. When she bends her knees and spreads her legs, she gives us a clear view of her swollen, wet pussy and I want to whistle in appreciation.

I contemplate Nate for a moment, and an idea pops into my head. "Nate, what do you think is Emily's biggest complaint about you in the bedroom?"

NATE

I stare dumbfounded at Aiden, but can't maintain eye contact with him. What the fuck? Heat rushes from my core up my neck, and into my face while I cringe in humiliation.

Emily squeaks and props up onto her elbows so she can look at us. Was she talking about me behind my back and saying I sucked? Am I bad in bed? Wouldn't I know by now?

My arms drop to my side as my face burns. My throat is too dry to form the words so I shake my head, no, towards Aiden.

Out of the corner of my eye, Aiden nods towards Emily. "Do you want to tell him Doll, or shall I?"

Oh, fuck. I'm already naked, but I feel like Aiden can see straight through me. I want to flee, but I can't move. Why is he doing this?

Emily whimpers, and Aiden continues. "Looks like I get to be the bearer of bad tidings. Nate, you don't fuck her hard enough. She doesn't like how gentle you are all the time."

A squeezing sensation in my chest makes me a little dizzy.

"Emily, tell Nate the truth. Is he too gentle with you?"

Her soft, "Yes," is like a knife to my gut.

Aiden's voice is firm and controlled. "Nate, it's not the end of the world. I'm going to teach you to fuck Emily exactly how she likes it."

A rush of lust zings through me at his words, and my cock pulsates. I didn't like the humiliation, but as soon as he flipped it around to him controlling me, it turned me on. Should I find this hot?

Thinking about fucking Emily while he tells me what to do has my cock twitching as a thrill rushes from my head to my toes. Emily moans as if she's anticipating what Aiden is going to order me to do, and I'm desperate to crawl between her legs and lose myself inside her.

Aiden hooks an arm behind him, around the chair, and leans back. "Do what I say, Nate, and everything will be fine. Now get on the bed and fuck your wife."

I eagerly turn towards Emily and realize her hand is between her legs and she's rubbing her clit. I groan as I get on the bed and cover her. Since Aiden told me to fuck her, I don't wait for further instructions and slide my cock between her wet folds. We both moan as I sink down and stop, fully ensheathed in her warm, tight, cave. Emily rocks against me, trying to get me to thrust, and I grit my teeth from the pleasure.

"Now Nate," Aiden's voice rings out. "I want to see you pound against that pussy as hard and fast as you can. Make her scream, and don't even think about coming without permission."

Emily's eyes lock onto mine, and I can tell she's almost out of it. I'm so desperate to come, I'm afraid I'm going to lose it the moment I move. Can I do this? She gives me a soft smile and mouths, "I love you," and my cock throbs in response.

Aiden bites out, "Nate..." and I don't wait for him to say anything else.

"Understood, Sir. I'll fuck her hard, and no coming." God, I hope my body cooperates.

I pull out of Emily and slam back into her as roughly as I can. She cries out, "Fuuuuuck, yes," and thrashes underneath me as I jackhammer into her, trying to bury myself as deep as I can.

The pleasure threatens to consume me, and I try to think of something else to stop me from coming. I stare at the wooden headboard and remember the last time I saw it. They don't know that I spied outside the window watching Aiden fuck Emily, and now it's me in the bed with her. I groan and almost lose it again. Shit. I try to focus on Emily and stop thinking about how fucked up and hot it was to watch her cheat.

Emily grips my shoulders and pushes against me with every thrust. Each whack against her pussy makes her magnificent tits bounce—god, I love her tits—and if Aiden wasn't controlling the show, I'd slow down and bury my face in them and inhale her unique scent that always relaxes me. But I'm Aiden's sub and I want to do as he commands, so I keep fucking her vigorously.

Aiden voices encouragement but I barely hear his dirty coaxing. I'm focused only on Emily and using her responses as a guide. She's moaning and crying out in ecstasy with every sharp plunge, and knowing she's enjoying this drives me closer to coming. Her tight pussy is like a vise and I wish I could savor it, but the need to make her happy, while also pleasing Aiden, is more important than my orgasm.

When she chants, "Fuck me harder," I light into her pussy, drilling with everything I've got. She screams out my name when she comes, and I almost climax with her.

Fuuuck, I barely stop myself in time, and her pussy clenches as I fight for control. I keep a steady pace while she rides out her orgasm, and I watch her face contort in rapture.

I almost don't realize Aiden is talking to me when he says, "Isn't she lovely when she comes?" and it takes a moment for his words to register.

I'm uncertain whether he expects an answer, but it makes me

inspect her. Emily is flushed, and beautiful. She's relaxing as she comes down from the peak, and she's lost in subspace.

"Yes, she is," I pant out and grimace from the painful pleasure of holding back my orgasm. Each pump into her wet pussy is exquisite torture and I'm reeling towards ecstasy.

"Good boy...now come for your Sir."

As soon as he tells me to come, a massive surge of bliss hits me and I cry out as my orgasm slaps me in the face while stars flicker in my peripheral vision. I unload ropes of cum and paint her cave walls with the strongest orgasm I've ever had. My entire body tingles as pleasure ripples through me and I keep fucking her until she's quivering and whimpering.

Knowing she's probably sore and sensitive, I withdraw and collapse on the bed next to her, and watch Aiden climb up against her the other side.

"Nate, look at me," he demands.

I'm stunned and shaking, and have a difficult time meeting his gaze.

"Nate, that was perfect. You're such a good boy."

I flush from the compliment while I'm flooded with mixed emotions. That was so amazing, but I don't like thinking I might have hurt Emily with how rough I was.

Aiden snuggles up to Emily and reaches across her to rub my cheek. "Relax, Nate. Stop thinking and enjoy the moment. Look how happy she is."

Glancing at her, I see she has her eyes closed and the corners of her mouth are turned up. She's glowing from within, radiating satisfaction. Aiden's right, she loved it rough.

Aiden caresses my arm and shoulder while I cuddle against Emily and relax. Sighing, I close my eyes and drift.

~

EMILY

I'm fuzzy brained, and snippets of emotions float through me. I'm a kaleidoscope of thoughts and feelings and it's difficult to grasp onto one to examine it. Tonight was incredible. Who knew Nate could fuck me that hard?

My eyes are heavy and I don't think I can open them, but when Aiden pets my cheek, I murmur, "Thank you," in his general direction.

"You're welcome, Doll," he whispers, and love for both my men warms me. How did I get so lucky?

The End

OWNING NATE

AN MMF ROMANTIC BDSM EROTICA SERIES

CHAPTER
ONE

I'm so focused on painting the finishing touches on my latest creation that I don't hear Nate come into the house.

His casual, "Hey," from the doorway to my craft room startles me and I almost drop my paintbrush.

Despite the near accident, I'm not angry. My heart races while I grin at him. "Holy heck, don't sneak up on me like that."

Nate moves behind me and kisses my neck. "I'm sorry, love. What're you making?"

Nate was outside working on our lawn and garden. He smells wonderful: a little freshly cut grass, a little sweat, and all man. He leans over my shoulder, and I inhale softly, enjoying his scent and the closeness.

"It's another clay fairy garden. See?"

I set the paintbrush down and turn the painted house around so he can see the little fairy door on the front side. It's finished, but the paint is still wet so I can't pick it up.

"Wow, you're really getting good at those."

The praise warms me, and I turn my head for a quick kiss. "It's good you like them since we're going to end up with a ton. They're really fun to make."

"We'll find a spot for them, or we can buy a special shelf."

God, I love my husband. I'm so fucking lucky he didn't demand a divorce when he found out I cheated on him with Aiden. Since I'm stiff from painting, I roll my shoulders under his hands to loosen them. I didn't realize how long I'd been focused on my project. Wait, what time is it?

My eyes widen, and my heart rate increases even more. "Oh shit, are we late?"

We're meeting up with Aiden today, and if we're not there on time, we get punished. Not that I don't enjoy the punishment. I've been purposely tardy a few times in the last month just to get spanked. It's not fear making my heart patter.

Nate laughs. "Not late yet, but I need to take a quick shower before we can go."

"Okay, love. You shower, and I'll clean up."

"Sounds good."

We blow each other kisses, and he leaves the room while I put the craft supplies away. It's been two months since Nate began his training with Aiden, and it's amazing how much has changed. A small part of me wondered whether I would still be attracted to Nate once I saw him submit to Aiden, but watching Aiden take control over us both is so fucking hot. I've also gotten more chances to experiment with being domme, with and without Aiden.

The nights that Aiden is with us are the best, though. It's a head rush when Aiden doms me and tells me what to make Nate do, and then I control Nate like he's my sexy little puppet. The mixed sense of power with being both a sub and domme at the same time makes me instantly wet. I want to demand Nate service me with his head between my legs while begging for Aiden's cock.

My pussy twinges at the thought. Okay, so that happened on more than one occasion. What can I say? I'm just a slut for Aiden's cock.

When I'm done putting away my craft supplies, I hear the shower shut off, so I know Nate will be ready in a few minutes. I hurry into our walk-in closet and remove my clothes. Aiden told me to wear the leather body harness I recently purchased. As I slide it on and adjust the straps at my shoulders, a tremor of desire ripples down my spine.

I don't know what Aiden has planned for us, but as I tighten the studded black straps, I instantly become submissive. The harness circles my breasts and waist, forming a V between my legs and running along my pussy and then up my back. It's as if I'm bound, and I know from experience that if Aiden tugs on the leather between my legs, he can edge me and turn me into a crazed fucktoy who will do anything he asks.

I'm struggling to tighten the straps on my side when Nate comes into the closet, fully clothed and ready to go.

He whistles at me. "I love that on you. Here, let me help."

Nate pretends to help me tighten the straps, but I can tell he really only wants an excuse to fondle my breasts. He tweaks my nipples gently, and I can't stop myself from moaning and swaying towards him. I feel myself growing wet.

Ugh. We really don't have time for this.

I swat his hands away from my breasts. "Hey, focus. We need to leave."

Nate gives me a playful, "Yes, Mistress," and finishes strapping me in. Lust simmers inside me at his words. Ohhhh, he's playing with fire, and he knows he is. It's easy for Nate to trigger my domme the more I explore that side of me, but Aiden can turn me into a mindless doll with a snap of his fingers. What Aiden wants, Aiden gets, and him requesting this body harness tells me he's going to turn me into a submissive mess tonight.

Nate grabs our overnight bag while I slip on a long, cotton sundress to cover the harness. I don't wear anything else under the dress, since there's no point. Everything but the harness is coming off as soon as we get there. We've taken to spending the night with Aiden whenever we all play together, so I put a change of clothes and panties in the overnight bag. Sometimes Aiden comes to our house, but tonight he said he wanted us to come to him. He needed time to set something up.

My entire body tingles in anticipation as we get into the car. What does he have planned?

～

AIDEN

It's five minutes past the time I told Emily and Nate to be here, which suits me perfectly. It's going to be easier to fuck them up if I start with punishment. When they let themselves in the house, I wait in the living room for them. Their instructions were to come into the house and strip before joining me. They're whispering, and by the amount of fumbling and cries of "ouch" I'm hearing from Emily, it seems like they're rushing. They have to know they're already late. It's pointless for them to hurry now, but knowing they're working themselves up turns me on. I've been hard most of the day while setting up the living room and imagining how tonight will go.

They both scurry into the living room but pause at the entryway, as if they're shocked. Zane, the owner of the bar I work at, recently gave me a raise and a bonus. I put the extra money to good use and bought a Saint Andrew's cross and a spanking bench. My living room is now a makeshift dungeon.

"Um...Sir?"

Emily's voice is soft, and I study both of them without speaking. Emily is gorgeous in the leather harness. Her nipples are hard pebbles just begging to be smacked—because come to find out, Emily has a tiny streak of pain slut in her after all. I could get lost in her breasts if I let myself, and the leather straps emphasize her curves.

Nate is fully naked, like I requested, and his cock is already standing to attention. He's been working out more often recently, and his abs have a sexy definition. He doesn't know it yet, but I also bought him a toy with my bonus...but that's for another day. I can see the lust in their eyes as they look at me. My bewitching submissives are already turned on.

"You're late."

It's time to show them no mercy, and Emily's eyes widen at my tone.

Nate is the first one to speak. "I'm sorry, Sir."

I'm always amused at the differences between Emily and Nate. Emily usually gives excuses, while Nate only apologizes. This is going to be fun.

"Doll, what do you have to say to your Sir?"

She glances down at the floor before speaking. "Sir, we got stuck in traffic. It wasn't our fault."

"Wrong answer."

She makes a face, and when it looks like she's going to speak, I hold my hand up. "Doll, what have I told you about leaving a few minutes early in case there is traffic?"

I don't really care that they're late. This is all just to mess with them.

"You said to plan to be here ten minutes early so that we won't be late so often."

Her voice is quiet, and I can tell she's reciting my instructions from memory.

"And did you do that?"

She looks down. "No..."

Sighing dramatically, I turned to Nate. "Do you think I should punish you two?"

Emily gives a tiny squawk, which I ignore, while Nate answers, "Whatever you want, Sir."

This is the part I love the most. Nate is such a good boy, and the more Emily plays with her switchy side, the more of a brat she becomes. Nate fulfills my need for total submission, while Emily gives my brat-tamer something to conquer. They really are the perfect pair for me.

"Emily, come here."

There's fire in her gaze and her stride is defiant.

"Kneel for your Sir."

She hesitates for a split second before gracefully dropping to her knees in front of me. I'm wearing a t-shirt and sweatpants. My cock throbs and strains against the fabric as I imagine face-fucking her as punishment. I've got other plans for her. There's a new spanking bench that needs its first naughty submissive on it.

I tip her chin up towards me. "Doll, you were late, and you're going to get punished. Understand?"

A shiver runs through her while a tiny smile tugs on the corners of her lips. "I'm sorry we were late, Sir."

Her tone of voice was not contrite when she said, "Sir." Bratty Emily needs a spanking.

"Doll, you don't sound like you're sorry...yet. Get up on the bench."

She glances at the bench, and I can tell she's apprehensive when she doesn't move.

"Now, Emily. Don't make me say it again."

She swears under her breath as she stands up and moves to the bench. The one I bought is fairly simple. It has a padded knee rest and then a padded platform for her to bend over. I measured and adjusted it to be the perfect height for me to fuck her from behind after I spank her. Something tells me Emily is going to be using the bench often.

"Nate, my good boy. Come over to the Saint Andrew's cross. You're going to watch from here."

Nate obeys immediately, and a surge of power in my brain causes my cock to twitch. I feel myself letting go and my surroundings fade as I become hyper-focused on Nate and Emily. A Saint Andrew's Cross always brings out my sadistic side, and as I strap Nate to the cross, I imagine using a flogger on his backside. We've gotten together without Emily a few times in the last month while Emily was at work, but Nate has yet to ask for more pain. I still sense that in him, so it's only a matter of time. I hope he does soon.

It only takes a few minutes to strap Nate's wrists and ankles to the cross. He's got a glazed look, and I can tell that he's heading towards subspace just from being restrained.

I stroke his cock slowly and whisper into his ear. "If Emily apologizes and means it, I'll let her come over here and suck you off."

His cock jumps in my hand and leaks some pre-cum. I stroke the moisture into his velvety skin before moving back to Emily.

"Well Doll, this is what's going to happen." I love telling them what I'm about to do. It always works them up more. "I'm going to spank your ass five times per cheek and then you're going to apologize. If I think you truly sound apologetic, I'll let you suck on Nate's cock."

Emily doesn't respond and braces herself on the bench. Her hands clench the edges of the platform. She's tense and ready for her spanking.

I stand back and study the scene. Nate is staring at Emily with a yearning in his eyes. I hope he's imagining it's him about to be spanked. He's such a good boy, he hardly ever does anything that requires discipline. With the new bratty Emily emerging, I'm expecting him to become a brat once he realizes he craves punishment. He's going to want what I'm doing to Emily. I'll be ready for him.

I love the studded harness on Emily. We need to get Nate something similar. My pets both deserve sexy outfits.

When I move close to Emily and caress her ass, she jumps. Yeah, my sassy girl wasn't expecting softness.

"I want you to count out after every spank."

Her, "Yes, Sir," is quiet, and it makes me smirk. She'll be singing loudly soon.

Emily and Nate were so focused on the Saint Andrew's cross and the bench, I don't think they noticed the new wooden paddle sitting on the coffee table. I pick it up, and Emily looks over her shoulder to see what I'm doing a moment before I give her a light test spank with the paddle. I almost smile at her gasp. Yeah, she didn't see the paddle.

"Ohhh, one."

I give her other ass cheek a soft spank.

"Two."

She wiggles her ass and repositions herself on the bench before I spank her a little harder.

"Three."

Another thud on her ass, but this time she gasps.

"Four."

I pause my spanking and run my fingers over her pussy lips, pushing aside the leather strap. She's soaking wet, and she moans as I brush my fingers over her swollen clit. Knowing she's turned on clicks something in my brain, and I sink further into my dominance.

Standing back, I spank her harder.

"Five—fuck."

Another whack.

"Six—oh fuck," she whimpers.

Each time the paddle hits her ass, her soft flesh jiggles and makes me want to fuck her in that position. I light into her ass for seven and eight, and she's moaning continuously.

For the next one she groans, "Nine—oh god," and I give her one final hard spank.

"Ten!" she cries out while her entire body shakes. Her ass is a bright pink, and I have to stop myself from biting it lightly. It looks so tempting.

"Now apologize to your Sir."

She immediately spews out, "Oh god, I'm so sorry. I was a brat. We were late, I'm so sorry. We messed up and didn't leave on time. It was my fault. I'm so, so, so sorry."

Yeah, the spanking worked like I knew it would. I've tamed the brat. I pull my sweatpants down and step out of them before removing my t-shirt. Dropping it to the floor, I move it aside with my foot. My cock is hard, and I'm ready to fuck someone.

Standing behind Emily, I grip my cock and trace along the leather strap covering her pussy. Nate's watching us intently, and I smile at him.

"Nate, do you think Emily sounded sorry? I'd like to fuck her, but I'm not sure she's sorry enough to deserve my cock."

Nate licks his lips and clears his throat before answering. "She sounded sorry to me, Sir."

I pull upward on the leather strap between her legs, letting the harness dig into the tender flesh of her pussy. She moans and shimmies her hips, causing the leather to scrape against her. She's so beautiful when she's at my mercy and desperate.

"Doll, you're in luck. Your husband thinks you deserve my cock."

She releases a loud breath and relaxes against the bench. My fucktoy has apologized, and now she gets her reward. Pushing aside the leather, I lodge the tip of my cock against her opening and tease her without pressing in. When the head of my cock is nice and wet, I sink into her silky heat.

She moans deep in her throat, and the need to hear her scream makes me pull out before slamming into her roughly. Her body welcomes me and her hips rise as I fuck her with deep, steady strokes. Her pussy clenches and ripples around me, and I grit my teeth to hold back from coming.

"Ohhh god, fuck me harder—harder!"

I increase the speed and hammer into her as the pleasure builds. She's so fucking wet and tight. I fight the rush building inside me and focus on making her come before I lose myself in her softness.

Grabbing onto her hips, I pull her back towards me, slapping her wet skin against me and driving my cock in as deep as it can go. She finally tips over the edge and screams out in pleasure. I keep fucking her through her orgasm. Her cave walls ripple around me as she writhes and whimpers with each powerful thrust.

My balls tighten, and I fight for control. When I'm moments from coming, I pull out and move around the bench and stand in front of her face. Her body goes limp but she lifts her head up as I stroke my cock inches from her.

"Open your mouth."

She tips her head back further, opens her mouth, and closes her eyes. I'm tempted to fuck her mouth, but it's too late. Her obedience is my undoing. Every muscle tenses, and my cock pulses. I explode with a growl of pleasure. One spurt hits close to her mouth, but then the next three go wide and hit her cheeks. She keeps her mouth open and I slide my cock between her lips.

"Clean up your Sir."

My voice is rough, and I'm reeling a little from the intense orgasm. She swirls her tongue around my shaft gently, cleaning her juices off my cock. When I get too sensitive, I pull out.

"Good girl."

Reaching down, I wipe the splatters of cum off her face with my fingers. She finally opens her eyes and smiles at me.

"Thank you for your cum, Sir."

I gaze down at her with love. She really is a good sub, and I like her newfound brattiness. I enjoy taming her.

"Doll, it's Nate's turn now. I want you to kneel in front of him and make him come. He's been patient and deserves a treat."

Emily scrambles off the bench and moves in front of Nate. She kneels down and runs her hands up the inside of his thighs. Nate jerks against the binds, and I almost laugh. Yeah, that's just like Emily to torture him a little.

My cum still coats my fingers. I move over to Nate, and bring my fingers to his mouth.

"I've got a treat for you as well."

He opens his mouth without me telling him to, and I slide my fingers in one at a time. He runs his tongue around each digit, and I can tell the moment that Emily starts sucking on him because he groans. When he's done cleaning me, he closes his eyes as the pleasure overwhelms him. I step back and lean against the spanking bench so I can enjoy the show.

Emily is throwing herself on his cock enthusiastically, and she's making a mess. I smile at the scene. It has to be on purpose. She's letting saliva drip down, and she's using her hands to smear excess wetness down his shaft and around his balls. Nate thrashes against the binds and pumps his hips towards Emily's eager mouth.

"Take him all the way in, Doll. I want him to blow his load deep in your throat."

She gives a happy little hum and sinks her lips all the way to the base of Nate's cock. Nate's groan of, "Oh, god," tells me he loves it. Emily works her throat around his cock, and Nate cries out with his orgasm. His entire body spasms, and Emily happily sucks on him until he's done shaking.

"Good girl. Good boy. Now clean him up, like the little cum-addicted slut you are."

She licks him clean before wiping the drool and cum off her face. She sits back on her heels and looks at me expectantly. It's been a long day, and now that I've come, I just want to cuddle with them both. A nap will do us all good and then I can make my subs play together while I watch. I tell Emily to undo Nate's ankle straps while I free his wrists. Nate sways a little, and I can tell he's still dazed.

"Doll, help Nate to the bedroom. I'll be there in a minute. Take off your harness before getting into bed."

"Yes, Sir."

I smile at her obedient tone. They're about to leave the living room when I call out to them. "Tell me, you two...who owns you?"

They both reply, "You do, Sir."

"Good little subs. Now get into bed."

I get a perverse pleasure from making them say I own them because Nate admitted to me that he tells Emily she owns him when she goes domme. I assured him he can be owned by both of us. They have a life that doesn't include me. I don't expect them to serve me when I'm not around. A pang of yearning hits me, and I push it aside.

I've had too many failed relationships. I'm probably going to be alone for the rest of my life. As long as I have a submissive to play with, I'll be fine.

I'm just their dom. I won't let the D/s bond get confused with actual feelings. That isn't in the cards for us. Though it's getting harder to say goodbye to them when we play. I've grown very attached to Nate, and I already know I love Emily. But this works out for everyone, and they belong to each other. They're obviously talking and communicating better, and I'm glad I had a small part in making that happen.

I force myself to concentrate on getting food and head into the kitchen. I grab three bottles of water and their preferred snacks. Nate likes almonds and Emily always asks for little packages of cheese and crackers. I take an extra pack of crackers for myself.

When I get to the bedroom, they're under the covers and snuggling. Nate is in the center of the bed, so I climb in behind him. I pass out the water and snacks, making sure to open the packet for Nate before handing it to him. He always fumbles with the wrapper and needs help opening it after an orgasm. We eat and drink in silence. I can tell they're both drained and sleepy.

I let my dom voice drop. "Pass me your bottles and the wrappers."

They hand them over, and I set them on the nightstand. We all snuggle in together. As I spoon Nate, my soft cock fits against his ass and he wiggles against me. I kiss his shoulder and smile to myself. Oh, Nate. You'll get that soon. But not today.

~

NATE

When I wake up the next morning, I'm alone in bed. I find Emily and Aiden at the kitchen table eating cereal. This is normal for us, and I don't ask permission before getting a bowl and spoon out. It's Sunday, so we can't dawdle long. I have to take my mom to church.

"Morning." I yawn as I sit down.

They both smile at me and Emily's "Good morning" is soft, while

Aiden's "Good morning, Nate" sends a shiver down my spine and my cock throbs.

Yeah, down boy. We don't have time.

I'm groggy, and Emily and Aiden are debating what the best type of dog is to have as a pet. It seems like they were talking about this before I walked in. I listen with half an ear while I pour the Honey Bunches of Oats into my bowl and reach for the milk. How much sleep did we get? We napped for a bit and then when we woke up, Aiden conducted the Emily and Nate Show while he made us fuck in a variety of positions. I swear he was just making up half the positions he told us to do. No way are those real sex positions.

Emily's voice breaks through my thoughts. "Nate, which do you think is better?"

"Sorry." I yawn again. "What are my choices?"

She giggles and looks at me with love. "French bulldog or golden retriever."

"Ooh, tough one." I think about it for a moment. My family had a golden retriever mix growing up, so they have a soft spot in my heart. "Golden retriever."

Emily snorts. "Figured you'd be on his side. That's fine, I'll just take my French bulldog and live by myself. I don't need you two!"

I imagine living with Aiden and waking up every day with him and a golden retriever in the bed with us. I like the thought more than I want to admit. My body grows uncomfortably warm, and when I glance at him, he's looking at me with a soft smile. Emily is just joking around. There's no way she'd know what direction my thoughts took from her simple jest.

I feel like I need to respond, so I tease her back. "You're not getting rid of me that easily. Besides, the golden retriever and French bulldog can be best friends."

She laughs. "Fair enough."

To change the conversation, I peek at my phone. "We need to get going. You know how my mom gets if she doesn't get to church early enough to get her favorite pew."

She sighs. "Yeah, and I need to get ready for work."

I speed eat my cereal while Emily cleans up her breakfast dishes. As we're getting ready to leave, Aiden and I sit on the couch in the living room and talk while Emily is in the bathroom. I rest my palms on my thighs, and Aiden reaches over and plays with my fingers while he talks.

"Emily says she has to work next Saturday. Do you want to come over for more one-on-one training?"

A zip of energy heads straight to my cock. I shift positions to give my growing shaft more room in my pants, and he moves his hand. Did he notice? I try to keep my voice neutral when I respond.

"That sounds good to me."

Good is an understatement. Every time I'm with Aiden, I want something more, but I can't figure out what it is. I keep hoping he'll do something and I'll immediately understand it's the missing piece. I'm curious to try anal with him, but I don't think that's what is missing...or hell, maybe it is. How would I know?

It's a sunny day, and light shines through the blinds and illuminates the spanking bench. I study it for a moment.

"Are you going to leave the bench and cross in your living room?"

Aiden laughs as if I said something funny. "Yeah, no one comes over except you guys. I can leave it out."

That seems risky to me. "What if someone sees it through the window?"

Aiden looks behind him and peers out the window. "Only the gardener comes around the side, so unless he's a Peeping Tom, I think I'm safe."

My stomach burns with disgust at myself when I think about how many times I was the one peeping in the window to watch Emily and Aiden. Shit, I should have admitted to them ages ago that I watched them, but it's too late now. I don't want to ruin what we've got going on. This is a secret I'll have to take to my grave.

When Emily joins us, Aiden kisses us both goodbye. His lips are firm and smooth. I want to melt into his embrace and continue kissing him, but we don't have time. I really am running late for church.

In the car, I make sure Emily's okay with me seeing Aiden alone next weekend. I've done it before, but I always want to check.

"Love, Aiden invited me over next Saturday while you're at work. Do you mind if I go?"

She rests her hand on my thigh and gives it a squeeze. "Nah, you have fun. You know I see him sometimes when you're at work."

That's true, she does. Her comment makes me feel better. This time she can be the one at work and all horny thinking about what we're doing.

After I drop her off, I'm whistling as I head towards my mother's house. It's a gorgeous day, and there's a definite pep in my step. My mother will probably think I got lucky this morning. How tightly would she clutch her pearls if I told her about Aiden? Yeah, it's best to keep this to myself.

CHAPTER
TWO

When Nate gets home from work on Tuesday, I'm in the craft room working on another fairy house. He says nothing when he walks into the room and immediately bends over me to give me a toe-curling kiss.

"Mmmm," I drop my tools on the table. I moan against his mouth as he swivels my chair so I'm facing him. Desire simmers in my gut as he drops to his knees and pushes my legs apart so he can get close to me. When he pulls up my shirt and kisses my stomach, my pulse quickens. Oh, hello. My panties grow wet at his obvious hunger. I don't know what got into him, but I'm loving it.

He murmurs, "I need you," against the sensitive skin of my belly as lust burns through my brain.

As I look down at him between my legs, a sense of power overwhelms me. I enjoy him kneeling for me, but this won't do at all. I want to ride him.

I untangle his arms from around me and press my foot against his chest to propel my office chair away from him. He captures my foot and admires my pretty red toenail polish for a moment before kissing the top of each toe. My feet are ticklish, and a shiver of delight runs through me. My pussy clenches with need, and I pull my foot out of his hand.

I give him my best no-nonsense voice. "We're going to the bedroom...now."

He grins and follows me out of the office. When he tries to tickle my sides, I giggle and sprint towards the bedroom. He gives chase, and we're both breathless and laughing. We tumble onto the bed, tearing at each other's clothes while kissing deeply and trying to keep our tongues in each other's mouths. I don't know the last time he's been this turned on when he got home from work, but I hope this side comes out more often.

We only get my pants off and his cock out before he's underneath me. I'm poised with his shaft in my hand and holding the tip against my wet slit. We both moan as I press down. Once he's buried to the hilt, I take total control by grabbing his hands and pinning his wrists to the bed.

I'm like a madwoman. I rock my hips back and forth with no consideration for him. He may have started this, but I'm going to take my pleasure from him. As I slam against him, I grind my pussy on his cock. He's my slut tonight.

Pleasure builds in my core, and I'm fucking him so hard the headboard rattles. "Do you like being my fucktoy?"

"Yes...god, yes," he moans, and writhes underneath me. "Use me."

Oh, I'm going to use you all right. I'm flushed and panting as I keep him trapped underneath me. Tension coils low in my belly as I spiral towards my orgasm. He tries to flex his hips up towards me, but my frantic pace makes it pointless. He has to just lie there and get fucked.

When I finally come, I explode and stars flash along the sides of my vision. I throw my head back and cry out from the rush of delight. I continue to ride him through my orgasm. He's moaning and thrashing, so I can tell he's going to come soon. I watch his face as it contorts with pleasure. When he focuses on me, his eyes bore into mine.

"Slap me," he pleads, his voice a desperate mewl.

What? My mind blanks for a moment, and he continues to beg.

"Smack me hard, like you did that one time. Please? I need it."

I can't hit him. I felt horrible last time. Why is he asking this of me? I feel a rush of anger, and I bounce furiously on his cock.

"No." I don't hide the annoyance in my voice. "Come for me, you little slut."

He cries out, "Oh fuuuuck!" as he shudders with his orgasm and coats my core with his warm seed. I slow down my movements. When I can tell he's unloaded everything into me, I climb off of him and lie on my back, staring at the ceiling.

What fucked up shit was that? He can't just ask me to smack him without a discussion first. Hasn't he learned anything from Aiden? The first time it happened was a horrible mistake. I didn't expect him to ask for it again.

I roll onto my side, intending to talk to him about this. His eyes are closed, and he's smiling slightly. His chest rises and falls at an even pace. What the fuck? He's asleep already?

I can't give him what he wants. I don't enjoy losing control and hurting him. We obviously need to talk, but now isn't the time. He looks so peaceful and happy. My anger drains, and I snuggle against him and yawn. Yeah, we can talk about it tomorrow.

The rest of the week is busy, and I never have time to bring up the smacking conversation. Nate is being all mysterious and weird about this upcoming Saturday with Aiden, and I see him researching stuff on the computer, but he closes the browser window whenever I'm around. *Whatever dude, it's not like I care what kinky shit you're looking at.* Plus, I could just check his history later if I cared that much. I doubt he deletes it.

When Saturday rolls around, I drop Nate off at Aiden's house before going to work. He said Aiden would bring him home later. I'm grumpy at work, and I tell my coworkers I didn't get enough sleep. I'm actually cranky because I want to be at Aiden's house with Nate, but I know they need this time alone. A part of me doesn't like sharing Aiden. Even though I know it's wrong, I still consider him MY dom. The real problem is that I love two men, and I'm afraid I'm going to lose one of them. What if they spend time together and find out they don't mesh well and Nate wants to stop everything we're doing? If I'm around, they're less likely to have conflict or I can head off any disagreements and smooth everything over.

This shouldn't be affecting me, but my stomach is in knots. Work is busy so that isn't helping. What are they even doing together? Neither of them invited me over to Aiden's tonight once work was done, so does that mean Nate is going to be home by the time I get off work? Why didn't I ask when he'd be home? I think Aiden is right and our communication sucks.

Since Nate was extra horny this week, he probably was thinking about whatever is happening right now. Does Aiden have Nate strapped to the Saint Andrew's cross? Is he going to paddle Nate's ass? I'm an odd mix of turned on and jealous. I just want to be there with them.

Fuck, I need to concentrate on work. This is going nowhere, and I'm just making everything worse. I plaster a smile on my face and head to the front of the store to take my turn at the register.

~

AIDEN

Two weeks ago, I questioned Nate about his sexual history with guys. He said he's only had oral sex once. At least he has some experience, and he's not walking into this surprised that he finds guys attractive. I'm definitely too damn old to play with someone who feels ashamed about being bisexual.

Nate seems to have come to terms with it. He said he never really admitted it to anyone, but deep down he knew. Emily is taking this gracefully as well. I haven't sensed that she's upset that her husband likes to suck cock, and she gets more horny when she watches Nate deep throating me. I think this is going to work.

On Tuesday, I texted Nate and told him I planned to fuck his ass on Saturday. I wanted him to be thinking about it for days and working himself up. I don't know if I actually will. It was mainly to see his reaction. His quick reply of, "Yes, Sir," pleased me, but this isn't a step I take lightly with a sub who has never had anal sex before. I enjoy fucking my sub's ass occasionally, especially with a guy, since it usually gets them to a deeper level of submission. Plus, it feels fantastic for both of us. But it has to be the right time, and I'll evaluate that as the night progresses.

When Nate gets here, he lets himself in and comes to the living room. I didn't give him any instructions for tonight, but he's comfortable enough with visiting and he knows I'm usually sitting on the couch waiting. He pauses in the entryway and sets his duffel bag on the floor. Even when he's not spending the night, he usually brings a change of clothes with him, so I'm not surprised that he has a bag.

I hide my smile when I see his outfit. He's wearing similar clothes to what I usually wear: a t-shirt and basketball shorts. I don't think he owned any before meeting me, because the light moisture-wicking fabric of the shorts fascinated Emily. She commented Nate was more of a sweatpants type of guy. Doesn't matter to me though, they both come off easily.

He stands there awkwardly after dropping his bag and swings his arms. "Hi."

Since he doesn't greet me by calling me 'Sir', I silently study him for a minute. I'm intentionally scrutinizing him to put him in the right frame of mind to please me. When he shifts his weight from foot to foot, I finally speak.

"Hello, Nate."

"Hi, Sir."

That's better. I've been thinking about fucking Nate all day, and I've been in a constant state of arousal. Tonight needs to go well so that he has a positive experience and wants more of whatever happens—hopefully my cock in his ass.

"Um, Sir?"

Nate shuffles his feet. He's being adorably shy. I almost tell him to come sit down so I can put him at ease, but I'm curious about what he wants to say. "Yes?"

"I, uh, prepped before I came over."

Well now, this is interesting. "You prepped for anal sex?"

I want to hear him say it.

He glances down at the floor, and his face goes pink. "Yes."

"Nate?" I pause until he meets my gaze. "What do you want tonight?"

He doesn't hesitate. "I want you to do whatever you want to me."

My cock pulses at his words. It's enough for now.

"Then take off your clothes and get on the bench. I want to fuck you."

~

NATE

Aiden's tone is caring but dominant. "Are you ready for this?"

I'm not sure what to expect, but so many people wouldn't do anal if it didn't feel good. I'm kneeling on the lower level of the bench with my stomach flat on the padded upper part. Turning my face, I lay my cheek against the padding. "I'm ready."

Aiden stands behind me, and I hear the squirting of a bottle of lube a moment before his finger applies a generous amount to my ass. Oh god, this feels better than me fingering myself this week to work up to this. He works the wetness into me, and I groan in pleasure at the unfamiliar sensation. I'm not hating this.

"Nate." His voice is gravelly. "Ask for it."

I can't bring myself to say the words and ask. I want him to just shove it in me. When I hesitate, he reaches around and grips my cock, stroking it slowly.

"Be a good boy and ask me to fuck you in the ass."

My head spins. I want to be his good boy.

My voice is hoarse, and I have to clear my throat before I can speak. "Please, Sir, will you fuck me in the ass?"

Jesus, asking is so damn dirty. This must be what Emily feels like whenever she has to ask him to use her.

"Good boy. I'll give you what you want."

He rubs the tip of his cock along the crack of my ass for a moment before pressing against the entrance.

He pushes the tip in slowly, and I moan from the painful pleasure as he fills me. His cock is thick, and he's going slow enough that I can feel every inch of him sinking into my ass. He pauses and lets me adjust before he eases his full length inside.

My head rolls back as I moan loudly at how good it feels. Shit, I should have asked Emily to use a strap-on ages ago. The full feeling is a pleasure unlike anything I expected.

I hold on to the bench while he fucks me with long strokes. My muscles tense and my ass tightens around his cock, making him catch his breath. When he runs his fingers down my spine, I moan from the pleasure. Everything he's doing feels like heaven, but I want more. His gentleness is making me crave a hard fucking. I want him to get lost in me.

"Sir? Fuck me harder, please."

I cry out when he slams his hips forward and deepens his thrusts. My body jerks against the padding, and I grip the edges of the bench firmly so I can move my hips and meet his thrusts. The pleasure builds in layers, and it's difficult to think. I can tell Aiden is still holding back, but his strokes are steady and deep. It's enough this time.

"I'm the first one to fuck your ass. This means you're mine," he growls.

I whimper, "Yes, you own me."

He stops moving completely, and I press my hips back, trying to get him to fuck me again. Why did he stop?

"Do you want to come?"

I whimper again. "Yes, Sir."

He pushes his twitching cock further into my ass. "Stroke your cock and be a good boy. Come for your Sir."

Oooh, yes. Stroke my cock. Be a good boy. Come.

I reach down and jerk my shaft quickly as he starts fucking me again.

"Tell me how much you love my cock in your ass," he demands.

Before I can answer, he drives deep and I gasp. "Love it. Feels so good. Can't think."

"No need to think. Just take my cock and come like a good boy. You know you want to."

I stroke faster. "Want to come, Sir. Need you to fuck me harder."

"Beg for it."

Spikes of pleasure tingle through my body, and I'm reminded of Emily again when I hear myself begging. "Need you to fuck me hard. Don't stop. Please, don't stop. I'm gonna come."

"Good boy," he growls as he plows into me.

The ecstasy builds until I can't take it anymore. My cock pulses, and I explode with an intense orgasm, coating my hand with cum. I cry out and buck my hips, meeting each thrust with a loud grunt. The sounds echo through the apartment, and I wonder if someone could have heard me next door.

Aiden continues to fuck me, and my brain is mush. He's balls deep in my ass when he comes with a groan. He jerks and unloads everything in my ass before slumping against me.

After a few moments, I feel Aiden easing out of me, and I close my eyes as wetness runs out and down my leg. Oh god. That was amazing.

Aiden rubs my back, and when he speaks, his Dom voice is gone. "Are you okay?"

I'm too mentally fucked up to say anything but, "Yes."

He chuckles. "I think someone needs to lie down after we clean up."

I don't argue with him. He's right. I'm having problems forming complete thoughts, so I drift in a sea of fuzziness while he takes care of me.

He helps me up and leads me to the bathroom. I lean against the counter as he starts the shower. When the water is warm enough, he surprises me by getting in the shower with me.

He takes control of helping me wash up. I've only ever showered with women before, and having Aiden's soapy hands on my body is more intimate than his cock in my ass. His strength is such a contrast to Emily, and I let myself ease into his arms and he hugs me while the warm water cascades over us.

He pulls back so he can look at me. "Tell me you're okay."

I search his face, and the lines on his forehead and the concern in his eyes make me smile softly.

"I'm fine. You just fucked me so good I couldn't think straight."

He grins, and says, "That's what I like to hear," and kisses me. His lips are smooth and firm, and a gentle happiness swirls in my gut. I might be addicted to him.

He ends the kiss and turns the water off. Within minutes I'm dry, bundled into his bed with him, and munching on almonds. His phone on the nightstand dings, and he checks his messages.

"Emily just got home from work and is exhausted. I'm going to tell her I'll bring you home in the morning."

I set the empty almond package on the nightstand and snuggle down into the pillow with a yawn.

"That's fine."

It's odd to be sleeping here without Emily, but as I watch Aiden type out a reply to her, an unexpected emotion makes me close my eyes.

Oh fuck, I love him.

CHAPTER

THREE

NATE

I'm an emotional mess in the morning. How did I let myself fall in love with Aiden? Emily is going to hate me. Oh god, what am I going to say to her? I don't think I should even tell her. This is going to fuck everything up.

I barely say anything to Aiden as we eat breakfast. He keeps sneaking looks at me, and I can tell he's thinking something, but he doesn't talk so I don't either. Emily messaged back last night and said she'd pick me up instead of Aiden bringing me home. We're finishing breakfast when Emily breezes in.

My thoughts are a swirl of disjointed fears, and I barely say hello to her when she leans over and kisses me before giving Aiden a peck on the lips as well. She's wearing my favorite pink sundress of hers. The one she wore the first time she physically cheated on me with Aiden.

She stands next to Aiden with her hand on his shoulder while he fingers the fabric. "Doll, I love this dress on you. It's my favorite. You look enchanting this morning."

My mind freezes for a moment. The room tilts, and I get the insane urge to laugh. I feel like we've come full circle. We're all here together, she's in this dress, and it's both our favorite. I have an uncomfortable need to spill my guts, and I bark out a loud laugh. They both look at me, startled.

"What's wrong, love?"

Emily's concern makes me laugh harder, and I speak without thinking.

"You wore that dress the first time you guys fucked. Of course he likes it."

The room goes dead silent.

Oh, shit. Did I really just say that? I look from one to the other. Emily's eyes grow wide, and Aiden has an unreadable expression.

Emily's voice quivers. "How do you know that?"

"Uh…"

I close my eyes for a moment before opening them again. I wish I could rewind the last two minutes. Why in the fuck did I say that? I open my mouth, but nothing comes out.

"Wait." She holds up a hand. "Don't you dare think about lying to me. Tell the truth."

Her voice is deadly calm—she's too controlled—and I can hear the underlying anger. I'm still at a loss for words.

Aiden's voice is firm. "How did you know, Nate?"

I swallow the lump that formed in my throat. "I was here and saw it."

Emily sucks in her breath and jerks her head as if I slapped her. "You fucking knew from the beginning?"

"Yes."

There's no point in lying now.

Her eyes blaze as she paces around the room. I peek at Aiden, and he looks sucker punched.

When he notices me looking at him, he finds his voice. It's his Dom voice, and a shiver runs down my spine.

"You guys said you were talking things through and communicating."

Emily's voice is quiet. "I thought we were."

Aiden takes a long look at me and then turns to Emily. "Not good enough."

~

AIDEN

When I look at Nate and Emily, a red haze of fury blinds my vision and it feels like someone's fist is squeezing my heart. I'm done. This is the deal breaker.

I stand up and clear the table, keeping my back towards them while I try to get my anger under control. When I know I won't blow up, I face them. Tears roll down Emily's cheeks, and Nate looks like he's about to cry as well. Watching them both close to losing it is like a knife to my gut. I can't do this.

"You two need to leave, go home, and talk. We're done here."

Emily tries to speak. "But—."

I interrupt her, and another surge of anger makes my voice harsh. "You two broke the most important requirement of being my subs. We are done. Don't make me say it again."

She sputters, "You can't mean it. There has to be another way."

I shake my head and leave the kitchen. I go into the bedroom and gather everything they've left here over the weeks. It only takes a few minutes, and I hear her sobbing while I stuff everything into their duffel bag. I wish I could comfort her, but I can't. This relationship is over, and I need to take care of my mental health first. They weren't talking and working things out like they said they were. This was one huge fucking lie right from the beginning.

When I bring the duffel bag into the kitchen, Nate looks shell-shocked and Emily's tears have turned into anger. I can tell it's directed towards Nate.

"Here's your stuff. It's time to say goodbye."

Nate stands up, takes the bag from me, and woodenly says, "Good-bye, Aiden."

He walks to the front door, and the anger deflates from Emily as she gives me a tearful glance before trailing after him.

She's shaking, and I hesitate for several seconds before I rush to catch up with her. Gripping her upper arm, I stop her from walking out the door while Nate continues out to the car.

I soften my voice. She needs to hear this. "Doll, I'm sorry it ended this way. Do one last thing for me, please. Promise me you won't drive until you're sure it's safe."

She sniffles and gives me a sad smile. "I promise. I'm sorry too."

When she leaves, I close the door behind her and lean my forehead against the cool wood. I don't notice I'm crying for a few moments until wetness hits my chest. I can't fucking believe Nate kept that secret. What was the point of not telling us he knew from the beginning?

I'm sick to my stomach and force myself to move to the living room. I sit on the couch and stare at the wall. This is messed up. I was right, and they were my kryptonite couple. It was too good to be true.

But the really screwed up part about everything is that last night in the shower I realized I loved Nate, as much as I already loved Emily. How in the fuck am I going to get over both of them?

EMILY

Nate and I sit in the car, not talking, for a good 15 minutes until I pull myself together enough to drive home safely. I don't know what to say to him. He might have just ruined our marriage unless he has a really good reason for not admitting he knew.

I'm emotionally numb when we walk into the house. He follows me into the kitchen, and I set my purse and keys on the counter before turning to him.

"Why didn't you tell me?"

His mouth opens and closes twice before he speaks. "I don't know."

His reply strips the numbness away. My pulse speeds up and my stomach hardens as the anger returns. "If you don't know, then I don't know that I want to be married to you."

Hurt flashes in his eyes and he whispers, "Fair enough."

What the fuck? Who says 'fair enough' when their wife is threatening divorce? I didn't know I wanted him to fight for me until his shitty response.

I flatten my lips and glare at him. "I'm moving my stuff upstairs while I think about what I'm going to do. If you ever figure out why you didn't tell me, you know where to find me."

I'm shaking and close to losing it as I blindly toss clothes and toiletries into a wicker hamper to take upstairs with me. There's a pounding in my ears as I navigate the stairs with the cumbersome basket in my arms. I don't know where Nate went, and I don't care.

When I get into the room, I drop the basket and sit on the edge of the bed. A wave of exhaustion rolls over me, and I lie back and close my eyes. I can't think anymore. Maybe if I go to sleep, I'll wake up and realize this was all a bad dream.

One can always hope.

The End

LOSING AIDEN

AN MMF ROMANTIC BDSM EROTICA SERIES

CHAPTER
ONE

AIDEN

It's been almost a week since that horrible day in my kitchen when I told Emily and Nate to leave. I've been walking around work like a zombie, and my coworkers are starting to give me the side-eye. I'm usually better at hiding my emotions, but every time I pass a mirror, my reflection tells me what everyone else is seeing—exhaustion, and a haunted look.

This breakup differs from any other I've gone through. Nothing prepared me for this kind of pain.

As I walk into work, I plaster on a smile and hope it looks realistic. I just need to get through today and then I have two days off. I can do this.

The bartender gives me a hesitant hello. I'm not faking my issues as well as I need to. Giving him a jaunty salute, I beeline for my office. I'll just hide in here all night and pretend I'm number crunching.

While I turn my computer on, I'm distracted by thoughts of the confrontation with Emily and Nate. Could I have done things differently? I'm just their dom. No matter my own emotions, their relationship together is far more important than anything I feel.

My chest tightens with annoyance as I replay the event in my mind. The more I think about it, the hotter my face gets, and my breath quickens. Why weren't they talking things through? And why was Nate hiding that he knew about Emily cheating from the beginning?

I'm jolted out of my reverie when the phone on my desk starts to ring. I answer it and hear Zane, my boss, on the other end. "Okay, you want to tell me what's wrong? I've had three people text me saying they're concerned about you."

Yeah, I knew I wasn't hiding it. I work with some really great people. I should have realized they would eventually contact Zane. Since I don't know what to say, I stall for time to think.

"I'm fine. I'm just tired. The two days off will do me some good."

"Hmm." Zane sounds skeptical. "No, man, really. What's going on? You've helped me with tons of shit in my life. Is Emily giving you trouble?"

Zane is much more than just my boss, he's also a fabulous friend. I don't know why I feel the need to keep secrets from him. Nothing bad would happen if I told him, and it might make me feel better.

I take a deep breath before spilling my guts. "It's trouble with Emily *and* Nate. I broke it off with them."

"Oh, shit," Zane says sympathetically. "I'm sorry. There's no fixing it?"

I sigh heavily, tears stinging my eyes. "I don't think so."

Zane listens quietly as I tell him the entire story of last weekend and what happened in the kitchen. As I tell him, I can feel the anger coming back. My hands ball into fists and heat radiates from my skull, hot and feverish. My reaction to the situation might seem lame to an outsider, but communication was always the most important agreement with them. They'd assured me they were talking, but obviously they hadn't kept up their part of the bargain.

"So, what are you going to do?"

Zane's unexpected question catches me off guard, and my heart rate speeds up. What can I really do?

"I don't know. Get over them? Do I have a choice? They're married, and I was just their dom."

His reply of, "I suppose," sounds doubtful again.

I don't want him worrying about me, so I brush the issue aside. "The two days off will help. I just need some time to think."

I know Zane well enough that when he replies, I can tell he wants to say more, but he's reining it in. "Okay, but if you need more time off, just let me know. I can ask Dave to step in for a bit. He'd love a chance to fill your shoes."

More tears prickle behind my eyes from Zane's kindness, and I'm quick to reassure him. "Nah, I'll be fine after the two days."

I need to get off the phone before I end up blubbering like a baby. Emily and Nate have a firmer hold on my heart than I realized. I've never broken down publicly over a relationship before.

Zane and I say our goodbyes. He tells me the offer of time off is always open, and I thank him before hanging up.

Sighing, I set the phone down. I'm just tired since I haven't been sleeping well. Once I get a few nights of good sleep under my belt, I'll be fine.

I keep repeating that to myself for the rest of my work shift, hoping it's true.

~

NATE

It's been two long weeks of not sleeping in the same bed as Emily. My loving wife has turned into a cold mistress—distant eyes and a sharp voice that's like daggers tearing through my heart every time we speak. The messed-up part about it is the more uncaring she is to me, the more I want to sink to my knees and beg for forgiveness. I'd promise her the moon if it would fix what I did.

I really fucked up bad. I should have told Aiden and Emily that I knew they were cheating all along. But the confession isn't just about knowing—it's that I liked it. I don't want to be like my friend at the gym who calls himself a cuck and seems proud of it. Whenever I peered through the window and watched Emily and Aiden together, my heart ached with shame and hurt, yet I can't deny the tingling arousal. Hell, I masturbated over her cheating. Even now, the thought still turns me on.

It's the second Sunday since the breakup, and I'm taking my mom to church again. I've been trying to act normal around her, but last week she was giving me sidelong glances on the drive home. Ugh, I need to pull my shit together this week and act like everything is perfect. I'm not ready to admit that my marriage is possibly ending, since I haven't given up hope yet that Emily and I can work things out.

My mom is having one of her rare good days, and she's chatty and happy all the way to church. I can't concentrate on anything she's saying, and a couple of times she has to repeat a question. Fuck, I'm not doing too great on holding my shit together here.

As we slip into our normal pew at church, my shoulders tighten from anxiety. I focus my breathing and hope to find some solace in the moment. No serenity comes. Usually I can find inner peace, but not today. The organ music reverberates throughout the sanctuary as people sing off-key and congregants shuffle their feet. Worry and uncertainty gnaw at me until the service is finally over. I let out a deep sigh of relief as we leave. I'm not fit company for anyone today.

Mom is quiet on the drive home, and she doesn't say much until I've got her settled into her recliner with water and a snack of Goldfish crackers. At least I did one thing right today and took her to church. I can feel good about being a dutiful son.

Right before I go to say goodbye, she gives me a long look and points to the recliner that used to be my dad's favorite chair.

"Sit with me for a moment."

Shit. She's going to ask me what's wrong. I don't want to talk to her about my problems, so I make an excuse. "Sorry, mom, I really need to get home."

Before I can say anything else, her voice turns firm. "Nathaniel, you sit your butt down. We need to talk."

There's no arguing with her when she takes that tone. I plop my ass on the chair. She sips her water while she studies me. Since my dad died, she's seemed like she's on the decline, but today her eyes are as sharp as ever.

"Are you and Emily fighting?"

I want to say that someone has to talk to me to fight with me, but I keep that thought to myself.

"Yes."

She settles back in her chair, looking pleased with herself. "I thought so. You've got that hangdog look your father always got when we fought. He should have dragged me to bed and settled our differences there. It would have made life easier."

My mom's words make me choke on nothing. I cough a few times before I catch my breath and croak out, "I don't think that would work with Emily."

Mom pops a cracker into her mouth and grins at me as she chews. "No, you're right. Emily seems to wear the pants in the family."

My head spins at how my mom is speaking. Am I living in the Twilight Zone? Is she losing it? I've never heard my mom speak about sexual matters so bluntly. My face scrunches up. Wait, she thinks Emily wears the pants?

She laughs at my expression. "Nate, I'm joking—mostly."

My mom doesn't do much these days except go to church and play bingo. What are the ladies at the bingo parlor teaching her? Is she picking this up from a TV show?

I'm on edge and can't sit still. This conversation is bizarre and doesn't seem like my mother. My stomach muscles tense, and I stand up, desperate to get out of the room.

"I need something to drink."

As I head to the kitchen, I swear I hear her mumble something about me needing more than just a drink. What has gotten into her?

I stand at the sink and take a huge gulp of water, draining my glass before refilling it. How much should I reveal? I study the tile on the countertop my father installed before he got sick. They had a long and successful marriage. Hell, maybe mom would have some good advice.

Within a few moments, my head is clearer and I'm back in the recliner with my glass of water. Fuck it, I'm going to tell her part of it, but not everything.

I face my mom squarely. "Do you know what an open marriage is?"

I'm assuming she knows, but I'm not so sure of anything right now regarding her.

"Yep," she replies, but doesn't elaborate.

"Emily and I tried it, and it didn't work. We might get a divorce."

She stares at me for a moment. "Emily can't handle you liking guys too, or are you gay?"

My mind screeches to a halt like a record scratch. Um, what? She thinks this started with me wanting to be with a guy? Confusion and disbelief war inside me, and I want to blurt out Emily cheated on me.

I don't reply, and she continues. "Don't look so shocked. Your uncle Pete liked the men. No matter how much our father tried to beat it out of him."

What is this? Fucked up family confessional time? I'm not in the right headspace to process everything she's telling me, and my thoughts are a swirl of confusion. Her brother Pete died when I was a kid, and suddenly I'm not so sure I know how he died. All I heard was that he was sick for a long time, but nobody talked about it much.

My mom's words snap me back to attention. "So, which is it?"

"Neither."

"No? Interesting." She takes a sip of her water and chews on another cracker, clearly waiting for me to continue.

I've never seen my mother act this way, and a small part of me feels the need to share everything with her. As we sit there, not speaking, the grandfather clock against the wall slowly measures out each second, as if it's counting down the moments left in our lives. I'm all she has since dad died. The clock was always comforting in years past, but today it's like a signal reminding me I should tell her something because she might not be around too much longer.

I finally can't take it anymore, and I blurt it all out. "Emily wanted an open marriage, so we gave it a go. Then I got involved as well. It was all of us together."

My mom doesn't look shocked, but I can't tell what she's thinking. Though she's the one who thought I was possibly gay, so it's no wonder she isn't surprised.

Her voice is quiet. "So what happened?"

Oh God, what DID happen? I struggle to figure out what to tell her. How do I admit this is all my fault?

I take another sip of water and guilt washes over me. "I was an idiot and lied about something and ruined it all."

She snorts. "If you lied, you WERE an idiot. So go fix it."

Yeah, I don't think that's going to work. I don't bother arguing with her. "I can try."

She smiles at me as if we've settled the matter. "Can you bring me my knitting basket before you go? I suppose I should stop knitting baby stuff for you and Emily until I hear otherwise. I'll make some hats for the homeless shelter."

I cough to hide a bark of laughter. What the fuck? We aren't even trying to get pregnant. I hope she's joking.

I get up, bring her the knitting supplies, and refill her water before bending down to give her a kiss on the cheek. "Mom, I'll call you in a few days. I love you."

She sounds satisfied with herself when she says, "I love you too." She probably thinks she weaseled some great mystery out of me.

Right before I open the front door, she calls out. "What's his name, anyway?"

My mouth drops open in surprise, but I hide it when I turn to look at her.

"Aiden."

"Aiden..." She mulls it over like she's thinking about something. "Do you love him?"

My heart constricts. Damn, she's playing hardball today. "Yes."

Her smile is sad. "Life's too short, my dear boy. Make it work. I'd like to meet this Aiden."

My pulse races, and my palms grow clammy as I stammer, "Okay," and practically stumble out of the house.

I sit in my car, trembling in shock from what just happened. Did someone body snatch my church-going mother? Hot tears burn my eyes, yet I laugh out loud. Shit, Emily is going to crack up when she hears about this.

Oh.

My stomach roils. I won't be telling Emily because we're not speaking. Well, fuck.

～

EMILY

I get home from work on Monday after what has been the shittiest two weeks of my life, and Nate's car is already in the driveway. Excitement stirs in my stomach before I remember it doesn't matter. We're not speaking to each other, because he's yet to explain why he didn't tell us he knew about the cheating all along.

I huff out a sigh and trudge inside. As I enter the kitchen, my heart skips a beat when I see Nate. His toned body is exposed by a pair of low-slung sweatpants that hug his muscular thighs nicely. Droplets of water glisten in his damp hair, as if he's just showered. He's facing away from me with a dishtowel slung over one shoulder, vigorously stirring something in a bowl.

My pussy hums alive. I want to rush to him, wrap my arms around his waist, and kiss him until we both forget we're fighting. I love him so damn much that it's almost a physical pain to stay away from him. The way my body is reacting to him reminds me I haven't gone without sex for this long since meeting Aiden. Someone needs to remind my pussy that we're unhappy.

I'm an odd mix of horny and upset, and the conflicting feelings make me sound angry when I speak. "Are you ready to talk to me yet?"

Nate looks over his shoulder, his eyes filled with uncertainty. He shakes his head slowly. "No."

I can't suppress my exasperation. My teeth are clenched as I fight to contain the anger bubbling up inside me. I want to yell at him, but instead, I bite my tongue and stomp my foot. Scorching heat burns my cheeks. "We can't keep doing this. Don't you think it's time you told me why?"

He sets down the mixing spoon in a controlled motion before turning to face me with an expression that seems chiseled out of stone. "I don't know," he says with cold detachment.

His answer infuriates me further, and my entire body flushes. He motherfucking knows why and just doesn't want to talk to me. An angry sob breaks free from me as I rush out of the kitchen and head straight upstairs to the spare room where I've been sleeping since the fight.

Why won't he talk to me? I almost don't care about the reason—it's more about his lack of communication. Flopping on the bed, I hug a pillow and bury my face in it. I want so badly to call out to Nate and apologize and make up. But that still doesn't fix things with Aiden. I love them both, and now I'm losing them. Jesus, this blows.

And why does he have to be so damn sexy when I'm angry at him? I take a few deep breaths. I need to be Zen Emily again, or I'm going to end up on blood pressure medication at this rate.

Once my heart calms down, my thoughts drift back to how sexy Nate looked in the kitchen. A rush of heat courses through my veins, and my pussy gives a little buzz. Yeah, I love sweatpants on guys. I could easily tug them down and get to his cock. My nipples harden, and I snort. God dammit, I'm supposed to be sad, not turned on and fantasizing about fucking him.

I punch the bed to release some pent-up aggression before rising to remove my work clothes. I strip naked, shivering as the cool air coming through an open window brushes my skin. All my nerve endings hum with pleasure, and I give in to my urges. I don't bother putting clothes on and lie down on the bed, spreading my legs. This feels so wrong to do while I'm upset, but maybe if I can make myself come, it will help?

I dive my fingers between my legs, working circles around my aching clit as I move my other hand to tease my nipple. I moan with pleasure as my mind wanders to the last time Nate, Aiden, and I were together. Aiden strapped Nate to the St. Andrew's cross, and I was on the spanking bench. I tingle with excitement as I relive the evening in my mind. Aiden knew exactly how to drive me crazy. My thighs quiver with delight as I imagine him spanking me and pulling on the leather strap of my bodysuit, making it dig into my pussy. God, that's a glorious memory.

My clit swells as my hand moves faster and faster while I continue to daydream about Aiden controlling Nate and me. I slip a finger inside myself and moan as the Aiden in my head tells Nate to lick my pussy. I imagine I can feel Nate's firm tongue swirling around my clit. Hot waves of pleasure ripple through me. My leg muscles tense, and I put my feet flat on the bed so I can finger fuck myself harder. I whimper loudly as I imagine my fingers are Nate's tongue moving in and out. I need to come so badly.

Tugging on my nipples, I moan as I think of Aiden's mouth at my breast. He's sucking and pulling, and pleasure swirls in my gut. The bliss builds in layers. It's not enough. I need to feel something new.

Without thinking, I give my breast a sharp slap like Aiden has done to me before. Pain shoots through me and electrifies my body. Every nerve in my pussy ignites, and I'm on the brink of an explosion.

I speed up the movement of my hand, and just when I think I'm going to come, the memory of Nate's sad face in the kitchen intrudes on the fantasy, and I deflate.

God damn it! I can't come while things aren't settled between us. I'm breathless and my body cries out from the stolen orgasm when I pull my hand out from between my legs. There's no way I'll come now. Fuckity, fuck, fuck, fuck.

I kick my heels in frustration as I study the ceiling and seek inner peace. I shouldn't have even started touching myself. This was such a bad idea. My heart still aches from what's going on, and now I'm crazy horny on top of being sad.

Sighing, I snuggle into my pillow and close my eyes. Maybe I need a nap. I'm sure everything will be better tomorrow.

It can't be much worse.

CHAPTER
TWO

AIDEN

I'm a fucking mess. I spent my two days off with my head in several pints of mint chocolate chip ice cream, hoping to forget Emily and Nate exist. Ice cream can't fix my life. All it did was make me sick from too much sugar.

Even though I told Zane I didn't need more time, by Monday morning I admit defeat and call him. I hold in my tears, but I can detect a quiver in my voice when I ask for the week off.

"Don't worry about work," he says gently. "Take all the time you need."

His words make me cry silently, and I tell him, "Thank you," quickly so I can hang up before he knows how upset I am. I'm so damn lucky to have Zane as a friend.

I mope around my apartment most of the day, uninterested in doing anything. How does one get over two people? Now that I don't have work to think about for a week, my brain plays back a slideshow of my times with Emily and Nate. It was a fun ride while it lasted. I've never had a sub like Emily, and I loved her switchy side that was coming out.

Nate was the icing on the cake. That last night with him was more intimate than I've ever felt with another man. Which shouldn't surprise me since I fell in love with him.

The air conditioner kicks on in the background, breaking the silence. I curl up on the couch and try not to think of them, but it's impossible. One of my favorite memories is the first time we were all together. Nate hadn't admitted he wanted more yet, but I could tell he wanted to be on his knees for me. Emily was sucking my cock beautifully, but it was Nate I was watching.

As I daydream, my cock stiffens, and I don't stop myself from running my hand down my bare stomach and stroking my shaft through my shorts. It's been so long since I've wanted to touch myself that the stimulation is electric. The pleasure builds as I continue to daydream about other times I was with Nate and Emily. I recall Emily's lips engulfing my cock while Nate was sucking on my balls. God, that was another great night.

It almost feels wrong to get turned on by thoughts of them since we're not together, but it also feels so right. These memories are all that I have left of the relationship, so I might as well enjoy myself.

I moan and caress my shaft more quickly. My legs tremble, and I arch my back and thrust into my fist, imagining that I'm fucking Emily's wet pussy. I can feel her tight walls around me as I hammer into her, making her moans of delight and Nate's groans of approval fill my mind.

When I picture Nate on his knees waiting to serve us, I come hard and fast with a pulsating wave of pleasure as cum spurts onto my shorts and across my stomach. I gasp, still ensnared in the fantasy of us together as we find our bliss.

The rapture crests and recedes, leaving me limp as my breathing slows. In its wake, I'm struck by an unbearable loneliness, like a pit in my stomach that threatens to engulf me. Lying there, surrounded by emptiness, I realize what I'm missing out on—the closeness and the connection with another human being.

I don't realize I'm crying until I feel tears dripping from my chin and landing on my chest. Grabbing a tissue from the table next to the couch, I wipe away the tears before cleaning the cum off my stomach. The reality of my situation hits me like a truck and leaves me hollow.

I'm all alone and missing the two people I love. Nothing feels right without them.

~

NATE

Emily doesn't work on Tuesdays, and she's in the kitchen making herself dinner when I get home. We've been eating separately, and I don't want to get in her way. I'll make food when she's finished. She's got earbuds in, and I assume she's listening to music. She doesn't hear me, so I pause in the doorway and watch her for a moment.

She's wearing a T-shirt and black yoga pants, and the way they stretch across her ass reminds me of all the times we fucked in the kitchen. My cock pulses in response. Shit, I can't be getting turned on right now. She's angry at me, and this is a quick road to nowhere that ends with me sad wanking while thinking of sinking into her wetness.

When she bends over to get a bowl out of a lower cabinet and sways her hips in time to the music, I almost groan. Before the blowup, I could have walked behind her and surprised her by rubbing my hand over her ass while she was bent over like that. Now all I can do is watch and ache. Yeah, this is torture.

I leave the kitchen before she realizes I'm there and head to the bedroom to change into my customary sweatpants that I wear after work. As I remove my clothes, I let them fall to the floor in a messy pile at the end of the bed. I'll pick them up later, or maybe not—this is the level of care I have for anything right now. Life sucks.

I'm naked. and I'm about to put on shorts when the image of Emily bent over pops into my head again. My cock pulses, begging me to stroke it. Fine, sad wanking it is. I can't feel any worse after an orgasm than I do right now.

I lie down on the bed and imagine my hand is Emily's mouth. I keep my strokes slow at first, but as soon as my mind adds Aiden in the room directing Emily on how to suck me, I speed the movement up. Tingles run up and down my body as the pleasure builds.

I didn't know I'd fall in love with a guy while still loving Emily, and the sexual satisfaction I felt with Aiden that last night surprised me. Groaning, I remember how it felt to have Aiden's cock sliding into me, igniting my body with a firestorm of pleasure until my eyes rolled back into my head. I ache to feel Emily's warm wetness surrounding me while Aiden grasps my hips and sinks his cock into my ass.

The pleasure intensifies with every passing second, my thighs quivering uncontrollably. I'm aching to come when a sound startles me. My eyes snap open while my hand freezes against my shaft, and I look towards the bedroom doorway.

~

EMILY

Since I couldn't orgasm last night, my body is still humming with arousal the today. I had hoped that a satisfying orgasm would give me several days of not wanting to rub against the nearest cock, but no such luck. Now it's only made things worse, and I can't stop thinking about fucking Nate and Aiden at the same time. My mind has fixated on the one thing out of my reach and can't seem to let it go.

I'm listening to music through my earbuds and making dinner. I don't know why the fuck I'm making twice as much food as I'll eat—well, okay, I know. Nate is going to be home soon, and the plan is to offer him dinner. We need to talk, and maybe if I fill his belly with tasty food, it'll break down the fortress he's built around himself. Not that I think it's actually going to work, so I don't know why I'm going through the effort. But I've got to do something, since waiting for him to open up is getting me nowhere.

Part of dinner includes a salad kit I bought at the store. I'm swaying to the music as I grab a bowl from the lower cupboard and dump the lettuce in it. How do I even start the conversation? Every time I attempt to talk to him, I can hear how accusatory I sound. If I were him, I wouldn't want to open up and talk about my feelings.

I'm stewing over how to word things as I rip open the packet of dressing. Thick, creamy ranch squirts out and splats onto my shirt. I groan and look down at the white stripe running down my front. I instinctively swipe at it with my finger to clean up the mess but just end up smearing it worse. Snorting, I lick my finger before using a wet paper towel to dab at my shirt.

Well, shit. This isn't working. I'm just making more of a mess. Since Nate isn't home yet, I'll sneak into our bedroom and grab a clean shirt. I still need to cut up the cold deli chicken to go on the salad, but it'll be fine if I'm not totally finished when he gets home. He won't get pissy if he has to wait five minutes for a dinner he's not expecting.

I abandon the salad and head to the bedroom. My mind is elsewhere—contemplating how to start the conversation with Nate—until I step into the room and notice a heap of clothes near the foot of the bed.

And then I hear a familiar low moan.

What the—Nate is naked and stretched out on our bed, rubbing himself. His eyes are closed and his head's tipped back as he moves his hips in time with his strokes. The look of raw pleasure on his face is unmistakable. He's home? *And* masturbating?

His hand moves faster, and my pussy clenches in response as I watch him getting close to coming. I swallow hard and stand still, feeling like a voyeur in my own bedroom. I should leave, but I'm transfixed at the glistening moisture on his cock. Mmm, saliva pools in my mouth. I think that's pre-cum and not lube.

His fingers slide along his length, and I imagine it's me stroking him. The rhythmic slapping sound and his heavy breathing are the only things that I can hear, and I'm fascinated to be an observer. I've never watched him stroke when he wasn't aware I was in the room.

Wait, he's not too upset to masturbate? He's the one not talking to me, and now he's finding the release that I can't. Anger begins to simmer in my stomach. His pleasure enrages me, and I feel an intense need to punish him for getting off while I'm still unsatisfied.

I take a deep breath, telling myself to step away before I do something crazy. But it's too late—the energy building in my brain is taking control of my body. I need to stop him, but how?

I zero in on his slippers next to the pile of clothes on the floor and snatch one up. He's so far gone, he doesn't even hear me rustling around. You know what? Fuck him.

My rage gets the better of me. I felt guilty for masturbating last night, and it ruined my orgasm. If I can't come, then neither can he. I take aim and throw the slipper at Nate. It strikes his chest with a soft thud. His eyes fly open in shock, and his hand pauses mid-stroke.

For a second I'm motionless and can't think, until a surge of adrenaline kicks in. I square my shoulders with determination and lift my chin.

"Why are you touching yourself?" I ask in what I hope is an authoritative tone.

Nate looks stunned, and he takes a few moments to compose himself before he speaks.

"I—I don't know," he stammers out, and his answer sends a shock wave of fury through my body.

"You don't know," I repeat, anger lacing my voice as my hands shake uncontrollably. Him and that fucking 'I don't know' bullshit. I clench my fists in an effort to keep my temper in check. "That answer isn't good enough."

He licks his lips before meeting my gaze. "Because I can't help it," he whispers, his cheeks blazing red with embarrassment. It's a fragile plea of desperation, begging me to understand.

He continues to look at me, an intensity brimming behind his gaze that makes my breath catch. I study him for a moment, getting more angry with each passing second until I'm practically vibrating. My heart pounds and I'm flushed, but the angrier I get, the more Nate's eyes glaze over with lust. I realize then that he's still hard, and his cock twitches.

Something inside me snaps.

A strange feeling blooms in my chest. I don't recognize it at first, but then it comes to me—it's lust mixed with a need to make him pay for all my suffering in the last two weeks. This might not be the first time he jacked off. He might be polishing his pole and living the high life every night while I'm miserable.

But as fucked up as my emotions are, there's also a craving for my gorgeous man who is so willing to submit himself to me, even if he only does it briefly in this moment.

I peel off my shirt, toss it to the floor, and take a step closer. He glances at my chest, and my nipples harden into painful peaks.

"Nate, look at me."

He does as I command, and his eyes reflect the same desire that rages inside me.

I speak in a deep and sultry tone. "I'm going to fuck you, and you better not even think about coming before I do. Got it?"

"Yes," he practically moans, and his cock sways again, teasing me.

Oh yeah, I'm going to take what I want. I'm so pissed at him, he better hope he can come fast. If he doesn't blow his load when I orgasm, I'm going to climb off of him and leave him aching. Tonight is for me. This is more than just sex. This is my need to dominate him. If he won't talk to me, he doesn't deserve to come.

With that thought, I eagerly pull off my yoga pants and panties. I'm desperate to feel him slide inside me, and wetness leaks down my inner thigh as I climb onto the bed and straddle him. Without hesitation, I impale myself on his cock. Pleasure overwhelms me as I sink onto his hardness, and I gasp in delight as I stretch and mold around his shaft. Fuck, I've missed this. It's almost like my pussy forgot how good he feels inside me.

When Nate moves his hands up to my hips to control my movements, I become irrationally pissed off. He doesn't understand this is about my pleasure.

"Stop." My voice is harsh, and he stares at me in surprise as I continue. "You're my fucktoy tonight. You're going to just lie there. Don't you dare move."

He responds with a hungry nod as I rotate my hips faster. I bounce and grind into him, savoring the exhilaration of taking what I want. My mind spins with pleasure, and I let out a groan. Resting my hands on his chest, I use the leverage to fuck him with wild abandon. Each movement brings me closer to an exquisite explosion.

He's still beneath me, doing exactly what I asked of him—being a good boy and enjoying every second—and that only turns me on further. I shiver in delight when his cock throbs inside me. His eyes are hooded with desire, but also something else...surrender.

I move faster, pushing into him with more and more intensity. My skin is slick with sweat as I ride him, and he grasps the sheets for purchase. He's not fighting me—he's loving this. He closes his eyes, and his chest heaves while his legs thrash. A pained expression crosses his face, and I can tell he's focused on making sure he doesn't come.

The power inside me shimmers and expands until it's an all-encompassing dominance. He's mine. I don't know why I ever thought about giving this up.

I'm slamming against him at a frenzied pace as the pleasure overwhelms me. My movements become erratic as I seek my bliss. I thought I wanted any cock, but in reality, it was his cock I needed. We fit together, and it feels perfect.

When I move one hand between my legs to brush my clit, the added sensation shoots me over the edge. I cry out in euphoria as I continue to ride him to prolong my orgasm. I'm so lost in the pleasure that I almost don't notice he's coming.

His groans echo off the walls, and his body tenses with pleasure as he arches up into me. His hands dig into the sheets, and his pained expression melts away as I feel him shudder and spasm inside me. A satisfied ache replaces my earlier urge to make him suffer. He needed this just as much as I did.

I slow down until I'm rocking against him gently as we both come down from our high. His eyes are still closed, and I'm not sure if it's because he's blissed out or if he doesn't want to break the spell and come back to reality. Either way, I feel the same way he does, and I ride him for longer than I would have otherwise.

When I can tell he's too sensitive, I roll off of him. We lie side by side, panting while we catch our breath. Nate is the first one to break the silence.

"That...was intense."

I laugh softly, relief flooding through me. I turn my head to look at him and find his gaze focused on me, his eyes full of something else—something that makes my heart skip a beat. He's looking at me with love.

The powerful urge to dominate him evaporates, leaving me on the brink of tears. Fuck, I love this man. All of our problems melt away as I nestle my head into his chest and let out a sigh as his muscular arms encircle me. His gentle caresses fill me with a safe warmth that I've been missing for weeks. I feel like nothing else matters, and we savor our moment together.

His voice is deep and a little uncomfortable when he speaks. "I didn't tell you because I was embarrassed," he confesses.

What? I pull back so I can look into his face. His cheeks are flushed from more than just sex. He's having a hard time making eye contact with me, but he seems to be trying his best.

I need to understand, and ask, "What do you mean?"

NATE

Emily looks confused, and a rush of love and fear swirls inside me. I want to explain myself better, but I'm not sure I can.

"I was embarrassed because watching you with him turned me on," I finally say, my voice shaking slightly.

Her eyes widen. "You were turned on seeing me with another man, or were you jealous?"

Oh God. I close my eyes briefly before opening them. I have to tell her the truth. "It was both," I admit with a sigh. "But mostly I was getting excited by your cheating." My stomach tightens with shame. She needs to hear this. I rush to add, "I hated it, and yet I loved it. I'm messed up."

I can tell she's contemplating everything I said, and my mind spirals. She's going to hate this side of me. She likes dominant men, and I just admitted to her I might be a cuck. Why did I tell her?

Her gentle laugh breaks me out of my thoughts. She leans in and gives me a peck on the lips. "We're both messed up, don't you think?"

Hope blossoms in my heart, and my voice is thick. "But did we ruin our marriage?"

Her fingers caress gentle circles on my chest, and I want to beg her to say she still loves me.

After the longest ten seconds of my life, she sighs. "I don't know."

My stomach drops as panic grips me and a tear slides from the corner of my eye. We did fuck it up. She wants a divorce.

I'm bewildered when her lips brush against my chest. What's going on?

Her voice is soft. "I don't think we ruined it, but I definitely think we need therapy. Will you go with me?"

The lingering gloom in my brain lifts, and I capture her in a tight embrace. She squeaks, though I can tell it's out of joy. I kiss her deeply until we're both breathless.

When we finally stop, she giggles. "So I take it that's a yes?"

I kiss her all over her face before answering. "That's a hell yes."

She laughs again and then sobers a little. "I think Aiden was right. We need to work on our communication."

A pang hits my heart when she says his name, and I push it aside. We definitely need to communicate better, but tonight isn't the time to tell her I fell in love with him.

"Yeah, we do."

She snuggles back into my arms, and I hold her, enjoying the moment until we both fall asleep.

THREE

NATE

The next morning, Emily is still cuddled into my side, sleeping. God, I missed waking up with her. I breathe in her scent and feel at peace. My alarm hasn't gone off for work yet, and I'm careful not to disturb her as I use my phone to message my boss that I'm sick and staying home.

As soon as I set my phone down, she stirs and slowly opens her eyes. A small smile plays at the corners of her lips, and my heart skips a beat as she looks up at me. I can see the love emanating from her, and I'm overwhelmed with my love for her—and lust. It's been a long two weeks.

My cock twitches in response to the delicate silk of her skin against mine. With both of us already naked, pushing her onto her back and burying myself deep inside her is a natural instinct.

Her eyes brighten as I bottom out, and she purrs in satisfaction, "This is quite the way to wake up."

God, she feels so good. I thrust a little harder, and she gasps before pushing at my chest. "Hey, wait. Don't you need to get ready for work?"

Her pussy is so tight and wet it's difficult to hold on to the thread of the conversation, but I want to drive her crazy. I don't respond, and continue stroking in and out quickly.

Her eyelids flutter from pleasure, and she moans as she struggles to not get lost in the sensation. "No, really, what about work?"

I keep my thrusting at a steady pace as my pleasure builds. "Nope, I called in sick. I've got all day to fuck you."

She arches against me, and her nipples grazing my chest make me lean down and take one into my mouth.

She moans loudly as she pants out, "Since this feels so good, I'll let you fuck me."

After watching Aiden control us both, I've learned a few tricks. I might not be a dominant man normally, but it might be fun to see what Emily does if I take control.

I pause my strokes long enough to grab her wrists and pin them to the mattress above her head. Her eyes widen, a spark of excitement igniting in their depths. Her breath catches as our gazes lock.

I deepen my voice so I sound commanding. "*Let me*? If Aiden were here with us, would you be *letting him* fuck you?"

My heart stops as his name slips from my lips. Shit, why did I say that? There's an immediate response from Emily. She mewls out and rocks against me, trying to get me to fuck her harder.

My jaw tightens as I hold back the need to get lost in her. I wish Aiden really was here controlling us both, but since he's not, I'm curious to see how desperate I can make her. I continue to fuck her slowly, making her gasp with every stroke.

Thinking back on how hot it was to watch Emily and Aiden together, I hear myself talking dirtier to her more than I ever have before.

"You loved being Aiden's little slut, didn't you?"

She moans, "Yes," and closes her eyes.

I keep her hands pinned above her head, enjoying being the one with the power. I have no idea what the fuck I'm doing, but I imagine Aiden across the room telling me what to say.

"You loved it so much that you cheated on me with him, didn't you?"

She whimpers another, "Yes."

"And now you're my little whore. Do you like being owned?"

I feel her body tremble under me as her hips jerk. This is exactly what I wanted. Her warm tight walls gripping my cock with each thrust bring me to the brink of pleasure. It's taking all my control not to come.

She pushes against me, and her voice is a desperate cry. "Oh god. Fuck me, please."

I smile down at her, and her eyes open wide. My imaginary Aiden whispers in my ear and I feel myself channeling him. I fuck her faster, as waves of ecstasy build.

"I own your pussy, Doll. You belong to me."

I whack against her, causing her to bounce against the bed with each thrust. Her moans increase in pitch and intensity until she screams out my name as she comes. Her pussy clenches around my cock, and I almost come right then, but I want her to get as much pleasure as possible.

I slow down my strokes. When I can tell her climax fades, I release her wrists, finally letting myself get lost in her tight wetness. Now I don't have to be anyone but myself.

I catch her head in my hands and kiss her softly as we surge together. She wraps her arms and legs around me right before I explode. Pleasure pulses through my body as I fill her. I lose track of everything but the incredible sensations as shudders wrack me from my head to my toes. I'm mindless from the bliss and stay locked against her until my orgasm fades.

After a few minutes, I roll to the side and pull her into my arms. She buries her face into my neck, and I cradle her to me, kissing her hair.

I really don't know what just got into me, and I'm not sure I could do that again. Aiden is the missing piece between us. With him, we both found the fulfillment we needed.

As if she could read my thoughts, she sighs. "I miss Aiden."

"Me too." I kiss the top of her head.

She looks up at me, her expression earnest. "Did you fall in love with him?"

I freeze, my mind blank, and she smiles gently. "It's all right if you say you did. I fell in love with him, too. I love you both."

When she admits she loves him, all my tension drains and I pull her closer to me, crushing her to my chest. "Yes, I love him."

She wiggles in my arms and pushes at me playfully. "Hey, I can't breathe!"

I loosen my grip, and she rolls over so we can spoon. We hold hands, our fingers twined together, and she plays with my wedding ring.

Her voice is soft. "So, if we both love him, what're we going to do about it?"

Can we do anything? My brain whirls with vague ideas, but nothing concrete comes to me.

"I don't know. I don't know if he would want to be our dom again."

Being with him but treating him like our dom isn't enough anymore. I want him to be with us all the time.

She voices my thoughts. "Maybe he'd want to be more than our dom."

Emily's words stun me. I never imagined she'd really want that. I proceed carefully, not wanting to seem too eager. "You'd want that?"

She kisses my hand, her breath a soft puff of air. "Yes."

My love for her almost overwhelms me, and I brush my lips against her shoulder. "I want that too."

She yawns and wiggles her ass against me. "Then after a nap, we should figure out how to win our man back."

This is absolutely crazy, and yet it feels right. I kiss her head again. "Yes, Mistress."

Her soft giggle soothes me, and I'm able to relax and drift off with my arms around her.

～

EMILY

I wake up before Nate does, and the sunlight filtering through the shades matches my mood—the world is bright again. Today is going to be a great day! I slink out of bed as quietly as I can and pull on some shorts and a tank top. My stomach growls since we missed dinner last night, and I head to the kitchen to find food. Yeah, the salad is long dead.

I pour myself a bowl of granola with milk and take it to the office.

It's time to plan how to win Aiden back, but the first step is to find a local marriage counselor—one that isn't opposed to a thruple. Just thinking of potentially seeing a counselor with both of them gives me a thrill.

While I'm eating, I search online and find a few excellent possibilities. I bookmark the info in my browser and move on to looking up information on being a domme. Aiden could help me with my questions, but I'm still uncomfortable with how I feel while I'm domme. I don't like hurting Nate, but if I don't get this under control, I'm afraid I will—especially since he keeps begging for it.

An article catches my eye, and I start reading about dom drop, which is apparently also known as top drop. Oh shit, I didn't even think about sub drop issues nor dom drop issues. We might have all been struggling with it and not realizing—well, I assume Aiden would have known, but it still sucks.

My stomach churns as I think about Aiden. I hope he's okay, but there's no way to know unless I can get him to talk to us. He's talked in the past about his boss, Zane, and how he was a close friend, so maybe Zane helped him if he needed someone. Ugh, I wish we hadn't broken everything off so abruptly, but it was his decision. I tense up the more concerned I get, and I'm scanning the website for what to do about dom drop when Nate walks in.

He comes over and kisses my head. "How are you feeling?"

I hesitate, wondering what I should say. I decide to go with honesty. "Actually, I was feeling pretty great until I found something online. We need to talk to Aiden."

Nate reads over my shoulder quietly for a moment. "How are we going to get him to talk to us?"

I glance at the website again. "I think we've got the answer right here."

He massages my shoulders, and some of the tension eases from them. I tip my head up for him to lean in and give me a brief kiss, and I murmur, "It's time to at least try."

～

AIDEN

On Wednesday, I drag myself off the couch and to the gym. No more wallowing in my own pity party; it's time to detox from the four-day junk food binge.

I'm sluggish at the gym and exhausted when I make it back home, but I'm feeling better than I have in days. After my shower, I throw a handful of vegetables and some berries into the blender to make a green smoothie. Eating healthy helps lift my mental fog, so doing something beneficial for my body empowers me. I can get through this.

I take my smoothie to the living room to watch a show, but I can't focus on anything. Emily and Nate keep popping into my head—did they talk it out or are they breaking up? I'm not sure if I'll ever know unless I reach out again. God, I miss them.

I need to occupy my thoughts so I don't dwell on the two of them. With a sigh, I set the remote down and stretch out on the couch. A nap will do me good. I can't think about them if I'm asleep.

A sound jolts me awake, and I'm disoriented. What time is it? The sunlight peeking in through the window tells me it's still daytime. My phone vibrates with a message, and I realize that's what woke me up. It's probably Zane checking on me.

I pick it up, intending to tell him I went to the gym and that I'm fine, but when I see the message is from Emily, I freeze. My hands start shaking and my heart rate speeds up as I swipe the message open.

EMILY

We need to talk. Can you come over on your next day off?

My chest tightens up, and I feel sick. I can't go through this again. I consider not responding, but I'm not that type of person.

AIDEN

I don't want to drag this out, I'm sorry. The answer is no.

She replies quickly.

EMILY

Please?

Fuck. What should I do? As I'm about to type back and tell her no, again, another text message comes in. This time it's from Nate.

NATE

I'm concerned about Emily. Can you come over as soon as you can?

That was all I needed to see. My stomach twists in knots as I type back to him.

AIDEN

I'm on my way.

I'm out the door and in my car in less than ten minutes. I keep a death grip on the steering wheel the entire drive there. With them texting me separately, it seems like they didn't work out their issues. I hope Emily is okay. I park in front of their house and see another text from Nate.

NATE

The door is unlocked, come in.

Walking into their house when I'm not their dom feels strange. It was uncommon for me to come over without intending to fuck one of them, and my cock gives a little throb like he's expecting good times. Yeah Buddy, sorry, that's not happening.

When I close the door behind me, Nate calls from the living room. "We're in here."

Creeping down the hallway, my heart pounds. I peek into the kitchen as I pass the doorway. It's a little messy, but everything else seems normal. My shoulders are tense from anxiety as I approach the living room. If they're both in there together, that means they're communicating at least a little. Could they actually be getting along?

When I turn the corner, I'm completely taken aback. Blood rushes to my head, and I feel dizzy. They both have on shorts and T-shirts, kneeling with their hands on their knees while they look at the floor.

The sight of them both in supplication knocks the breath out of me, my body reacting quicker than my mind can comprehend. Adrenaline courses through me, but I soon feel a wave of fury. What the fuck do they think they are playing at? This type of shit isn't funny.

My voice sounds cold. "You have 10 seconds to explain yourselves before I walk out the door."

They both lift their heads and look at me, and my heart sinks down into my stomach. They have the same expression of sorrow, and my gut unclenches as I feel myself giving in.

There's no way I'm going to be able to walk away from them.

The End

COLLARING THEM

AN MMF ROMANTIC BDSM
EROTICA SERIES

CHAPTER
ONE

AIDEN

My heart hurts as Emily and Nate kneel in front of me. My hands are shaking, my fingernails digging into my palms as I calm down from the initial wave of fury. They better have a damn good reason for wanting to see me because right now it seems like they tricked me with their text to get me over here. Nate said he was concerned about Emily, but they're obviously in this together.

A heavy silence falls upon us as I try to moderate my reaction. Heads down, Nate and Emily exchange a glance, their faces full of regret.

Finally, Emily focuses on me and speaks up. "We didn't keep to the agreement about being open with our communication. I'm sorry."

Nate lifts his head long enough to chime in quietly, "I'm sorry too," before he looks down at the floor again.

Now that my initial anger has faded, it's easier to assess the situation. I see two people who are hurting and in need of comfort. But did they just bring me over here to apologize and get closure for themselves? They could have texted me and kept me out of the drama. I can't be their dom anymore, not with how deeply I care about them. Conflicting desires war inside me as I struggle between wanting to rush to them and hug them or walk out and never see them again.

I'm uncertain how to act, and it makes me sound cold. "I accept your apology, but it doesn't change anything."

Emily peeps out a tiny protest. Her eyes shine with unshed tears and her face is flushed with emotion when she says, "I love you and miss you."

Time slows to a crawl, and it's so quiet I can hear my heart pounding in my ears. Nate meets my gaze with a fierceness that sears through him. His eyes reflect a burning passion that speaks louder than words ever could.

His voice shakes. "I love you, too. Please stay. We need to talk."

I already knew I wouldn't be able to walk away from them as soon as I saw them kneeling, and the vulnerability radiating from Nate pierces through my defenses. Leaving them isn't an option. It wasn't just them who fucked up—I've made mistakes as well. It was easier to be angry at them than to take accountability for my part in what happened. I reacted badly, and a lot of our pain in the last two weeks is my fault.

It's only a few steps until I'm within arm's reach of them. I don't want to be standing above them for this conversation, and I kneel to their level. Taking a deep breath to steady my nerves, I let it out before speaking. "I'm sorry," I say quietly, extending a hand out towards each of them. "We should have talked instead of me just kicking you out that day. What I did was wrong, and you deserved more from me. Can we talk now?"

Emily takes my hand, and Nate does the same. Neither of them answers immediately, and they eye each other with an expression I'm not sure how to interpret. My shoulders tense, and I prepare myself for the worst. If they don't want to talk, what am I doing here?

Eventually, Emily speaks. "Yes," she whispers. Nate nods in agreement, and I let out a sigh of relief.

"But first..." Emily's voice is hesitant. "Do you feel anything for us beyond being our dom?"

A wave of love for them washes over me. God, I'm so stupid. I should have told them straight off that I loved them—more proof that I'm not perfect. My throat closes, and I have to clear it before I can answer. "I love you both," I admit sheepishly, "And I was an idiot not to say it before now. Am I forgiven?"

NATE

Emily launches herself at Aiden and squeals out a, "Yes!" mirroring how I feel but am unable to express the same way. She kisses him deeply, and I watch, feeling overwhelmed until Aiden breaks off the kiss and tugs on my hand.

His voice is gruff. "Get over here."

I fall into his embrace, and his lips slide against mine with just as much passion as he had for Emily. My head whirls as he deepens the kiss and Emily's arm slides around my side. When we break apart, the three of us kneel together, wrapped around each other with our heads touching.

We stay quiet for a few moments, and Emily is the first to speak. "Aiden, we love you so much, and we want us all to be together. We don't want you to be just our dom."

Aiden gazes at me with adoration in his eyes. "Do you feel the same way?"

"Yes," I whisper, feeling my heart jump into my throat. "I want that more than anything."

He tightens his grip around us, and his voice is gruff again. "I want you both forever."

I feel a surge of joy as my heart skips a beat. I have the urge to confess everything since I'm the one who got us into this messy situation by not being totally honest when given the chance.

My words tumble out. "Emily and I talked about this, but you need to know as well. I didn't say I saw you two together, because I was ashamed by how much it turned me on."

Aiden grasps my shoulder firmly, and his voice is solemn. "I understand. That's a lot to deal with."

I lean into his strength and murmur, "Thank you." He might be more dominant than I am, but I can tell he really does understand.

Aiden kisses us both again. "I knew you two were still new to the lifestyle. I should have been a better dom."

Emily pipes up, "You were a great—," and Aiden cuts her off. "Don't make excuses for me. I fucked up, and I'm sorry."

A hint of a smile plays on Emily's lips. "Okay, no excuses. You were kind of an ass." I almost laugh at her audacity, but she continues. "If this is confession time, I have something to say."

She sits back on her heels, and her face turns pink like she's embarrassed. I extract myself from Aiden's embrace, and we both glance at her. I love the soft side of her when she's being vulnerable, and I want to scoop her up in my arms and tell her everything will be fine. She can't confess anything worse than what I said.

Emily fiddles with the hem of her shirt before sighing. "Um, I sort of enjoy taking control and punishing Nate with sex."

I suck in a tiny breath as my entire body tingles. Okay, I wasn't expecting that. My cock twitches as I think back to last night when she threw my slipper at me, climbed on top of me, and took what she wanted. I figured she enjoyed being domme a little since she kept switching on me. My cock throbs, and I shift slightly to give it more room in my shorts.

Aiden chuckles, and his dom voice is back in full force. "That doesn't surprise me, Doll. What do you like most?"

His tone immediately makes me feel submissive, and I peek at Emily, curious at what she'll say. I can see her nipples harden. She squirms and directs her response to Aiden. "I like it when you tell me what to do to him."

"That's because he's a good boy who likes being controlled." Aiden looks at me. "Don't you?"

My body warms and a ripple of desire runs through me, and I sigh, "Yes."

After the experience last night, when I was imagining Aiden telling me what to say to Emily, I now understand why she enjoys it so much. If they told me to crawl for them, I would, but there's something else that needs to be said first.

"Will you be our dom again, but also be more than just our dom?"

Aiden hums as if he's thinking, and then his voice is firm. "Only if we all make a promise. No more secrets."

"I promise," I say with a smile as relief floods through me.

Emily's voice is solemn. "No more secrets."

"Also." Aiden's voice deepens, and his tone pulls at my gut. I really would do anything for him right now. "I can't always be dom, so we'll need to come up with something that works for all of us."

Emily nods, and before I can agree, Aiden continues. "But we can talk about that later. Right now, I want to teach Emily something."

Emily sits up straighter. "Yes, Sir."

"Doll, I want you to repeat after me."

She nods.

"Say, 'I fully embrace my desires, and it's perfectly natural to want to take control.'"

Her voice is a velvety purr that makes my cock throb when she repeats it. "I fully embrace my desires, and it's perfectly natural to want to take control."

It's hard to breathe while they are talking about both of them domming me. Christ, this is hot. My cock is so hard it's ready to burst, and I want to please them both.

Aiden smiles at Emily. "Now say, 'But I'm still Aiden's fucktoy who'll do whatever he wants.'"

She giggles. "I'm still my Sir's fucktoy who'll do whatever he wants."

I half expect him to tell her she didn't say exactly what he wanted, but he smiles indulgently. "Good girl. If you enjoy this dynamic, there's no reason we can't have fun with it. Nate can be both our sub whenever we all want to play." He turns to me. "Is that okay with you?"

I trip over my answer in a rush to get it out. "Y—yes."

"Good." Aiden rises and sits on the couch. "Now I want to see my subs play together. Doll, you ready for some fun?"

～

EMILY

I snap to attention as a thrill runs straight to my pussy. Oooh, HECK yeah, I'm ready for some fun. Beaming a smile at Aiden, I keep my voice low and seductive. "Yes, Sir."

I blow a kiss towards Nate, and I can already tell he's halfway to fucked up mentally. The freedom I feel from both of them being fine with me expressing my true nature is liberating. I'm still not sure I want to hurt Nate again by smacking him, but Aiden can teach me how to better rein in my impulses. I'm sure there are plenty of ways to torment Nate sexually when he's misbehaving.

Aiden rubs his chin as if he's thinking, but the devilish sparkle in his eyes tells me he's already got plans.

"Doll, I want you to strip Nate and then rub his cock. Make him nice and needy."

A mental image of doing exactly that pops into my head, and I give a throaty moan. "Yes, Sir."

Standing up, I tower over Nate and give him a soft smile. "Get on your feet."

He immediately obeys, and I grab the bottom of his shirt to remove it. He raises his arms so I can slip it off. His chest radiates warmth, and I relish the soft fuzz of the hairs that cover it as my palms skim down to his hips and below his shorts. He's already rock hard, so I give him a small caress before easing his shorts off, sliding them down his legs. Oh yeah, he definitely needed some attention. I clasp my hand around his cock and start to pump up and down, glancing at Aiden for approval.

He nods at me slightly. "Go on."

I missed this—being able to do what I want with Nate while still being obedient. It's perfect.

Nate spreads his legs apart as I massage the length of his cock and use my other hand to cup his balls. They're always so sensitive to the touch. I give them a gentle squeeze, taking delight in his moans of pleasure.

Aiden stirs on the couch and pulls his cock out of his pants. Fuuuck. Now I'm desperate to touch him too. Nate's cock surges, and

I'm tempted to give him a firm tug, but I don't want to make him come too quickly. I want all of us to enjoy this for a while longer.

Aiden's voice is low and commanding. "Doll, bring Nate over here so you can stroke us both."

Being told what to do makes me feel submissive, but when I look at Nate, his haze of submission stirs my domme side, and I want to toy with him. Excitement surges through me, and I grip Nate's cock and lead him to the sofa. Aiden didn't tell me exactly what to do with Nate, so I make the decision. "Sit down next to Aiden," I tell him firmly.

He quickly sits. He's close enough to Aiden that the men's thighs are touching. Dropping to my knees, I reach for both their cocks. They're both erect and leaking pre-cum, ready for me to explore. I glide my fingers up the length of Aiden's shaft, watching his reaction. His cock is thick and full of veins that feel wonderful beneath my fingers.

The moment my fingers contact Nate's cock, I experience a powerful electric shock, as if an unseen force is binding the three of us together. I've never felt anything quite like it, and I feel connected to both men. The sensation is addictive.

While I slowly stroke them both, Aiden turns to Nate and kisses him deeply. I massage the pre-cum into their shafts and wish I could take them both in my mouth at once. I can see their tongues twirl together. This is so fucking hot.

Aiden breaks away and says, "Suck my cock. I want to feel your mouth around me."

Oh yeah, that's what I want too. I reposition myself between Aiden's legs and take his cock in my mouth. As I lick up the underside of his shaft, I roll my tongue around the tip. His moan gives me confidence, and I reach over to stroke Nate again while I suck on Aiden.

The two men groan in unison, and I know I'm pleasing them. The heat in my core increases, and I wonder if I should push things further. Maybe I shouldn't tease them any longer...

My mind drifts as I continue sucking Aiden and playing with Nate's dick. My head goes fuzzy, and I sink further into a state of submission. I daydream about the men filling all my holes.

Aiden says something, but it seems far away and I don't understand.

All I can focus on is sucking and rubbing. When Aiden pulls on my hair gently, I lift off his cock and grin at him. "Yes, Sir?"

"You're an excellent slut. It's time we moved to the bedroom."

I practically jump up, and Aiden leads us both to the master bedroom. We've been in here before with him, and it's surreal to be back, knowing that we all want this to last forever.

Aiden's presence fills the room, and he directs us. "Nate, lie down on the bed. I want to watch Emily ride you."

When Nate obeys, I kneel next to him and stroke his cock a few times before straddling him. My back is to Aiden as I guide Nate's cock inside me. As I slide down his thickness, my body shivers in pleasure, and our moans fill the air. His hips buck upwards, pressing against mine with each thrust, and his fingers wrap around my waist.

I rotate my hips, feeling myself become overwhelmed with bliss, and we both stare into each other's eyes in mutual ecstasy. I lean forward and push my breasts against his face until he takes the nipple into his mouth while caressing my ass cheeks with his hands. His movements bring me closer to the edge, and desire rushes through me like a storm.

I relish the sensation of Nate sliding inside me—every inch intensifies our connection, and I welcome the pleasure. I grind my hips in time with his upward thrusts, coaxing us both closer to ecstasy. Nate's grip on my buttcheeks tightens, and he stops sucking my nipple as we both moan louder in unison.

The bed dips as Aiden gets into position behind me. I hear the squeeze of a lube bottle and I almost giggle. He must have picked it up from the dresser. I glance over my shoulder at Aiden briefly and then look back down at Nate. His eyes are closed tightly, and I know he's lost in the moment. I tighten my stomach muscles and piston my hips faster. I want to make him come.

"Slow down, Doll," Aiden murmurs as his lubed-up finger dances around my asshole.

Oh, god. Am I finally going to get them in both holes at once? I ease up my pace until I'm barely rocking against Nate's cock and I feel Aiden grab ahold of my hips.

"Ready?" His voice is strained, and I gasp out, "Yes."

He slowly pushes a finger inside my ass. I moan in pleasure as he works the lube inside me. The sensation makes me clench around his finger.

"Damn, Doll. Your ass is so tight."

My head spins when he removes his finger, and I feel the head of his cock press against my ass. I grind down on Nate's cock as the tip of Aiden's becomes a glorious pressure as he slides into me.

"Oh fuuuuck," I cry out as a painful pleasure builds.

"You're doing great," Aiden breathes. "Let's just take it nice and slow."

His words are calming, and I try to relax as he eases himself inside me. I whimper as he gets deeper and deeper, stretching me further than I thought possible.

When he's all the way inside me, I feel the urge to rock against both cocks. I shift my hips, and Aiden helps me glide up and down on Nate's cock while he fucks my ass. Nate grunts his approval, and I continue to ride him. My orgasm builds, and the double onslaught of pleasure is almost too much. I'm panting and mewling, and every thrust from Aiden forces me down onto Nate's cock.

Waves of ecstasy sweep through me, and I can tell I'm going to come at any moment. I focus on breathing while I rock back and forth on Nate's cock. I'm continuously moaning as Nate's cock swells inside me.

I lose track of everything around me except for the pleasurable sensations coursing through my body. Each thrust from Aiden and the rhythm of my riding Nate sends shocks of pleasure through me. My thighs begin to spasm, and I'm so close to coming.

When Aiden speeds up his thrusts, I can't take it anymore. I cry out as my orgasm hits me. "Yes, oh fuck yes!"

I'm like a madwoman, riding both their cocks as the waves of bliss electrify me from my head to my toes. The orgasm seems never ending, and the rapture peaks again as both cocks massage my cave walls.

I'm lost in euphoria when Aiden growls, "Come for us, Nate," and both men explode almost at the same time.

Bursts of hot cum coat my insides, and the filthiness of it makes me shiver in delight. Nate's eyes are closed, his face is distorted in pleasure, while Aiden gives a final plunge into my ass before releasing my hips and sliding out. I collapse onto Nate's chest, gasping for breath.

Holy fuck. I'm going to need more of that.

I stay molded to Nate's chest for a few minutes until Aiden stands up and pulls off his clothes. He climbs back onto the bed and tugs me off Nate so I can cuddle between them. The room smells like sex, and I'm sticky from sweat, but I don't care. I want to bask in the afterglow of our shared pleasure.

"That was incredible," I chuckle softly.

They both agree, and my body is still tingling with post-orgasmic pleasure while we spend some time kissing and touching each other.

CHAPTER

TWO

AIDEN

We each take turns cleaning up in the bathroom before snuggling into a pile and falling asleep. When I wake up, I'm spooning Nate and Emily is sprawled out on her stomach next to him. Moonlight filters through the open blinds, and I'm not sure how long we napped.

I lean over and kiss Nate's shoulder. His skin is warm and smooth. When I inhale, enjoying his scent, my cock stirs. I press against his firm ass, and I shift so that my shaft can nestle along the crack of his butt without waking him.

He moans in his sleep, and I grin to myself. Waking up with both of them beside me every morning is a pleasure that I could certainly get used to.

Emily shifts onto her side, facing Nate, and her sleepy eyes meet mine. A small smile appears on her lips as she murmurs softly, "I like seeing both of you here."

A warmth spreads through my chest. I'm about to agree with her when Nate shifts, pressing my stiffening cock deeper between his ass cheeks, and I suppress a groan. I reach my hand across Nate and Emily twines her fingers in mine. Nate's hips rock just slightly, and I bite back a growl. Is he awake?

Kissing his shoulder again, I'm close enough to get a peek at his face. The corners of his mouth are turned up, so either he's smiling in his sleep or he knows exactly what he's doing.

As I tug on Emily's hand, she looks confused, but snuggles closer to Nate. She presses her tits against his chest, and I let go of her hand and trail my fingers up Nate's shoulder. I point at her and then tap his neck. She grins and leans forward to kiss him where I indicated. She sucks on Nate's skin gently, and Nate wiggles his ass against my cock. Oh yeah, he's awake.

Clasping his hips, I give a few tiny thrusts to dry hump against him. When he cups one of Emily's breasts and plays with her nipple, she coos, "Ohhh," softly.

I smile down at them as I reach around Nate to caress his hardening cock. He thrusts into my hand, sending a wave of heat through me, and Emily stops sucking on his neck and focuses on his mouth instead. I hadn't intended to fuck both their asses today, but Nate writhing against me pushes me ever closer to the edge with each passing second. My cock throbs in anticipation of my own pleasure, as I imagine sinking into him.

My voice is still gruff from sleep. "Emily, get on your back."

She murmurs, "Yes, Sir," and immediately obeys.

As my dominant side wakes up fully, my cock pulses and I give a few more thrusts against Nate before getting off the bed to grab the lube. Emily is close enough to the edge of the bed that when I walk by her to set the bottle on the nightstand, I can easily reach her leg. I grab her ankle, lifting it up and stretching her open.

She plays with her nipples, and I smile down at how slutty she looks. Her pussy is glistening and I'm tempted to taste her, but I have other plans. Nate's stroking himself, and I almost tell him to stop, but decide to let it go. We all deserve as much pleasure as we can get after the last few rough weeks.

"Nate, I want you to fuck her and make her moan."

He replies with, "My pleasure," and when he positions himself between her legs, I let go of her ankle and she rests it on his shoulder.

She moans as Nate sinks his cock into her. I watch them fuck for a few minutes as I stroke my cock. Emily's cute little sighs mingle with Nate's as they surge together. I don't want either of them coming yet, but they don't seem in danger of that.

Cracking open the bottle of lube, I pour some in my hand and rub it along my shaft. I moan from how good it feels, but I want more. I bring the bottle with me and get on the bed behind Nate. He's on his knees, pressing into Emily, and I squeeze the lube out onto my hand and rub it between his ass cheeks. He sighs and speeds up his thrusting as I push a finger inside him.

This is perfect. I moan with pure pleasure as my cock slides into Nate's ass. He gasps as I guide my shaft into him, stretching his tight ring. I revel in the sensation of his warmth wrapping around me like a silken glove. The pleasure intensifies as he quickly realizes that he can control the thrusts from both sides. I groan out, "Good boy," as he goes wild. I hold on to his hips, and all I have to do is stay still while Nate rocks back and forth between me and Emily. He's jackhammering into her, and every time he pulls out, I slam into his ass. All I can focus on is the raw pleasure coursing through my body.

Emily's cries of rapture intensify as he slaps against her pussy with each thrust. Nate's doing all the work, and I'm enjoying the ride. My eyes almost flutter closed from the bliss, but I love watching those two together. Nate is a beast, pounding into Emily, and her mouth is open as she moans louder and louder. The room is filled with the wet slapping sound of Nate hitting her pussy, and I almost come from the pleasure of Nate's frantic movements.

I grit my teeth to hold off my orgasm and smack Nate's ass. He jumps in surprise and clenches his butt muscles, giving me more plea-sure. I spank him again, and he groans but doesn't slow down his thrusts into Emily. I'm enjoying the game, so I rain smacks on his ass repeatedly until I can't stand it any longer.

The pleasure is building up inside me, and I want to see them both come before I let go. When Nate partially withdraws from Emily, I lean forward close to his ear. "Make her come."

Nate grunts in response and starts slamming harder into Emily, with me still buried in his ass. The harder I press against Nate, the deeper he plunges into Emily until she finally screams out with her orgasm. Nate shudders, and I growl, "Come for me," to him as he explodes.

We all cry out together as the bliss overtakes us, and with a loud groan, I shoot rope after rope into Nate's ass. When I'm done unloading everything I've got, I pull out. Nate collapses on top of Emily, panting, and I lie down next to Emily and snuggle against her side.

We're a sweaty mess and we all need a shower. It might be fun to see if we can all fit in there, but I need a few minutes to recover first.

Nate rolls to Emily's other side, and I reach across for his hand, linking our fingers and resting them on Emily's stomach. As Emily slips her hand over ours and squeezes, an unexpected emotion hits me: I feel like I'm where I belong.

~

NATE

I'm exhausted from the sexual workout but also exhilarated. The double pleasure was even better than I imagined it would be. Emily clearly enjoyed it as much as I did. I'm not sure I've ever heard her moan that much.

We cuddle together for a bit and then decide we need a shower and food. When I get up, Emily gives me a sultry smile that tells me she wants more. She takes both our hands and leads us to the bathroom.

Our shower isn't small, but it's not designed for three people. We manage to fit in, but it's laughter, then gasps of pleasure as Emily makes sure Aiden's and my cocks are both clean. Emily is being extra cute as she tries to tempt us into fucking her by rubbing her soapy body against us, but my growling stomach means I need food more than sex right now. She's going to have to wait.

As we dry off, I contemplate a renovation of the bathroom. A longer vanity with a third sink would be awesome. We have a large house and no kids, so we could probably steal space from the room on the other side of the bathroom and put in a bigger shower. This might be putting the cart before the horse, so I don't voice my suggestion. I'm not sure what Aiden is thinking in terms of the future. Loving someone isn't the same as living with them, but I want to wake up with both of them all the time.

Aiden catches my eye in the mirror and gives me a sexy smile that makes me flush. I get the crazy feeling that he can read my thoughts. If so, good. Maybe he can help us choose the tiles.

Thinking about the expansion reminds me I never told Emily about the conversation with my mother the other day. I rub a fluffy towel along Emily's body to dry her off and tease, "Hey, by the way, my mom was knitting us baby stuff."

Emily groans, "Oh, God," and I laugh, "Don't worry, I convinced her to make hats for the homeless shelter instead." That wasn't exactly how the conversation went, but close enough.

I'm enjoying the carefree atmosphere that's been missing between us for weeks. When Emily's sufficiently dry, I take Aiden's towel from him and run it along his back. I can't help skimming my fingers along his clean, soft skin, and his muscles jump under my fingertips. I kiss his shoulder and decide to tease him as well. "My mom also wants to meet you."

He peers over his shoulder at me with surprise written on his face while Emily responds, "Wow, what? She knows about Aiden?"

Her round-eyed expression makes me belly laugh. "Let's find food, and I'll tell you all about it."

Emily perks up and says, "I vote we make breakfast for dinner," and we quickly agree.

Aiden and I keep grinning at each other as we cook scrambled eggs, sausages, and toast. He looks happier than I've ever seen him since most of the time he's in his dom mode when I'm around him. Tonight he's relaxed and bantering with us. I want more of this.

I tell them about what happened during the conversation with my mother, and Emily is amazed at my mom's open attitude. Aiden is quiet, and I'm guessing it's because we haven't worked out the details of our relationship yet.

When we sit down to eat, Emily is the one who finally brings up the topic that's probably on all our minds. "We need to discuss our future."

I nod eagerly, and before I second guess myself, I blurt out, "I want us to be in a committed three-way relationship."

Emily radiates love, and I already know this is what she wants. My heart pounds as we wait for Aiden's response.

Aiden glows, and he swallows his bite of food before he responds. He reaches across the table and takes our hands, giving them a squeeze. "I would like that too."

Emily's chirp of happiness matches the joy spreading inside me as I realize that this is it—we're finally complete.

EPILOGUE

EMILY

Nate and I kneel, naked, before Aiden in the re-decorated mother-in-law apartment on the top floor of the house. Aiden moved in two months ago, and we turned the room into our play room. Aiden joked he had a Saint Andrew's cross and a spanking bench that needed a home, which inspired us to redecorate. We added a sex swing and a few other toys. We painted the walls a dark red while the floor is now vinyl to make cleanup easier.

I came up here earlier to light candles around the room, and the scent of vanilla hangs in the air. It's romantic, and there's a hint of anticipation from all of us because we know we're going to play soon.

"Are you two ready?" Aiden asks, and a tingle runs down my back as Nate and I both nod. He's wearing his customary basketball shorts, and I admire his sculpted legs and back as he picks up a black leather collar with a silver heart from the dresser next to him. "Then let's begin."

Aiden told us we can make our collaring ceremony whatever we want, but in all our hearts, it's more than just Aiden being our dom. We're affirming our commitment we all made to each other. Happiness swirls in my stomach as Aiden pauses before putting the collar around my neck.

"Emily, this isn't just a collar. This is a symbol of our relationship. This is a bond of love and trust that we all share. By accepting this, you will be my submissive. I will protect you and lead you on your journey. Do you accept my collar?"

My voice is barely above a whisper, and I'm so excited that I can hardly speak. "I accept."

Aiden smiles and leans over and kisses me. Our tongues swirl together, and pleasure pulls at my core. When he breaks off the kiss, he picks up the second collar and stands in front of Nate. I trace my fingertips along the supple leather encircling my neck, its presence an exquisite reminder of my bond and love for both Aiden and Nate.

Nate's collar is wider than mine and has a silver loop to attach a leash to it. We both chose what we wanted, and I have a hunch that Nate's going to find he's leashed at some point soon. Hell, maybe I'll be the one who does it. I wouldn't mind a pet Nate to lead around.

Aiden has to clear his throat before he speaks again, as if he's choked up, and I focus back on our ceremony. He starts off the same way he did for me. "Nate, this isn't just a collar. This is a symbol of our relationship. This is a bond of love and trust that we all share."

When Aiden pauses, I know he's waiting for me. Aiden and I planned this without Nate's knowledge. I rise gracefully and stand next to him and smile down at Nate. My voice is soft and sensual. "Nate, by accepting this collar, you'll be both our submissive."

Nate's eyes widen, and I can see desire and love reflected in them. Aiden lays a hand on my shoulder and squeezes before he takes over again. "I will protect you—probably from an overeager switch," Aiden winks at me before looking at Nate again, "and lead you on your journey. Do you accept our collar?"

Nate doesn't hesitate. "God, yes."

Aiden takes my hand and puts it on the collar, and we both wrap it around Nate's neck. Nate trembles, and I bend down to kiss him softly before Aiden gives him a more passionate kiss.

"Stand with us," Aiden says and helps Nate to his feet. "You had a request for something tonight. Ask again, and I'll give you it."

Nate's mouth drops open, and I inwardly smile. I knew this part was coming as well. Nate's eyes dart between us, then he takes a deep breath and blows it out before asking, "Will you flog me please, Sir?"

Aiden's face hardens, and his back straightens. I can see he's going into his dom mode at Nate's request. A shiver of anticipation runs through me. Nate's been wanting to experiment with more impact play. I don't think I'd ever want to be flogged, but the idea of watching excites me.

Aiden takes Nate's hand and leads him over to the Saint Andrew's cross. Nate looks over his shoulders at me, and his eyes are glazed with desire as Aiden straps him to the cross so his back is to us. Aiden runs his hands down Nate's torso and over the curve of his ass before leaving Nate and coming back for me.

I almost want to giggle at poor Nate. He's going to be waiting for the kiss of the flogger to happen while Aiden does whatever he plans with me. This starts the part of the night I know nothing about.

Aiden takes my hand and leads me over to the bed. "Lie down on your back, Doll."

I obey, and he grasps my wrists firmly, one at a time, securing them to the iron bed frame. The coolness of the restraints against my skin sends a jolt of electricity through my body. My breathing speeds up when I feel a familiar warmth awaken between my thighs as he attaches my ankles to the frame as well, ensuring that I'm a captive audience. I can easily see Nate across the room, and a sudden surge of pleasure races through me as I realize I won't be able to touch myself during this erotic experience.

Aiden goes over to the dresser and opens the top drawer. I'm assuming to get the flogger, which he brings out, but he has something else as well. What's that? I can't see it clearly, but it fits in the palm of his hand.

He walks back to me with a devilish grin on his face, and my nipples harden. Oh no, it's for me. My pussy clenches and wetness leaks down the crack of my ass as I test the strength of the restraints on my wrists. Yep, I'm not getting away unless I safeword this.

I'm breathing rapidly as Aiden stands over me. He sets the flogger on the bed, and I study the black leather handle and long tassels while he plays with whatever else he brought with him. Aiden pulls strips of elastic out of the pocket of his shorts, and I'm confused for a moment until he attaches them to the thing in his hand. I get a better glimpse and moan. Oh god, I'm fucked. It's a purple butterfly clit toy, and those are straps to keep it in place.

He bends over me and places the toy between my legs. I raise my hips to help him run the straps under my ass before bringing them to the front and clipping them onto the toy. He tightens the straps, and I wiggle around to see if I can dislodge it. Nope, that sucker isn't moving. I stop struggling and gaze into his eyes as the room spins. The anticipation of him turning that on is probably worse than what it will do to me.

His voice is rough. "Now, my little slut. You're going to watch me play with Nate. If you close your eyes, you're going to get a hard spanking."

Ugh, shit. My voice sounds breathy. "Yes, Sir. No closing my eyes. Got it."

He fiddles with the toy, and as soon as the buzzing starts, I bow my back and cry out from the intense pleasure.

"Ohhh, fuck."

He's got it on a high setting, and I'm immediately flooded with a sharp pleasure that borders on pain. I take it back. This is so much worse than the anticipation.

"Enjoy your toy," he says as he picks up the flogger and moves to Nate.

Oh shit—oh fuck. The vibrations are so intense that my orgasm builds quickly. I'm moaning and squirming as the toy buzzes against my clit.

Lust blurs my vision as I watch Aiden whisper something into Nate's ear before he steps back. I'm mesmerized as Aiden starts out slow, lightly slapping the tassels along Nate's ass and shoulders. Nate makes little moans of delight, and I can tell he's enjoying the beginning stages of the flogging. So far it doesn't seem too bad; maybe I'll ask for it some-day. The buzzing between my legs makes it difficult to think though, so it's possible I'm just fucked up and thinking anything looks good right now.

I can feel the vibrations from my toes to my fingers, and my legs tremble as the pleasure builds in layers. I rotate my hips, wishing I had a dildo inside me and not just a vibrator against my clit, as I watch Aiden's arms rotate in a figure-eight pattern with the flogger.

"Ohhh, god," I cry out as the vibrations build.

Aiden lets out a short, sharp laugh. "Doll, count out each time you come."

Wait, he isn't going to stop this once I come? Imagining how sensitive I'm going to be tips me over the edge, and I scream out at the unexpected orgasm. I'm shaking, and the buzzing doesn't stop as waves of bliss roll over me.

"I didn't hear you," Aiden says sternly, and I cry out, "One!"

He chuckles. "Isn't she a good girl, Nate?"

"Yes," Nate groans, and Aiden picks up the intensity of his movements with the flogger.

"Fuck, oh fuck, that hurts," I moan.

"Are you going to come again?" Aiden asks and glances at me. I nod my head furiously, and he smiles. "Good girl."

No one touches the toy, but I swear the vibrations become even more intense. I can't stop myself from rocking my hips and imagining Aiden is fucking me. I cry out, "Two!" when another orgasm rushes over me. My clit is so sensitive I'm close to begging Aiden to make it stop. I'm on a never-ending rollercoaster of pleasure as Nate moans with each bite of the flogger.

I feel like I'm floating in a dream, and I have to force myself to keep my eyes open. Though, at this point, I'd welcome a few hard spanks. Fireworks explode along the corners of my vision when I come again, and the intensity of this orgasm makes me cry out nonsense. I think I said, "Three," but I'm not sure. I'm vaguely aware of Aiden pulling the toy off my pussy and removing the restraints. He must have released Nate from the cross because I hear Aiden telling Nate to fuck me.

Nate climbs onto the bed, and within moments, his cock is sinking deep into me. I'm so sensitive that I cry out with each thrust. Wishing I could wrap my arms and legs around him, I struggle with the binds until I give up and just lie there as Nate whacks against me.

I don't know how many times I've come—was it three?—when

another one hits me. My body jerks, and I cry out as my insides contract. My pussy clenches around Nate's cock, and he grunts as if he's trying not to come.

The bed dips by my head, and I realize Aiden removed his shorts. He's got his cock in his hand, aiming for my mouth. I part my lips as he slides inside, and I suck on him while Nate speeds up his thrusts. Living with Aiden means I suck his cock often, so I know what he likes. I keep a firm suction going while swirling my tongue along the underside of his shaft.

"Goddamn, that feels good. You're such a great cocksleeve," Aiden groans.

I increase my suction at his filthy words. He knows I love it when he degrades me. Even though Nate is only fucking me because Aiden told him to, I still feel gloriously used by both men.

Nate's rhythmic breathing and moans tell me he's about to come, and I try to arch my hips to force him in deeper. It's only a matter of seconds before Nate cries out and I feel him jerk inside me. His cum fills me as I moan and close my eyes in ecstasy.

After a few more strokes, Nate withdraws and collapses on the bed next to me. I lie limply as Aiden pulls out of my mouth and frees me from the restraints. When Aiden goes to the foot of the bed, I'm confused for a moment, until he hooks his arms under my thighs and pulls me down towards him. He flips me onto my stomach and yanks on my hips until I lift onto my knees. I have no energy, so I keep my face smooshed into the bedding as Aiden plunges into my pussy, straight to my core.

"Ohhhh god," I cry out as he hammers into me. I'm so sensitive that I fight the urge to crawl away. If I come again, I might pass out from the pleasure. I bite my lip to muffle my cries. He's not gentle as he slams into me over and over again.

"You're so wet," he pants, and his hips piston faster. "Your cunt is so hot and tight."

I whimper and tighten my inner muscles around his cock. I want him to finish quickly, but I also want him to last forever.

"Is my slut going to come again?"

When he asks that, I realize I am. "Yes, Sir!" I cry out.

His, "Good girl," makes me shiver and my body tenses. I moan, "Oh fuck, oh fuck," as he uses me exactly how I love it.

Aiden bends over me and wraps my hair around his fist, pulling my head up. I rise as he uses my hair as reins and fucks me. Nate is on his side, watching us, and when he gives me a soft smile full of love, I splinter with release and scream out Aiden's name.

"That's it, Doll," Aiden growls in a rough voice as he pumps himself into me. "Come all over my cock."

I cry out as waves of bliss pummel into me. Aiden groans, and I feel the spray of his hot seed coating my cave walls. He lets go of my hair, and I collapse back down onto the bed, completely spent. I'm trying to catch my breath when Aiden climbs between me and Nate.

Holy shit, that was amazing. I'm in a mental fog as I watch the guys kiss, and Aiden strokes Nate's cock, causing Nate to get hard again. I love being fucked, but I also enjoy watching my men together.

Aiden kisses down Nate's chest, and I give Nate a dopey smile when he groans as Aiden starts sucking on Nate's cock. Aiden's been having fun lately, forcing Nate to orgasm. One way he does it is by sucking on him until Nate's about to explode and then Aiden makes Nate come all over something—usually me.

Today Aiden surprises me by having Nate finish in his mouth. Nate groans when he comes, and when Aiden climbs back up the bed, he kisses Nate deeply. Oh yeah, Nate just got a mouthful of himself. No doubt about it.

As they continue to kiss, I roll over and stretch out and stare happily at the ceiling. My life is so crazy different from what it was a year ago. All three of us have been going to therapy together, and it's really opened up our ability to communicate and work through our differences.

This journey started in a rough way for Nate and me, but we've come through to a stronger and happier place. I wouldn't wish away anything that's happened, because it was necessary to bring us to this point.

I've come to peace with my switchy side in the last few months, and having Aiden living with us really does complete our lives. The collaring ceremony was just the first step. We've got custom rings on order, and we're planning a tropical vacation for a commitment ceremony on the beach next month.

My fingers brush lightly over my stomach as I daydream about the trip. It's good that we're taking it soon. We said no more secrets, but I'm waiting until the morning before telling them I'm pregnant. Maybe I'll get some light spanking for waiting a few days to share the news. I'm definitely fine with that.

I wasn't paying attention to the men, and I squeak when Aiden wraps his arm around me and pulls me closer to them for a snuggle pile. Nothing could make this moment better. I'm with the two men I love, and I've got a wonderful secret to share soon. A baby wasn't in the plan, but nothing that's happened to us was planned. We'll adapt and grow together as a family.

Smiling softly to myself, I try not to giggle as I think about Nate's mother. I guess we'll have to tell her she can start knitting baby stuff again.

The End

Want a more?

Get an ebook bonus epilogue and a bundle of bonus stories featuring
Emily, Nate, and Aiden at
https://books.april-cross.com/illicitdesires

About April Cross & Lacey Cross

I write erotic romances that are ghost pepper spicy, but are really just an excuse to write a ton of sex—preferably with a hint of BDSM power play.

I also write erotica as Lacey Cross and like to focus on freeuse, wife sharing, and BDSM erotic shorts. I'm all about the women experiencing as much pleasure as possible.

Website: https://www.april-cross.com/

If you like short and hot wife sharing or freeuse stories, check out my erotica books.

Lacey's books: https://lacey-cross.com/

goodreads.com/aprilcross

bookbub.com/authors/april-cross

facebook.com/aprilcrossauthor

ACKNOWLEDGMENTS

The Illicit Desires series was a year and a half in the making, and I'm incredibly proud of it. This wrapped up a long journey for me, as well as for Emily, Nate, and Aiden.

I really appreciate everyone who read the series and supported my writing dreams. Thank you.

And for those of you who were waiting a year and a half for the happily ever after, I hope you enjoyed the ending!

~

I don't want to forget to thank anyone, so here are the original acknowledgments per book.

FOR EMILY'S SECRET DOM

I'd like to thank two very special people.

This book would not be what it is without my editor, **Wordcat**. I appreciate all your help in bringing my visions to life.

Also, thank you **Alec Lake** for giving me clarity on how Aiden should talk and react to Emily. Your advice and help have been invaluable.

FOR MASTERING EMILY

Mastering Emily wouldn't be what it is without the help of **Wordcat**, my editor and friend. You are one of the biggest reasons I'm where I'm at in my writing career. You're amazing and I hope you know how much I appreciate everything you do.

Also, **Alec Lake**, thank you again for your continued input on the perspective of Aiden. It's wonderful having a friend looking over my shoulder to make sure I'm wording things the correct way. You're my champion, and I'm grateful for all the pep talks.

FOR CONTROLLING EMILY

I have two important people to thank for Controlling Emily.

Kristin Lance–You were amazing in helping bring this story to life when I was stuck at how to get from point B to C. Everything you do to help me is appreciated more than you realize. It's writers like you that make a difference for other writers, so thank you.

And as always, my amazing editor, **Wordcat**. You've been so wonderful when I've gotten behind and needed quick editing. I value your guidance and help more than you know. Thank you.

FOR OWNING EMILY

No book gets written without thanking my editor, **Wordcat**. I still don't think she realizes how much I appreciate everything she does for me, but someday I hope she reads all these acknowledgements and realizes.

Also thank you to K who made a request for Emily to do something specific in this story. I didn't originally plan the scene to go the way it did, but the addition made the scene hotter.

Thank you, Alec Lake, for your feedback regarding Aiden. Your help through this series has been invaluable.

FOR MASTERING NATE

My editor, **Wordcat**, you're awesome like always, but for Mastering Nate I really appreciate the time you took to verify some of the words I used really were what I intended to say.

And thank you **Alec Lake** for, once again, being my beta reader and cheerleader. You see how hard this series is for me to write because of the emotional parts, and I appreciate everything you do.

FOR AIDEN'S CONTROL

Anyone who follows my newsletters or Twitter knows that I struggle to write the Illicit Desires books. Tapping into the emotions of Emily, Nate, and Aiden drain me, which is why I take breaks between each book. I didn't expect this series to be as long as it is, and I have it plotted out to finish with book nine. I WILL finish it by book nine, even if that last book has to be 20k words to make it happen. I plan to bundle these all together as one story at some point, for anyone wondering.

Aiden's Control had things in it that I've never written before, especially not from a guy's point of view, so I want to thank a couple of writer friends for their input and guidance.

Alec Lake – I know I thank him every book, but Aiden's voice really is very much driven by input from him because...let's face it, I'm not a dominate guy, so Alec always beta reads the stories and gives me advice on how a dom would react. So Alec, thank you for taking the time to help me every single time I'm flipping out and stressing over Illicit Desires. I'm sure you know this already, but the book would be very, very different without your guidance.

Manus Dare – A new person to thank for this one. Manus, I really appreciate the help you gave me on a particular scene and it's so much better after your input.

And finally, I can't go without thanking **Wordcat**, my editor. You're amazing, and wonderful, and someday we're going to remember whether I wanted to capitalize the word dom without us having to look it up every time I write a BDSM book.

FOR OWNING NATE

Thank you to my editor, Wordcat. You caught some funny mistakes in this one and gave me a laugh.

Also thank you to Alec Lake. Your input on one scene in particular was invaluable. I appreciate all your help with this series.

FOR LOSING AIDEN

There's two main people to thank for this one.

My editor, **Wordcat**, thank you for all your help on this one and the series. I know it's a challenge to edit pieces of a story when it's been ongoing this long. You're a trooper and I appreciate everything you do.

Kristin Lance, thank you a ton for all the help with this part. You're a great sounding board when I'm feeling stuck and you always have great ideas.

FOR COLLARING THEM

I want to give a huge shout out to my cover design friend, SB. She helped me design all these covers when my photoshop skills were lacking. She had no idea it would end up being 12 covers by the time I did the single books plus the bundles. I really, really appreciate all the help and when I look at them all in a row, it warms my heart because they're so pretty. So, SB, you're awesome!

Also, a huge thanks to my editor Wordcat. This finale book was another one of mine with lots of moving body parts, so it's fabulous to have someone helping me to point out where it's difficult to tell whose hand is where. I appreciate all the hard work you put in helping me bring my dirty stories to life.